MotheRing

Stephanie Upton

Acknowledgements

A real family affair … I would like to give huge thanks to my husband, Jamie, for all his support, help, patience and motivational encouragement. A big thank you to my daughter, Petrina, and her friend, Chelsea, who are the beautiful models on the front cover. Also, a big thank you to my son, Jamie, for designing and taking the photos for the cover of this book. I am also grateful to my sister, Caroline, for organising our Dover trip, and massive thanks to her and Paul for letting me use the name of their award-winning Lancashire restaurant. (And thank you to Erasmus Darwin House, for allowing us to use your building for our photography work.)

I would like to thank everyone who has helped with the writing of this novel; both friends and professional editors. To everyone who has assisted, and there are lots of you, thank you from the bottom of my heart.

A special thank you goes to Val, Annette, and Sandra. I am also indebted to Siobhan Curham, and the many other professional editors who have guided me along the way.

Thank you also to Michelle Emerson for her proofreading and excellent publishing skills.

Dedication

This book is dedicated to my two wonderful children, who were both my inspiration for writing this story.

Contents

PART TWO

PART THREE

PART ONE

Two Families.

Two Time Periods.

CHAPTER 1

8th May 1946

Catherine Leblanc looked as though she was guiding the ferry safely on its way, she was tall and thin against the skyline, with her oval face to the wind and her copper plait soaring through the air. A wave swept over the deck and she grabbed for the rail. For one fleeting moment, she thought she was fighting for survival against the water. The wave regressed into the sea, and she breathed a sigh of relief. She'd survived a war; the sea was nothing in comparison. She glanced behind and saw the French coast disappearing as the morning mist buried the land in a shroud. She turned forwards, preferring to watch the high waves driving her towards her future, her return to Kent, her precious garden of England. She'd dreamt so much of this day and she'd never given up hope that it would happen. Her body rocked with the swaying movement of the boat as it plunged through the pounding waves. She closed her eyes, and her dad's dying words echoed in her head. "At last, I'll see your mother again. I hope life gets better for you."

"*Meilleure Vie,*" she said out loud, knowing she was heading for that '*better life.*' Her eyes flew open; she must stick to the story in her letters. She didn't want to upset her gran with tales about their involvement with the French Resistance. She continued to stare at the sea, focusing on her happy childhood memories. After a while she noticed the white cliffs of Dover, appearing like small teeth on the horizon. Her head lifted towards the water that sprayed her fair skin, and she breathed deeply, allowing the crisp salt air to fill her lungs. The boat seemed to be gaining speed as it pushed against the gale blowing across the English Channel. The grey sea now seemed to be lifting the cliffs, making them taller by the minute; they felt like a gathering of white angels welcoming her back with open arms.

The ferry took ages to dock before Catherine could finally step onto English soil once more. Through the gates of the harbour, she instantly spotted her grandmother. The tall, elegant lady with short white hair curled around her face had a grin that went straight to her heart. But Gran's frame looked thinner, her body older, and she had a walking stick protruding from her hand. Then she noticed that the laughter-lines around her mouth had changed into worry-lines. Catherine decided the war had altered everyone, and that included herself.

"Gran!" She dropped her case and ran to her, nearly knocking the old lady over as she pulled her into her arms. "Oh, Gran, *enfin.*" Squeezing the elderly, fragile body, she cried inwardly. Why had she gone to France all those years ago? She'd caused Gran such heartache and stress.

Gran pulled away. "Thank goodness you're home, my darling." It sounded wonderful to hear her gran's voice again. "I just wish I could have got here sooner," Catherine whispered as she looked into the old woman's tearful deep green eyes.

"Well, thank goodness those false French papers of yours were so good!" Gran took her arm. "And I'm pleased you finally sorted out your father's house. Poor Pierre, dying from another stroke like that." She nodded towards the car. "Let's get you safely back where you belong."

Catherine fought back her own tears. This feeling of protection was something she hadn't felt for such a long time.

"Nice to see you, Ma'am," said a voice in a very familiar Kentish brogue. Catherine turned to see Sam, the family chauffeur, returning from collecting her bags from where she'd abandoned them. His small body was now slightly hunchbacked, allowing his bald head to shine in the sunlight. Before Sam could open the car door for her, she threw her arms around him. As she withdrew, she recognised his sincere smile, but this time it revealed some missing front teeth. The surprised chauffeur's smile turned quickly into a look of concern. She knew she was a lot thinner than when she'd left as a teenager.

"I'm back," she said excitedly, trying to lead his thoughts away from her lean appearance. "It's great to see you, Sam. How is Anna? And how are your girls?"

"They're well, thanking you, Ma'am. Our girls are all hitched now, but they send their love," he said with real feeling in his voice. "Phyllis is the only one who still lives close."

"Oh, I'm glad Phyllis is still around," she said, appreciating Sam loved the fact that she and Phyllis had been childhood friends.

"Our Phyllis blossomed from your guidance back then." Sam's eyes sparkled. "You were so like your mother at that age, always so positive." Catherine saw Gran's face light up; any mention of Cynthia always did that.

"I'm not supposed to tell you," whispered Gran, "but Anna is busy making your favourite cakes."

"I've missed her cakes rock." Catherine grimaced. "Oh no, sorry, I've been in France for too long! I mean I've missed her rock cakes." Then she flashed her emerald green eyes towards Sam. "I guess we'd better get going while the cakes are still warm. I don't want your wife to be cross with us!"

Sam bowed his head and guided her into the car. As he helped Gran, Catherine could tell from his protective stance that he too was worried about her. Sam picked up his cap from the driving seat and Catherine sat back, inhaling Gran's familiar perfume with vigour. Her dream of being home was finally real. Sam drove along the small streets of Dover and Catherine's heart dropped; rubble and bricks stood in piles where buildings had once stood.

"They call Dover, East Kent's Hellfire Corner," Gran informed her. "The Germans bombed us because they thought Dover was the lock and key to England. On top of that, they used to release their bombs before flying home." Her voice dipped. "Lots of people lost their lives."

Catherine reached for Gran's slender hand and feeling the comforting touch of her ruby ring, she sighed. At least Gran hadn't been one of those who'd died.

The town seemed gloomy and different, so many buildings had been damaged, even the old theatre stood with half its insides ripped out. She'd loved that theatre. Gran had taken her to see so many pantomimes there, somehow it symbolised her childhood being destroyed by the war. Sam turned a familiar corner and drove up a narrow cobbled street towards the clifftop. The car bounced over the stones and Catherine's voice wobbled with the movement.

"This town still holds the key to my heart."

Gran gave an understanding grin. "It won't take you long to settle back into being an English girl."

Catherine nodded, determined nothing would ever take her away again. "I plan to stay with you forever." She pushed her dishevelled plait behind her. "But you do realise I'm not a girl anymore. I'm a twenty-five-year-old woman now."

"I know that dear," chuckled Gran, "and I also know you won't be with me forever." Her eyes turned to the floor. "Like your mother, you'll leave to marry and have children of your own."

Catherine sat back in her seat. She wasn't bothered about marriage. Men weren't worth it, and as for babies, why would anyone want that? The car reached their street, and she sat upright. "Oh, look." She pointed. "We're home!" The large Georgian house appeared tired, the garden was overgrown, and the paint was flaking from the wooden window frames. Catherine made a mental note that she would work on getting the house back to how it was before she left for France.

After lunch and a quick change of clothes, Catherine sat on her bed, contemplating how her room hadn't changed since she was a child. Even her mother's wedding photo still stood on her dressing table. She picked it up, and it felt as if her mother was smiling at her, glad she was back in the room they had both had as children. She gazed out of her bedroom window and watched the sea as it pushed its waves towards her. Just like her life, the storm seemed to have passed, and tranquillity was taking over. When she was in Normandy, the sea had offered her freedom, an escape route to England. She understood she'd been a different person then; she'd had to switch off her warm-hearted emotions to cope with the brutality she faced. She confirmed to herself that she'd never need to switch off her warm heart again.

"Are you ready yet?" Gran shouted up the stairs.

"Just coming," Catherine called back. Darting to her dressing table, she quickly tidied her newly plaited mane. Then down the stairs, she flew.

"Let's go, then." Gran waved towards the door. "Sam's waiting with the car."

Catherine grabbed another rock cake from the cake stand. "Thanks for lunch, Anna. I've missed your baking."

Anna, a cheery-faced woman, who had her hair twisted into a clip above her head, gave a broad grin. "And we've all missed you." She adjusted her apron around her generous waist. "And thank God you're back safely." As Anna turned to help Gran with her coat, Catherine caught a whiff of freshly baked bread; life had returned to normal, and it felt incredible.

As the car climbed the hill towards Dover Castle, Catherine looked out across the sea. The weather had cleared, and she could see the outline of the French coast on the horizon. She sighed with relief, her acting as a native French girl had finished some time ago. She'd been a good actress though, at the end of the war, even her resistance friends couldn't believe she was half-English and had lived there most of her life. She turned to look towards the miniature-looking Dover below; this was home; she had no wish to ever revisit France, the memories were too painful. Sam slowed as they drove under the large V.E. day anniversary banner that loomed across the castle entrance. He parked in the field that was designated as a car park and while he helped Gran, Catherine jumped out from the other side and walked around to assist. The noise of the band and the huge crowd indicated that the festivities were well underway.

"Hello, Win," a middle-aged woman shouted as she briskly ran towards them. "How are you?"

"Oh, Edna, I haven't seen you for ages," Gran replied. "Are you alright? You've not been to Bridge Club."

"I've been helping Greg; he's been suffering badly from his war injury," Edna said while staring at Catherine.

Gran nodded and turned to Catherine. "You remember Edna, Gregory Jones's mother?"

Catherine didn't have time to reply, as instantly, Edna Jones threw her arms around her.

"I'm so glad to see you're alive, my dear." Edna pulled away, and her eyes scanned Catherine up and down. "And you've grown into a very attractive young lady. I bet you'll turn the heads of a few young soldiers in the crowd today."

Catherine forced a polite smile. She'd seen enough young soldiers in her life, she wasn't interested, but there was no point in explaining. She stared back at Edna Jones, noticing the woman's strong jawline, which was the same as her son's.

"Is Gregory, alright?" Catherine asked in a half-interested voice.

But the woman didn't seem to hear. "Shall we try and get to the front?" Edna announced as she swept back her greying blonde hair and took Gran's arm. "You're just in time to see the opening of the fete," she added as she waltzed Gran forwards.

They walked in the direction of the rolling drums, and as they stopped, Catherine looked over the crowd towards the erected stage. The red, white and blue tent material was flapping at the back, while the attached little Union Jack flags waved wildly in the wind. A man with medals dangling from his blazer walked onto the platform.

The drums fell silent, and the man announced loudly, "Unfortunately, General David Lawrence is unable to open this event for us today. But I'm pleased to announce his brother, Colonel Aengus Lawrence, has kindly agreed to step in."

Catherine gasped, then she quietly left her gran and pushed forward; she needed to get a better view. A tall man in full-dress army uniform strolled to the front of the stage. Catherine thought the Colonel looked like Cary Grant, with his dark black hair, olive complexion, and piercing blue eyes. He appeared older than her, and as he spoke, she realised he had a deeply powerful Irish accent, that sounded strong and trustworthy. Surely this couldn't be the same Aengus who'd been Claude's British contact? Intrigued by the idea, she moved closer.

Then Aengus caught her eye, and in mid-flow, his voice changed as he started to talk about his Special Operations work in France. "I, er, I'm lucky because I have a photographic memory, I never forget a face," he said, appearing to be communicating directly to her.

Catherine had heard enough, this had to be Claude's SOE. Dispensing with his gaze, she forced her way through the wall of people. Aengus's speech ended, there was a roar, and she looked up to see him cutting the ribbon. She watched as Aengus left the platform, her eyes following him as he stopped beside the stage to listen to a woman. Then she noticed he seemed to be looking over the woman's head, scanning the gathering. She found a gap and circled behind him. He seemed to be the same height as her, yet he looked taller when he was on the stage. The woman had walked away, and now Catherine was close enough so, reaching across, she tapped his shoulder. As he turned, she held out her hand to shake his then she panicked, she couldn't risk anyone overhearing her, so she spoke in French.

"I'm Catherine Leblanc; my code name was 'Meilleure Vie' and …"

He ignored her hand and instead propelled his arms around her, embracing her with passion. Looking at her with outstretched arms, he whispered in French, *"I saw you in the distance once. Claude got you to distract the German soldiers while he smuggled me out. You were so young … it was such a risk for you to take."*

"It had to be done," she replied, shrugging her shoulders. "Besides, I'm a competent woman."

Catherine noticed Gran who, aided by her stick, was pushing her way hastily into earshot. Quickly, Catherine stepped away from his arms and spoke in English. "Aengus, this is my grandmother, Winifred Demore." With a faint voice, she added, "Gran, Aengus was in France, just for a short time during the war."

Aengus slightly bowed his head. "It's lovely to meet you, Mrs Demore." Then he looked at them both. "My code name of Aengus seems to have stuck with my work colleagues! But my real name is Joseph Jack Lawrence or just Joe to my friends."

"Joseph does sound quite formal," mocked Catherine.

He gave a deep laugh. "It's a good Catholic name, that's for sure."

9

"So, how do you two know each other?" Gran asked, clearly intrigued.

Joe replied politely, "Actually, we don't know each other; we just know *of* each other." His gaze moved back to Catherine. "Can I see you again?" he asked. "We could catch up on old times. How about tomorrow evening? Where do you live?"

"What old times?" enquired Gran.

Catherine felt herself blush. "That would be very nice," she replied while ignoring Gran's question. "I've only just returned to England," she said. "I live with my Gran at 21 Sea View Road."

Joe gave a wide grin. "My daughter and I have just moved to number 1 Sea View Road!"

"That's you?" exclaimed Gran.

"Yes, my house is on the corner, it's the one with the privet hedge."

Catherine stared at him; the location of his house wasn't what interested her. "You have a daughter and a family?" she said, unable to disguise her amazement.

He folded his arms. "I'm a widower. A German bomb hit my wife's car. She must have – have died instantly," he stuttered.

"I'm sorry to hear that," Gran interjected. "But how do you two know …"

Joe continued softly, "My wife and I had a daughter, Tia, who's three now. It's been hard, but my brother's been amazing, he's basically helping me to raise her."

Looking into Joe's oceanic eyes, Catherine murmured, "He sounds like a caring man."

"Tomorrow," he muttered as he unfolded his arms and stared at her. "I'll be home from work by five. How about you come to mine for dinner, then you can also meet my daughter. We usually eat about five-thirty."

Catherine looked at his face. His smooth features and playful smile gave him such a boyish quality. Her heart melted. "That would be perfect."

Gran was now leaning heavily on her stick. "Catherine, dear, how do you know this officer, did something happen in France?"

Catherine nodded to Joe. "I'll see you tomorrow then. Goodbye, Mr Lawrence." She linked her arm with Gran's. "We need to go and find Sam." As they walked away, Catherine knew it wasn't Joe's fault, but he was the reason she was going to have to tell Gran her nurtured secret. She leant towards her gran and whispered, "I'm sorry about that, it just wasn't the right moment to tell you about my life in France. Once we get home, I'll get Anna to make us a pot of tea, and then I promise to explain everything."

CHAPTER 2

7th April 1947

The bed covers felt hefty as Selina yanked them up to her neck, her head spinning with the positive and negative thoughts the new day could bring. She was relying on the hospital to help her to get pregnant. All she wanted in life was to be a mother, what's more, she wanted to be as good a mother as her mum had been to her, but would it ever happen? These thoughts weren't helping, sleep wasn't going to return. So, climbing out of her warm bed, she grabbed her old comfy dressing gown and wrapped it tightly around her delicate frame. Not wanting to wake Mark, she slid quietly across the room. Pushing the curtain slightly aside, she softly rubbed away the condensation from the window. The resulting clearness allowed her eyes to focus on the narrow, twisting street below. Church lane lay undisturbed except for the milk float sluggishly heading towards the little church that nestled beside their road. Gravesend appeared calm. Even the noisy airstrip, so busy during the war, had fallen silent. The grey light surrounding the Kentish town was becoming clearer as the sun forced the sky to redden. The day was waking up.

Mark's snoring wasn't easing off, so she moved away from the curtain and tiptoed out of the bedroom. She crept down the stairs, avoiding the squeaky floorboards as she went. Breakfast first, she decided, as she placed some bread under the grill. But then she felt her stomach churn as she contemplated the day ahead. Why were professional people so intimidating? She buttered the toast, at least Mark had been granted the morning off work, she needed him to be with her.

"Is that for me, love?" Mark's voice echoed from the doorway, and before she could answer, his left arm slid slowly around her waist. She sunk her tiny back into Mark's muscular body, his warm, solid chest gave her a sensation of security, which for a moment, replaced her fears. Without turning to face him, she put down her knife and gently stroked his arm.

"That army doctor was right about those exercises," she said as she held his flexed muscle. "Your arm's getting stronger now."

"Yep, I guess he knew his stuff alright," Mark whispered, gripping her even closer. "But I wouldn't have bothered with his stupid drills if you hadn't made me." Mark gently kissed the back of her neck, electrifying her nerves as his lips touched her skin. "So, how's me wonderful wife, today?"

She turned to stare into his coffee brown eyes. "You do know they might not be able to help us."

"Don't be silly, love. It's a London hospital, they'll sort you out." He broke away to reach for the toast. "But I'm glad your dad left us some money, these hospitals don't come cheap."

"At least he never knew we couldn't have children." She felt her eyes filling up.

13

"Stop it, love. They'll give you some stuff." Then, with a cheeky grin, he added, "And tell us to try harder, which can't be a bad thing!"

"You always make everything seem alright," she said with a nervous laugh.

Mark sat at the table and pulled her small body onto his lap, his large hands turning her head towards his. "We'll have our bab soon. After last night, you could be pregnant already!"

She giggled, but her body was still quivering, would she ever be pregnant? Once again wanting his protection, she pressed into his rugged physique. Her heart beat loudly in unison with his. She looked up and traced her hand down the scar on his face; his war wound seemed to add to the strength of his appearance. Then she brushed her hand through his oak brown hair.

"I want a son who looks just like you."

"Well, I want a daughter who's as beautiful as her mother, and as good-natured too."

Her fingers scraped back her sandy-blonde hair from her forehead, allowing it to tumble around her tiny face, framing it as if it were a painting. "All I ever wanted was to marry you and be a mother to our children." Her soft red lips lifted at the corners then fell again. If only she wasn't an only child, she hated the idea of letting her mother down. Her mum wanted grandchildren so much. She moved her hands onto her lap. "Mum found it difficult to get pregnant ..."

"Your mum had you in the end."

Ignoring his remark, she wriggled from his lap and pushed back her shoulder-length hair from her face. "I'll go and get ready," she said, dropping her head as she wandered towards the door.

Once back upstairs, Selina shivered as her breath vaporised into the chilly air of the bedroom. Winter had been exceptionally bitter, the long months of snow combined with the fuel rationing had not made peacetime survival easy. Spring was opening its eyes, but now that the substantial snow had finally melted the flooding was causing extra unwanted hardship. She slipped on her long-sleeved woollen dress and firmly hooked her cardigan buttons. Peacetime hadn't been as she'd imagined; she'd lived a life she hoped her children wouldn't have to face. She sighed. That was if she ever had any children.

*

As they entered the Victorian hospital, Selina saw a maze of clinical-smelling passages with drab-looking walls.

"This way, love," Mark said, taking her hand and heading towards a signpost marked 'Maternity'. He marched her down the long corridor, his stride seemed confident, his stature upright and positive. She couldn't help but walk with reticence in her step; she hated the thought of walking towards the Maternity Department. Why couldn't there be a separate department for infertility? She regarded herself as a fraud, a deep sense of shame came over her. She wasn't with child. Her heart beat faster as she thought of the pregnant women who'd be sitting in the waiting room with their bumps in front of them, she didn't want to see them. They entered the room just as a nurse appeared and called out a name. A woman stood up and eagerly stepped forward. Mark halted while Selina moved closer to the desk.

In a matter of fact voice, the receptionist asked, "Name please?"

"Mrs Selina Tozer," she replied with a shy smile.

The woman's eyes looked her up and down, as if to question her appearance, then she checked her list. "Take a seat over there. The nurse will call you when it's your turn."

Selina scanned the room. Yes, there were those elegant women she'd imagined, with pride glowing from their faces. She tried to steer Mark towards the corner, but he paraded them to the front row. She sat silently on her cold wooden chair. She didn't want to speak, the last thing she wanted was for the other women to know why she was there. Another name was called out, the wait was agony. Her mind returned to her wedding day when the vicar had discussed the importance of children. He'd seemed to have implied that the reason for marriage was to reproduce. What if she couldn't have children, what was the point of marriage then?

Her attention was alerted when the nurse appeared at the door. "Mrs Selina Tozer."

Mark stood up first and took her hand. They followed the nurse down another dark corridor, and finally, the nurse pushed open a door, indicating that they should enter.

"Mrs Tozer," the nurse announced, then she exited, and closed the door behind her.

The room appeared colourless, with only a small portion of light shining through the wired window. Selina's eyes tried to adjust to the darkness. A large old-fashioned desk loomed in front of her, and dull grey filing cabinets lined the walls. She saw the doctor dressed in his expensive-looking suit, with what looked like a real silk tie. He appeared to be in his late fifties, and he had that terrifying intellectual appearance about him. Selina glanced towards the two chairs that sat in front of him.

With a disinterested voice, the doctor said, "Take a seat."

They sat on the buff, worn chairs in silence. She could hear the clock ticking on the wall, its pulse much slower than her own.

The doctor looked over the rim of his glasses. "Well, Mrs Tozer, why have you come to see me?"

She pushed loose strands of hair behind her dainty ears. "About two years ago, my periods started to become less regular, and now they've stopped altogether. I want to get pregnant, and we thought ..."

"Have you experienced hot flushes?" interrupted the doctor. "Or night sweats?"

"I do get hot, and I often wake up soaked in sweat," she said, with her head bent low.

"I'm afraid it sounds like early menopause."

She was afraid he would say that. "Is there something you can give me to restart things?"

"I'm afraid not." The doctor looked her in the eye. "Early menopause is not unheard of, but it is unusual. You are not unwell; nature has just worked prematurely." He turned to reach for his pen. "Have you any other questions?"

She shook her head. It felt as if he'd shot her in slow motion. She couldn't speak, she just wanted to get out of this horrible place. Her future children were all she'd ever thought about, and now she wasn't going to have them. What was the reason for her life now? She didn't wish to hear him continue. She heard Mark's breath increasing as he reached for her hand, then with a gravelly voice, he muttered,

"But you must be able to do other stuff to help her to get pregnant?"

The doctor glared at Mark as if judging him to be stupid. "Your wife's ovaries have effectively died, they're sterile. There is no chance of her getting pregnant."

"There must be something …"

"There's nothing I can do for your wife." The doctor glanced at her with a look of disdain on his face; she guessed he'd judged her too impoverished for him to waste his time on. "She is unable to have children," he added sharply.

The walls of the room seemed to be moving, pushing against Selina's chest, squashing the breath from her body like a medieval instrument of torture. Letting go of Mark's hand, she stood up.

"Thank you," she mumbled, though she didn't know why she'd said thank you. Mark retook her hand, and as she gazed at the doctor, she could see he was already scribbling on her file. He didn't even raise his head in response to their leaving. She guessed his job was simply to deal with failing bodies, being an understanding person wasn't his role. Or perhaps he didn't care because he could tell they weren't rich and therefore they weren't of any importance. All she wanted now was to run away. As if he understood, Mark's hand squeezed hers tightly, and he guided her out through the door. She turned to see the doctor was already reaching for the next person's file.

Once in the open corridor, Selina felt tears streaming down her face. Mark wrapped his arms around her, pulling her close to his chest. She collapsed in his embrace, hoping he would stop her from crying. But her grief took over. It was as if their child had died, the child that they hadn't had and now never would. Her body shook as the devastation took hold. Howling like an out of control storm, she bawled into his muscular torso. She didn't know what to say or how to say it, and she could tell Mark didn't either, words just weren't there. After what felt like an eternity, she looked up at him for help. She needed him to take the lead. He responded by turning towards the exit. She hoped he remembered the way out. He took her hand, and with a positive stride, he moved her through the heartbreaking waiting room of mums-to-be, then he turned and charged her down the bleached passageways, towards their escape.

Selina braced herself as she stepped out of the hospital. "Mark, I love you, but you need a wife who can ..."

"Stop it," he said with force. "It's you I want to be with, in sickness and in health, till death do us part – remember."

"But what's the point in being with me if I can't give you children?"

"I ain't going to stop loving you just cos we can't have kids." He squeezed her hand. "We've got each other, and that's all that matters to me." She knew he meant what he said, but it didn't take away her feelings of uselessness. His hold tightened on her hand, and he moved forward. She followed obediently, allowing him to escort her towards the hospital gates. Once they approached the road, he whispered, "I don't think I should go back yet."

She strained to see Mark through her sore eyes. "But you have to go back to work. I don't want you to get into trouble."

"Look, there's a telephone box in the park over there," he said as he pointed. "I'll phone and ask if I can go in later this afternoon." He took out some coins for the telephone, and she nodded, feeling unable to argue.

Selina sat alone on the park bench and watched some toddlers playing on the wooden roundabout, their heads twirling like ballet dancers. She turned to watch a girl glide down the slide and another screaming from the swings. Wherever she looked, she could see children running and laughing, obviously glad to be outside in the spring air, while their mothers gathered together in small groups. She'd never be able to do what these women were doing; she'd never know how it felt to watch her own child play. Did these women know how lucky they were? Then, for no apparent reason, one of the women went over and clipped a boy around the ear. The woman proceeded to grab him by the arm and yank him forwards.

"Come on you lot," she shouted towards a group of children. "We need to get back to the orphanage."

Another child ran towards the woman and then about five others joined them. Selina sighed. Life wasn't always what it seemed. The war had destroyed so many families. Her attention turned as she saw Mark leaving the telephone box. She stared at him as he ambled back across the green grass, his chin resting on his chest and his arms drooping heavily by his side, his confident stride gone. She shuddered as he slumped down next to her.

"My boss told me he understood because ..." she saw Mark choke back his emotion. "He said he has a son, so he knows the importance of children." Mark's tears welled in his eyes, and he turned away for a moment. "Mr Moss said his wife's pregnant with their second child," he turned back towards her. "I know he meant well, but the thought of his wife being pregnant ... I ended up having to put the phone down as quickly as I could." He put his arm around Selina's shivering body and pulled her close. "Mr Moss said I could spend the rest of the day with you."

She knew Mark wanted to protect her from the heartache she felt. He wanted to take her pain away, the pain she knew he also felt but was trying hard not to show. She gazed up at him, and now she saw the agony in his face. Selina tried to speak, but it wasn't easy.

"Even though I'll never bear your child, it will always be alive in my heart." She was aware that sounded silly, but the dream had been with her for so long. "I had a name for our baby," she blubbered. "If it was a boy, I wanted Mark Junior, and if it was a girl, I wanted Maria." She gave a wistful smile. "I like Maria because I think it's a female version of Mark. It's like Mary but more foreign-sounding." Then her anguish became intolerable, and she cried, "Why can't we have children?"

"I know what you mean," he whispered. "We'd have made good parents." He held her tightly, almost as if he were trying to stop her from crying again.

"Mum's going to be upset." Selina sniffled as she cuddled into Mark's arm, then she looked up. "Dad wanted grandkids too, didn't he?"

"Eileen will be upset for you, and as for Harold, all he ever wanted was for you to be happy." He glanced up at the gloomy grey sky. "I think that's why your dad liked me; he could see I felt the same way about you."

She moved away and sobbed into her handkerchief. "I do miss Dad." Her face distorted as she looked at him, and her hand went to his arm. "We'll have to write to your parents and tell them about today."

"As if they'd care."

Selina looked away. Mark's parents had hardly been in touch since they'd moved to Stoke-on-Trent. She was aware that Mark's dad loved it there, and even his mum claimed to like the area. Well, his dad probably told her she liked it there!

Mark slipped his hand through his hair. "I bet they won't be in Stoke for long; Dad will soon be in another fight at work; he won't ever change."

Selina frowned; she'd never understood Mark's father. Using his two children as punch-bags had been unforgivable. As for Mark's mum, she hated what that man must do to her.

Mark turned and muttered, "Still it was great when they gave me Dad's job at the docks. At least checking for pilfering ain't difficult with me bad arm." He stared into space, and she guessed he was remembering the accident. She often wondered if that high ranking officer ever gave any thought to what had happened to Mark. "But my job will never pay good money, not like our Brian gets," Mark added despondently.

Selina blew her nose. "You'll have to tell your Brian we can't have kids." She stared at Mark, suddenly hating the fact his brother had kids, and she couldn't give Mark the same.

"Listen to me, I have everything I want, I have you. You're too good for the likes of me. You have a brain that's far better than mine, and you're gorgeous, sitting there staring at me with those big green eyes. I've always said your loving nature shines through that pretty little face of yours." He scratched his head. "You'd have had adorable kids. I don't half wish I could make the world a fairer place for you."

She didn't answer him. Instead, she sat in silence, observing the children as they ran around the park. This was the scene she'd always visualised for herself, but today a doctor had opened her body and ripped out her dreams. Mark pulled her into his muscular frame. She'd always relied on Mark to fix everything, but this time he couldn't. Her sturdy man must be feeling useless and defeated.

He whispered to her, "Remember, love, we had nothing when we were wed, all those shortages and rations, yet we had the best day. Sometimes you don't get what you want, but that don't mean you can't enjoy life." He softly stroked her hair, just like her mother used to do when she was younger. "Life is precious. That's why I saved that officer in the war."

Then she realised he'd felt useless and defeated before, his arm injury had shattered his strong male façade. Selina nestled under his arm.

"Oh, Mark, you've been through so much and now this." She stared up at him. "I can't imagine life without you, but I can't imagine it without kids either ... I'm never going to cope!"

"You'll cope cos you have me. I won't let you down, not ever. We'll have a good life together. I promise."

"But we both wanted a family," she moaned.

"Bomb!" a woman yelled. "There's an unexploded bomb," the woman continued as she ran towards the others in the park.

Selina squealed and grabbed Mark's arm. He was frozen to the spot, staring at the woman, who was holding her son's hand while pointing back towards a dilapidated hut by the woods. Like sheepdogs herding their sheep, the other mothers started calmly moving their children out of the park. Selina noticed there was no panic, just precise and controlled movement away from the park.

"This is London," Mark said. "They're used to it." Standing up, he added, "I'll go and talk to the woman who saw the bomb."

"No, Mark, wait …" but it was too late, he was running towards the woman and her son. Selina got up from her bench, her legs shaking as she moved quickly towards Mark, who was now listening intently to the woman.

As she reached the two of them, she heard Mark say, "It sounds like a doodlebug. I saw a poster in the telephone box with a phone number for the demolition squad." He put his hand in his pocket and drew out some coins, then turning to Selina, he said, "You watch the lad while we go and phone the army." His head jerked towards the hut. "And make sure you stop anyone from going near that hut." Selina nodded, proud that Mark always took control. Then she looked around at the empty park; she was alone. She felt a small hand wriggle its way into hers, and as she looked down at the little boy, she cried.

CHAPTER 3

9th May 1946

Catherine sat in the sitting room, wondering what Claude would have thought about her seeing 'Aengus'. Her gaze fell on the photo above the fireplace. She stood and strolled towards it. The photo seemed dated now, but her grandfather Charles still looked full of pride as he accepted the football trophy from the King. Her hand gently touched the soft white feather placed neatly below her grandfather's picture. She knew it helped Gran to think that white feathers were a sign that the dead were still around. However, Catherine didn't believe in any such nonsense. She smoothed down her wrinkled dress, straightened her straps, and moved to the window. At least Aengus wasn't like those men she'd pretended to like in occupied France; she needed to forget those memories.

"You look very elegant, dear," Gran announced as she entered the sitting room.

Catherine turned, the evening light outlining her jade-green dress. "This is very close-fitting." She ran her fingers down the silk. "Do you think it makes me look too tall?"

"You look like your mother just before … but I wish you'd untie that beautiful hair of yours."

"It gets in my way," Catherine muttered as she looked. at the grandfather clock. It was five o'clock. She bent down and kissed Gran. "I'd better go, it's time for me to walk up the road." She waltzed towards the sitting room door, but then stopped. "I'll probably be back late, so don't wait up."

Her gran glared. "That man could have sent you to your death when you were in France. I wish you would change your mind about tonight."

Catherine ran back and placed her arms around her gran. "I've told you; it was my choice to join the resistance. Anyway, I'm focusing on the future now, and that's being here with you, forever."

*

The privet hedge outside Joe's house was huge, but as Catherine reached the open gate, she could see a car on the drive. She stopped and took a deep breath before she strode to the front door. Why did she feel so nervous about seeing Joe again? He was just a man. She rang the bell, which didn't seem to make a noise, so she reached for the large, ornate knocker and banged it against the brass frame. An attractive girl dressed in a nanny's uniform answered the door. The girl scowled at her, so Catherine guessed the bell had worked after all. She was told to place her coat on the stand, and then she was ushered into the sitting room.

Catherine stood gazing above the fireplace; her eyes captivated by a portrait of a woman draped in a spaghetti-strapped evening dress. She noticed the woman's small, curvy body was in stark contrast to her own long, thin appearance. Her soft, tawny-brown curls were pinned in a smiling horseshoe behind her neck. The effect gave a friendly feel to the woman's beautiful round face. Suddenly, the door flew open, and Catherine turned to see Joe holding hands with a tiny child. The girl's azure-blue eyes shone against her olive complexion. Her beautiful curly black hair fastened in bunches encased a plump, round face that looked alert and knowledgeable. In the silence, the girl stepped forward.

"Hello, I'm Tia. Are you Catherine?"

"*Oui.* I mean yes, I am," Catherine said somewhat uneasily, and then she added. "Tia is a lovely name."

"Her name means aunt in Spanish." Joe shifted his feet and leant on the sideboard. "My grandfather was Spanish. His daughter, my favourite aunt, died during my wife's pregnancy." He nodded at the portrait. "We chose the name Tia in memory of my aunt."

Catherine went to speak, but Tia got there first.

"I like your hair," she announced with her cute little voice.

Catherine softened her voice to mimic Tia's. "I can plait your hair like this; it's easy to do. Shall I have a go now?"

"Oh, yes, please."

"While you do that, I'll go and tell Nanny that Tia is ready for her tea."

"Wow," announced Joe as he returned with the young nanny. "You do look grown-up." Tia grinned widely and stroked her hair. Joe turned back to the nanny, "After tea Catherine and I will put Tia to bed, that'll give you more time to clear up."

Catherine entered the dining room and was faced with a chandelier sparkling from the ceiling, a candela flickered on the table as it lit up the best china, and a record was playing soft, classical music.

"This is too much," Catherine said as she sat down. "I've been used to living a plain life while I've been in France."

"I wanted to treat you," Joe explained in French. "And it's my way of saying thank you for obeying my instructions – and not getting yourself killed in the process."

"You know we obeyed all of our British contacts." Then she giggled. *"But believe me, Joe, those days are over!"* It felt strange, even though she'd never met him in France, she'd shared a past with this man. She felt her body relax as he reached over for the bottle of Pol Roger's Cuvee.

"Winston Churchill described this drink as 'In victory, deserve it'."

"I think that's appropriate for our time in France," she replied in perfect English. Then she smiled as she remembered all the etiquette lessons Gran had paid for. Those lessons might not have made her into a lady, but they did help to improve her English.

"A penny for your thoughts," he said.

"I was thinking about how much I owe to my gran. She raised me."

"But I thought you lived with your father?" he said as he drank some wine.

"It's a long story."

"Go on, I'm intrigued."

She moved her fingers along the stem of her wine glass. "Well, it started when my father's firm sent him to Dover, where he met my mother, Gran's only child. They married just before he returned to Calais. Life in France was hard; Dad's family disowned them because Mum was English!" Catherine turned away; she hated prejudice. "But Gran would often come over, and Mum and I would regularly stay with Gran in Dover." She leant back as the nanny brought in their food.

"Thank you," Catherine said to the stern-looking girl. "I can see you're a good cook as well."

The girl didn't answer and silently left the room.

"Where was I?" Catherine continued, not wanting to make an issue of the girl's rudeness. "Mum died when I was only five, and at the same time, Dad's firm announced they were moving to Paris. Dad was worried about caring for me while he was working. So, Gran persuaded him, just until he was sorted, that I should return with her to Dover." Her French pleat fell forwards, and she tossed it back. She smirked. "But I loved my gran, and by the time Dad was finally organised, I'd settled here, and I didn't want to return to France. So, the compromise was that I'd visit Paris during all of my main school holidays." Her voice dropped. "In 1939, Dad had a small stroke, so I left the sixth form to go and care for him. I wouldn't listen to Gran, and I got stuck when ..." she sipped her cuvee. "I was half English, so we destroyed our papers, moved to Normandy, and Dad arranged new identities for us both." She looked at her plate. "So how did you end up here?" she asked. "You're obviously Irish."

"You're observant," he said with a teasing chuckle that made her heart flip. "Early in 1944, David, my brother, was promoted once again and posted here. He managed to get me withdrawn from Normandy to help him with the planning of D-Day." He gave her a wide grin. "Mum and Dad claim David has their brains, while I have their good looks." He brushed back his thick black hair. "David went to Oxford, yet surprisingly he's a Labour supporter, and recently he's got himself involved with politics." He grinned. "Anyway, he's single, so he says his niece is his child as well as mine." Joe looked at his plate. "I wouldn't have got through this without him," he added as he cut into his food. "Do you like children?"

"Yes, I do," she answered. "But I don't want any of my own." She swallowed a mouthful of fish while watching his mouth curl. She straightened her upper body and said, "Unlike other women, I don't feel the need to have babies. I don't like them; they scream a lot and need constant attention." She saw him grimace. "Besides, my grandfather and my mother both died from heart attacks. I won't risk passing on a disorder to a child." She felt his hand reach out to her, and she could see he was about to offer sympathy. She didn't want it. She pulled her hand away and added, "I'm happy with my decision, and once my mind's made up, I never falter." She'd had to tell him the truth, and it was best to be forthright. "However," she added softly, "as far as older children go, I do like them. When I first went to help Dad, and before I worked in the café, I was a nanny for a while. So, do tell me more about your daughter."

Joe put his spoon down and smiled. "People are usually trying to stop me from rambling on about her, but as you insist ..."

As Catherine listened, she realised Joe's love for his daughter was inspiring. Joe was interesting to talk to, as well as gorgeous to look at, and in her experience, it was unusual to find a good looking man who also had integrity and understanding. She woke from her thoughts as Joe started to talk about Claude and her colleagues from the resistance.

"I'll always be grateful to you for what you did," Joe was saying as Tia bounded into the room.

"Nanny says it's my bedtime," she cried.

"Already! We've been talking too much!" laughed Joe. He winked at Catherine, adding, "We'll have our dessert later!"

Catherine looked at the floor, confused by the new emotion she was feeling.

Tia grabbed her nightie and ran to the bathroom. Catherine stood and surveyed the child's bedroom. It had pink and white fairies flying across the walls. She guessed Joe had allowed his daughter to choose the decoration.

"This is a beautiful room it reminds me of my childhood in—"

"I'm back!" shouted Tia as she ran into the room. "Catherine can read me a story and Daddy you can sit over there." Tia went to her bookshelf, which was low to the floor so that she could reach everything.

"Tia identifies every book by its pictures," Joe said as he plonked himself down on the chair. "I think she's hunting for her storybook of fairy tales."

"This one's my favourite," Tia announced, as she turned the pages to Cinderella, but then she changed her mind and flipped the pages to find another tale. "I want this one." Tia's little face beamed as she handed Catherine the open book, then she leapt into bed. "You look like the sleeping princess in that picture, and Daddy, you could be the prince who wakes her up."

Catherine turned to Joe, and she went to speak, but the words fell away from her. She wanted him to kiss her. She wanted him to hold her in his arms and never let her go. She turned away, embarrassed. She had to control these unfamiliar desires.

Joe cleared his throat. "Tia, let Catherine read the story. Besides, you're not supposed to know the end before she's finished."

"Daddy, I know all the stories," Tia said as she folded her little arms around her chest.

Catherine parked herself on the side of the bed, and with a soft tone, she said, "*Ma petit fille*, you lie down, and I'll begin." As Catherine read, she could feel Joe's eyes upon her, listening to her every word.

"You have a lovely voice," Tia said, closing her eyes.

Joe whispered, "It's that soft French accent, it's entrancing."

After a while, Catherine glanced down and saw Tia was sound asleep. A protective instinct took hold, and she lightly kissed Tia's forehead. She stood up, surprised at the strength of her stirring emotions. Joe turned off the lamp, his hand entwining with hers as he pulled her quietly out of the room and onto the landing. Then she felt his arms enclosing her and feeling her passion welling up, she turned towards him. She liked this man in a way she had never experienced before. Their bodies melted into each other, fitting together perfectly. His head came forwards, his lips touched hers, so tender and soft, making her stomach roll with pleasure. In the distance, she heard the door knocker and the nanny welcoming someone into the house.

"That's David's voice," Joe whispered. "When I told him about you, I made it clear he wasn't to come around tonight."

"I'd like to meet your brother," she murmured.

Joe sighed as he moved his arms away from her. "I guess we have no choice."

Catherine entered the sitting room and saw a large man listening intently to something the nanny was whispering. He looked towards them and instantly, the girl stopped talking and turned and scampered out through the side door. The man's dark hair was brushed back from his huge forehead, and his scruffy suit hung from his broad frame. She felt her hackles rise as he eyed her from head to toe then, as his slate-blue eyes glared at her through his thick-set glasses, she felt a chill running down her back. There was something about him that made her feel threatened, and it wasn't his enormous size or his awkward stance.

"Hello, you must be David," she said, holding out her hand.

"You're young," he answered without acknowledging her gesture, "and tall."

She stared into his bulging eyes, magnified by the lenses in his glasses. "I'll take being tall as a compliment," she replied. "But as for being young; I've certainly experienced a lot in my short life which—"

"I bet you have!" he interjected, with disgust in his tone.

"David don't be like that!" exclaimed Joe.

"I just say it as it is, there's nothing wrong with that." He turned back to Catherine and snorted. "Joe hasn't got pots of money, you know."

"I'm not interested in Joe's money," she snapped, finding herself getting annoyed. This man wasn't what she'd expected.

Joe grabbed his brother's trunk-like arm. "David, stop it. What's wrong with you?"

"Honestly, Joe, how could you?" David yelled as he pulled away. "Hannah was a superb woman, no one could ever replace her." His thick lips seemed to be spitting out his words. "And what about Tia? It's not good for the child to have ladies come and go in her life."

"You know full well that Catherine is the first woman I've invited here since Hannah died." Joe's voice sounded fierce. "I'm not like you, chasing every woman in a skirt." He scowled at his brother. "David, I don't understand you, stop being so unpleasant."

"I won't see my niece hurt." He turned and glared at Catherine. "And I won't see my brother hurt either."

"I don't intend to hurt either of them," Catherine said, flashing her eyes at Joe. Then she turned to David. "I like your brother and your niece very much. And whether you like it or not, I intend to be their friend."

David shifted his gaze from her. His glasses slipped down his hooked nose, and he thrust them back up. He didn't speak, then he stared blankly at her.

"Are you not able to understand me?" she asked sarcastically.

"You're very feisty," he grunted. His gaze moved to the portrait above the fireplace, "Hannah would definitely not approve." Catherine stared into the woman's azure-blue eyes, and for a moment, she believed David. Then fixing on Joe, David added, "You're making a fool of yourself Joe, this girl isn't right for you, and you need to think about your daughter in all this. Mark my words, this will end in disaster." He raised his massive shoulders as he breathed deeply, and then with an arrogant strut, he headed for the door.

CHAPTER 4

23rd May - 14th June 1947

"Hello love," Selina heard Mark yell, as he ran through the front door, then before she had time to answer, his strong arm grabbed her tiny waist.

"You're drunk," she teased as she tried to ease him away, but knowing she'd lost the struggle to escape his tender grip, she fell into his chest, loving the feel of his secure physique.

He pulled back. "I've got something to tell you. Brian had a great idea in the pub tonight. He suggested we could try to adopt a child, then we'd have a family of our own." She felt her breath increasing, and Mark's face ignited with pleasure. "The child would be ours to love and care for. We'd be parents, we'd be a mum and dad."

She stared at him. "But they wouldn't let the likes of you and I adopt, would they?" she said hesitantly.

"Why not? We've a house with two bedrooms, and I bring in enough money to support you and a child. There's lots of orphans from the war who need new families." Now she could see the longing in his eyes.

"Mark, do you think … can we try?" Her hands raised to her grinning face. "Imagine having little hands holding mine and calling me Mummy." Her hands abruptly fell back to her side, and her grin faded. "But I'd never be the real mother, would I?"

"So what if the child ain't our flesh and blood. You'd be the mother who brings the child up and cares for it, ain't that what being a mother is about?"

She couldn't stop her grin from reappearing. "I guess you're right."

"You'll be a mummy, I promise. We will adopt a child," his voice sounded determined, and she could feel her desire building again. Could their wish happen? Could Mark really fix things? His face tightened. "I'll talk to me brother, he's clever. He'll help me find out how to sort stuff."

In a dreamlike state, she murmured, "So, we might have a family after all." Then her voice turned melancholic. "But I doubt they'll let us adopt. We're not respectable like others are."

"That's rubbish," he replied.

*

Two weeks later, Selina held Mark's hand as they walked towards her mum's new home. Selina found herself thinking about her dad's friend Cyril. He'd been such a help when Dad was ill, and now she was grateful to him for finding her mum such a perfect little house. It was positioned a few streets away from theirs, and right by a bus stop. Her dad would have been pleased her mum was sorted. She halted as her father's dying face returned to her memory. Mark's hand pulled her forwards.

"Come on, love, we need to hurry."

She walked on, deciding that at least her dad hadn't seen her recent heartache. She smiled. He would have been proud of Mark's adoption plans. Her thoughts turned back to her mother; Selina knew the infertility issue was hurting her mum, she wanted grandchildren. This adoption idea had given her mum new hope, and a vitality Selina hadn't seen for a while. She grinned, Mark had promised Dad he would take care of both of his women - Selina and Eileen – and now she knew he meant it. They arrived at her mum's front door, and Mark gave it a sharp knock. Instantly, it flew open. Her mum's best tweed skirt looked a little tight, while her beige, short-sleeved jumper hung loosely over her large build.

Her mum's eyes sparkled as they fell on her. "I hope Brian's right about this place," she said, holding her coat in her arms.

"Whatever happens, Eileen, we're all in this together, as a family," Mark said.

Selina's mum grinned broadly.

"Let's get a move on, the bus is due soon," Mark announced. He put out his arm to assist her mum.

While Selina sat on the bus next to Mark, she glanced across at her mum. She noticed her mum's rounded body was rigid, and her hands held each other like a belt fastening her tightly to her seat. One of her hands moved as she wiped her eyes, then it fell back to hold the other again. Selina understood that this adoption was a dream they both craved, and it would be a release from all the sadness they'd suffered. But she still felt they were living in hope and like before, their hopes could die in front of them. A new sense of strength took hold. For all their sakes, Selina had to make sure their hopes didn't die. Putting out her arm, she announced,

"Mum, ours is the next stop."

The office was easy to find, and the receptionist was extremely helpful. They were introduced to a Mrs Bartram who spoke to them for about five minutes. After leaving the building, Selina beamed as she stared first at her mum, then back to Mark.

"At least she agreed to give us an appointment to discuss the process."

"It all sounded positive to me," Mark said, winking at Eileen.

"Selina, love," her mum's short blonde-grey curls spun around her face as she turned. "I think that Mrs Bartram was interested in you and Mark. I know she was busy, but she did seem keen for you to return for that appointment with her."

Looking for reassurance, Selina glanced at Mark.

"Yes, I'm certain she wants us to apply to be adopters," he said, as he took a puff of his roll-up.

"I wish our Harold were here to share this news," her mum sighed before giving one of her meaningful laughs. "This is brilliant, love, just what the doctor ordered."

Selina couldn't bring herself to smile. In her experience, doctors weren't warm-hearted people.

Mark's eyes gleamed. "I'll write to me mum and dad and tell them our plans." He took another puff. "And when we get home I'll pop round to tell our Brian we have an appointment. He's going to be pleased, it was his idea, after all."

On the following Saturday, Selina walked into the room to see Mark's face was tight around his scar line, his eyes lost in thought.

"I've got a reply letter from me mum," he mumbled. He gulped his tea. "They're not happy about the adoption idea." Selina sunk down beside him. He held up the letter and read. *"It's not the same as having your own child, it wouldn't be yours, and it won't be a family member."* He smirked. "That's Dad's words, he's telling her what to write." He glanced back down at the letter. *"The child may come with problems, why would you want to take them on?"*

Selina stared at him, anger swirling inside her like a whirlwind. "All parents have to cope with whatever is needed," she cried. "Problems could come with children you give birth to."

Mark nodded. "My parents shouldn't be adding to our heartache. I can't believe they're being like this. There's a note scribbled at the bottom of the letter; it's written in Dad's handwriting." He read, *"Why waste your time and money on bringing up someone else's kid? You're not the real father and Selina ain't the real mother – of any child. Don't do it, son."*

Selina put her hands to her face. "If your parents can't accept us as the real parents, then other people wouldn't either."

"Don't say that, love. Other people ain't like them." But his disappointment showed through his eyes.

"It isn't my fault I can't have children," she sobbed. "All I want is to be a mother."

"They don't get it; they think they're giving advice. They can't see how cruel they're being. You have to ignore people like them."

But Selina felt so let down. Why couldn't his parents embrace the adoption idea like everyone else had done? Her mum was ecstatic about the prospect of having a grandchild, why couldn't his parents be like that?

Mark stood up and threw the letter in the bin. "This ain't a negative thing, it's a good thing, for the child and for us. Yes, love, I'm talking about our child, the one we will have!"

"But …"

"No more buts, if anything me parents have shown me that to be a father ain't a biological thing. Fatherhood grows from caring for a child, which is something me old man has never done, and that's why he doesn't understand."

"Mark, where do you get your thoughtful nature from?"

"I watched and learnt from Harold."

CHAPTER 5

2ⁿᵈ - 3ʳᵈ June 1946

Catherine felt a tender kiss on her lips, and her eyes opened to the light streaming through the curtains.

"Good morning," murmured Joe.

"The prince has woken me," she chortled as she kissed him back. "I've been asleep all these years, but now I think that's changed. In your arms, I'll never be cold again." She cuddled into his pyjamas, knowing that she meant every word.

He held her tightly. "I'm glad I've warmed your heart," he whispered. Then he laughed as his hand caressed her long silky nighty. Catherine jumped as the bedroom door suddenly flew open, and Tia ran in.

"I forgot to lock the door last night," whispered Joe as he tried to sink below the blankets.

"Oh, Catherine's here!" yelled Tia. "Move up and let me in." She jumped on the bed. "We're all together, and I like that," she said as she snuggled in next to Catherine.

Without thinking, Catherine uttered, "This feels like a proper family." Then she felt herself blush.

"Daddy is Catherine living with us now?" Tia asked.

Catherine sat bolt upright. "No, your daddy and I ... are just friends."

Joe looked Catherine in the eye. "You must know I'm in love with you."

She stared at him, then back at Tia. "I admit I too have fallen in love ... with both of you. I didn't plan to ..."

Joe sat up and took Catherine's hand. "In that case, will you give me the honour of becoming my wife? The war taught us both that life is short. I intend to live every minute as fruitfully as I can, and I can only do that if you're by my side."

"Yes," she stated, not moving her eyes from his. "I'd love to be your wife." She then kissed him passionately, her attention only taken away by Tia clapping her hands, while shouting with glee. Catherine whispered to Joe, "I never thought I was capable of loving a man, and as for being a *maman*..."

Joe bounded out of bed. "Well, then, let's get sorting." Grabbing his shirt, he said, "I need to let work know I won't be in today. Tia, you run to your room and call nanny to come and dress you. Catherine, up you get, we need to visit Win. I want to do this properly."

"You're right, Joe," Catherine agreed. "Gran has to be the first to know."

Tia hopped and skipped back to her room, shouting for her nanny to hurry up.

"She's excited because she knows she's about to get a mother," Joe said, doing up his trousers. "It's a shame she doesn't remember Hannah."

"I never thought I'd be a mother, but I'm looking forward to it now." Catherine laughed as her dress slid down her slender body.

"It seems I've made the right decision then," Joe said before giving her a long kiss.

Tia ran back into the room and flung her arms around her father's legs. "I'm so happy."

"I love my little girl," Joe whispered. Then he added, "And I love the tall, elegant woman standing beside her." He straightened his back. "So, do we have breakfast, or do we go and face Win?"

"Win first," Catherine and Tia said together.

Joe groaned. "I can see the two of you are going to be a forceful pair."

As they marched towards Gran's house, Catherine took Tia's hand. When they reached the gate to the newly tidied garden, Tia wriggled free and ran to the front door, pulling the cord to the bell.

Anna appeared instantly. "I'm sorry, Anna," Catherine said. "Tia pulled the cord before I had a chance to use my key."

"That's alright, my love," Anna smiled as she stood back to let them in. "Your gran's reading her morning mail," she said, pointing to the parlour. She turned to Tia. "Would you like anything to eat, my dear?"

"No, thank you," Tia replied shyly.

Catherine indicated towards the room. "We'll go and see Gran." Then taking Joe's hand, she nudged him forwards.

Gran stood up from her desk. "Hello, my darling and how lovely to—"

"We've come to tell you something," interrupted Tia.

Gran's body stiffened. "Oh, and what's that?"

Catherine noticed Joe fiddling with his jacket and his face looked edgy. She nodded at him, hoping to encourage him to speak.

He gulped. "Mrs Demore, I would like to ask your permission …" he gulped again … "your permission … to take your granddaughter's hand in marriage."

Catherine watched as Gran's face turned grey. "No," she responded sharply. She turned to Catherine. "It's so soon, and you promised you'd—"

"Gran, you didn't wait very long before you married Grandfather and you had a wonderful marriage together," Catherine interjected. "Now I've met Joe. I know he's right for me."

"I knew you would marry and leave me, just like your mother did, but honestly, already?" Gran turned to Joe. "You're a good man, and over the last month I have forgiven you for using my granddaughter in the war, but …" she fell quiet.

"Gran, you know how much your approval means to me," pleaded Catherine.

Gran continued to stare at Joe, then her expression softened. "I guess you had better make an honest woman of my granddaughter!" she said, shrugging her shoulders. Her focus turned to Catherine. "I suppose you will only be moving down the road, which isn't as bad as moving to France!"

Catherine gave Gran a huge hug. "I'll always be here for you." Then she took a deep breath, remembering her gran had organised a large church wedding for her mother. "Gran, a *petit* do at the registry office is all I want." She could see the disappointment in Gran's face, then she glanced at Joe, knowing the lack of a church would upset him too. With determination, Catherine added, "I don't believe in God, the war took away the faith that I had, so I don't want a *gros,* I mean big church affair." She sighed. "I just want to be … Mrs Lawrence and I want to get married as soon as possible," she added as she squeezed Joe's hand, hoping he would uphold her wishes.

Joe gazed at her for a while and then turned to Gran. "I can't force Catherine to marry in a church." His expression stiffened as he added, "I'm Catholic, so the church is vital to me, but it didn't protect my first wife from being killed! I want to marry your granddaughter, so I have to accept her atheist views, even though I will never share them."

Catherine inwardly glowed. Against his own beliefs, Joe had supported her, he'd given her what she wanted!

Gran looked at Catherine and chuckled. "Joe's discovered you like getting your own way!" Then she gave an understanding grin. "I respect him for putting you first. So, if that's what you want … but you'll still wear a wedding dress, won't you? And this little one could be a bridesmaid?"

"What's a bridesmaid?" asked Tia.

Catherine realised she had pushed Gran enough. "OK, Gran, I'll do that for you." She turned to Tia. "At the wedding, you'll get to wear a pretty dress like me. You'll have to *marche*, that is walk with me, and be my little helper for the day."

"Oh yes, I want to do that," Tia readily agreed.

"Right then," said Joe. "Let's go to the registry office and book a date." He winked at Gran. "We'll have our reception at Twelve restaurant, it's the best place in Dover." His face suddenly dropped, and he looked at Catherine. "We'll have to go and see Ada, Hannah's mother, and tell her we're getting married. I don't want her to find out from someone else, and then there's David, of course."

45

"I like Uncle David," Tia said, then she pulled a face at Gran. "But my Granny Ada isn't very nice. I don't like her."

Joe bent down to his daughter. "Tia, you know you mustn't say that. Granny Ada loves you."

"I'm hungry," Tia replied dismissively.

"Ok, Tia, breakfast first and then we will start our jobs." Joe stood up and looked at Catherine. "Ada isn't an easy woman, and she's not going to be pleased that I'm remarrying. We have a difficult time ahead."

CHAPTER 6

23rd June - 28th June 1947

As she put her shaking hands under her knees, Selina knew it wasn't the temperature of the room that was making her tremble. Today was either the start of a dream or the finish of a dream, and she wasn't sure which outcome it would be. Mrs Bartram's brunette hair, combed tightly in a bun, seemed to have the effect of pulling her slightly ageing skin behind her temples.

"Firstly," Mrs Bartram explained, "you need to know about the different processes you'll need to complete to become adoptive parents." Along with her rimmed spectacles and protruding chin, her genteel voice seemed to add to her distinguished appearance. "There are forms to fill in, interviews to have, and references to get before any decision can be made about adopting a child." She peered over her glasses at Selina. "Then you will have to wait for a child to be matched with you." This was more than Selina had bargained for, but at least once they had the child, it would all be over.

"We don't mind if it's a boy or a girl, as that's usually up to nature anyway," Mark said. Selina was glad he was doing the talking; Mrs Bartram was scary. "We'd consider an older child," he added, "but the younger, the better. In fact, if we had a choice, we'd prefer a baby." She didn't know how Mark could speak so boldly, she could never be as brave as he was.

Mrs Bartram's face seemed to tense, and her tone became abrupt. "You need to know that in the first few months of the child's placement, the mother can change her mind and take the child back."

Selina's heart broke in two, and she found herself whispering, "But I'd fall in love with the child straight away. To have it taken away during the first few months …"

"During the placement, you're only caring for the child." Mrs Bartram's nose seemed to turn upwards as she spoke.

Selina trembled. "I'm not sure we'd cope with losing our child back to the mother; it would be like a bereavement." Thinking about her father, she added, "And it's too soon to go through that again."

"You must appreciate that I have to explain what might happen," Mrs Bartram said, and her tone softened. "But the reality is that the child often remains with the adoptive family. It's just all part of the process you must go through." She gave an understanding smile. "I know it's hard for you, but we must give the mother a final chance." Mrs Bartram's tone became rigid again. "Then, after about six months into the placement, there will be a court case which, if all goes well, will make the child legally yours."

"Court?" The shock at this development made Selina's knees wobble.

"Yes, you will need to go to court. The law, since the Adoption of Children Act 1926, has become a lot more regulated. There's even talk of it becoming more formal in the future." Mrs Bartram's voice softened again. "But the good news is that the Act means that once the court decides the adoption can happen, you will be the child's permanent and secure parents, and then no-one can take the child away from you."

"So, the child would be our child, mine and Mark's?"

"It would be yours completely."

The idea of going to court sounded petrifying and not something Selina relished. But her dream of being a mother suddenly seemed within reach. She wanted it to happen right now; she'd done all her waiting already. "How long will it take … until this is all over and we're officially parents?" The word 'parent' was something she'd imagined being for such a long time.

"It may take up to a year to get you to the approval stage, then there's the placement on top of that. However, we have many orphans now. The war was cruel, and things are moving faster these days." A faint frown came over Mrs Bartram's face. "The demand for care outweighs the capacity that we have available. Our buildings are overflowing, and conditions are not always good." She looked tenderly at Selina. "But you must understand, we have a responsibility to do all these checks. We've learnt that some of the evacuated children had to cope with appalling things. Adults are not always the best when it comes to caring for others."

Selina uttered, "I'll be a good, caring mother. My mother was a good teacher." She felt Mark's hand on hers, and he clasped it encouragingly.

"We do understand," he said. "And we're sure we want to go through with all of this." Selina nodded, feeling too emotional to say anything else.

"In that case, I'll go through this form with you now, and then I'll explain in more detail about the processes. I just wanted you to understand that it's a long system to go through."

Selina felt Mark squeezing her hand again. "We want to be put into your system as soon as possible," he said assertively. Selina smiled. Mark was going to fix things just like he always did. But this time, it did feel different, as so many things could still go wrong.

"We need to reply to your parents' letter," Selina said as they returned home. "We have to tell them we're going through with the adoption." She went and took some writing paper from the drawer. "I'll do it, then I'll start making lunch."

After a while, Selina looked up. "Does this sound alright?" she asked, and then, without waiting for a reply, she started to read.

"Dear Mr and Mrs Tozer. We are writing to let you know that we are going ahead with trying to adopt a child. If we're successful, then the child will be ours forever. We hope you can accept this, as we will love our child unconditionally. Legally, our child will have your surname, and you will be the grandparents. We promise to encourage the child to love you, and we hope you both will respond likewise."

Selina looked across at Mark. "From now on, I'm going to fight for my future child."

"I can see that, love." Mark took the pen from her hand. "Give it here, and I'll add my bits." Mark busily scribbled his responses to his parents' previous comments and finished with,

"If you can't understand and support us, then I'll have no further contact with you. Regards, Mark."

He looked at Selina and sealed the envelope. "My parents need to understand, and their disapproving attitude has to stop." He stood up. "I'm off to the Post Office, lunch can wait."

*

It was five days later when Selina picked up a letter from the hallway. "I think this is from your mum." Her eyes grew wider. "I hope they've accepted our adoption plans now."

"You open it love," Mark said, following her to the sofa. "My eyes can't focus yet, it's too early on a Saturday morning."

She sat down, pulled open the envelope and read...

'Dear Mark and Selina. We still don't understand why you want to take on someone else's kid. You aren't ever going to be its real mum and dad.'

Selina stopped and glared at Mark, her eyes filling with tears.

"We told them the child would be ours," Mark shouted. "Why can't they see that biology ain't everything?"

Selina pushed her hair back from her forehead and wiped the perspiration from her neck. With a heavy heart, she continued.

'If you're still determined to go ahead with the adoption idea, then I will try to come to terms with it – even though your father still doesn't approve.'

Mark winced. "Dad's standing over her again; he wants us to know he isn't happy."

'If the adoption does happen, then we'll both have no choice but to try to support you.'

Selina rubbed her brow and muttered, "There's another scribble at the bottom."

"PS, Mark, I'll do what I can to get your father to come around to the idea." Selina's eyes remained fixed on the page, while her mind was consumed with sorrow.

Mark frowned. "Dad's walked away again." He touched Selina's hand. "At least they've said they'll try. But we have to face it, love, they don't understand." Selina felt his hot, damp arm around her as he drew her into a hug. "I'm telling you, I'm going to make sure you're a mother, and if they can't see that, then they're stupid. Nothing's going to get in the way of our dream. We'll be real parents one day. Who cares what they, or anyone else, thinks."

CHAPTER 7

3rd June 1946

"Catherine, is that you?" a voice shouted as Catherine and Joe walked across the restaurant car park.

"Angeline," Catherine yelled as her small friend charged into her arms.

Angeline looked up at her, eyes wide. "When Gregory Jones came back from the army he told me you'd died in France."

"How strange," Catherine replied, as she once again remembered Gregory. She'd hated it when the adjoining boys' school had their Latin lessons in the girls' building; boys were such a waste of time. Gregory had been a pest, but she'd never let that bother her.

Angeline flicked her sable-brown curls behind her shoulders. "I should have known you'd survive in France. You're a fighter. I remember how you used to sort out those bullies in school."

"Those girls needed sorting! I wasn't going to let them hurt you." Catherine smiled at her old school friend. "It's so great to see you! When I first returned to England, I did try to find you, but your parents had *deplaced* – moved away."

"Yes, they've gone to Thornton, in Blackpool. Oh, Catherine, please tell me you're home for good."

"I am, and I'm living back at my gran's." Catherine grasped Joe's hand. "Angeline Cotterill, I'd like to introduce you to Joseph Lawrence, my fiancé."

"Oh, congratulations." Angeline turned to Joe. "You're a fortunate man."

Joe shook her hand. "I am indeed and—"

"I'm going to be a bridesmaid," Tia interrupted, dancing around.

"This is my future stepdaughter," Catherine announced, as Joe reached to steady Tia. Then she noticed Joe glancing towards the car. "I'm sorry Angeline, we've got to go and visit someone now. Could we arrange a time to catch up properly?"

"How about you come to mine tonight?" Angeline asked. She reached in her handbag and scribbled her address on a menu card. "My two sons are only four and two and my husband, Saul, is working late. He's the head chef at this restaurant."

"He works here? And you have a family? I can't wait to meet them." Catherine glanced at the note. "Oh, that's not far from Gran's. I can cut down the alley that runs through the cliff." She turned to Joe, who was now appearing anxious to leave. "See you around eight, *mon amie*," she whispered as she hugged Angeline.

*

"Tia's fallen asleep in the back," Catherine announced, as she turned back to the front of the car.

Joe nodded while still concentrating on the road ahead. "Before we get to Ada's, I need to explain something," he said hesitantly. "The thing is, Ada's always blamed me for Hannah's death." He slowed down behind a tractor. "I suggested Hannah go and visit her mother while I watched over Tia." He accelerated and overtook the tractor. "Hannah was returning from visiting Ada when her car took that direct hit." He changed gear. "Ada lost her husband and her son in the war. When her daughter died as well, she felt like everything had been taken from her."

"I understand why your mother-in-law would disapprove of anyone taking her daughter's place, but ..."

Joe slowed down. "You can still see the crater in the road. They haven't mended it very well." He suddenly seemed a million miles away. They hit a huge dip in the road, and she realised that this must be the place where Hannah had died. She glanced around at all the fields and decided it couldn't have been a coincidence, the German pilot must have been aiming at Hannah's car.

With trepidation, she asked, "What would Hannah have thought about you and me?"

"She'd want Tia and I to be happy," he said, smiling across at her. Then he fell silent.

As they arrived at their destination, Catherine thought the house looked old and rambling; it was as if no one had lived in it for years.

"I'm not moving," screamed Tia. "I don't want to see Granny Ada." Joe reached in and pulled her out of the car. Tia was kicking and yelling at him. Catherine watched as Joe wrestled with his daughter while holding her in the air.

"Tia, it's always important to do what is right, and seeing your grandmother is the right thing to do," he said firmly. Catherine was impressed as Joe strode up the path while vehemently hanging onto his screaming child. With his free arm, he knocked on the door.

A woman with greasy, tawny-grey hair opened the door. Her shoddy blouse tucked into her unfashionable skirt made her look older than she probably was. "What's wrong with Tia? What've you done to upset her?" the woman snapped.

Joe seemed to ignore the bitterness in her voice. "I hope you don't mind us calling like this." He gazed across at Catherine. "Ada, I would like you to meet Catherine."

Catherine stretched out her hand, but Ada turned away as if she hadn't seen her.

"Come in," Ada said. "It's cold standing out there. I'll put the kettle on. Tia, I've a cake inside."

Tia stopped screaming, and Joe placed her down on the floor. She held his hand and sheepishly walked into the house with him. Catherine was one step behind them. It wasn't a place she wanted to be, but for now, it seemed the right thing to do.

Ada raised her cracked teacup to her thin lips and over the stained tablecloth, she asked Joe about Tia. The woman seemed to spend her time disagreeing or making derogatory comments towards Joe. Catherine sat back and remained silent. How Joe coped with this unpleasant woman was beyond her comprehension. Joe was a kind man, she wished she could be that reasonable. She could see she had a lot to learn from him. They finished their tea, and she watched Joe as he shuffled awkwardly in his chair.

"Ada, I have some news to tell you. Catherine and I ... plan to marry. We've just booked the date. We managed to get a slot on the 24th August, this year."

Ada's face turned red with anger. "What?" she snarled. "Why haven't you told me about this woman before now?

And David never mentioned you were seeing anyone, either."

"Catherine and I met recently," Joe responded, without appearing at all ruffled.

"So why the rush?" Ada asked, and then she shrieked, "Is the girl pregnant?"

Catherine marvelled at Joe's calm veneer as he answered, "No, Catherine isn't pregnant. We just want to get married." He took a breath and resumed, "Anyway, we're not total strangers, we knew of each other during the war."

"You knew each other in the war, when my Hannah was alive?"

Catherine held her breath while Joe replied. "We didn't meet when Hannah was alive. Catherine was in the French Resistance and for a very short while I was her contact. We only met last month, and now we're in love." He winked across at her.

For the first time, Ada turned to her and screeched, "You're French!"

"*Je suis fier de mon heritage.*"

Then Ada turned and snapped to Joe, "You're not even marrying an English girl."

He stood up. "Catherine, I think it's time to go."

Ada launched into an attack. "She," pointing towards Catherine, "will not replace my Hannah. How could you even think of marrying so soon, let alone to some young French tart?"

Joe signalled to Tia that they were leaving. Ada seemed to be getting more agitated.

"I won't be at this foolish wedding," she shouted. "How could you do this to Tia, a French girl bringing up my Hannah's child?"

Tia started howling, and Catherine felt her fiery personality bubbling to the surface. Her temper had taken over, it was time to speak her mind.

"Ada, firstly, my father and I fought with the French Resistance." She saw the woman was glaring at her, probably because she was now speaking in fluent English. "He, along with many other French people, sacrificed his life to keep France and may I add, England, free from the strong possibility of permanent Nazi tyranny. The Nazis were prejudiced against the Jews, can't you see you're doing the same towards the French?" Catherine's breath increased. "You're being prejudiced towards me, but I've also experienced French prejudice against the English. People can be cruel; these primitive tribal behaviours must stop!" Then she added sarcastically, "But you obviously think prejudice and hatred is a good thing!" Catherine looked across at Joe, who was busy trying to console Tia.

She turned back to Ada. "Secondly, as for Tia, I never expected to be a mother, and I don't intend to have any children of my own, so I aim to love Tia as if I'd given birth to her. However, I promise you I'll not allow Tia to forget her heritage. I will encourage her to learn all about her mother. I'll always try to do what is right for Tia because she'll be my child too. If you can't see that our marriage is a good thing for Tia, then I'm sorry for you. What worries me is that the person you'll be hurting the most will be Tia."

While staring at Ada, Catherine became aware that Tia had fallen silent. She found herself feeling sorry for Tia's grandmother. She was a lonely woman who'd lost so much. Her tone softened. "My gran has also lost her daughter and her husband. She always said that I was the one who gave her a reason to live. Tia could do the same for you." Ada scowled at her. "You should tell Tia stories about your daughter, just as my gran told me all about my mother. Grandmothers are vital, and Tia needs you, just as I needed my gran." She could see Joe was looking stunned. But she'd needed to take control, this woman required telling. She stared at Ada, but there was no response coming from the woman's lips. Turning sharply to Joe, she commanded, "Let's go now." Her eyes fell on Tia, who was starting to cry. "Joe, I think we should take Tia home to the nanny before we see David. I don't expect that's going to go well either and I won't allow Tia to get this upset again."

CHAPTER 8

19th March 1948

Selina scrubbed the kitchen floor, her apprehension pushing her hands faster. She stopped and stared at the tiles. What would the panel of dignitaries whom she'd never met be saying about her and Mark today? She hoped their application form, Cyril's reference, and their interviews with Mrs Bartram had been good enough for them to be accepted as adopters. Her wet sponge dripped soapy water onto the floor, but she sat upright. What gave these intellectual people the right to decide if she and Mark were capable of adopting a child? She scrubbed at the stone tiles again. Why couldn't Mark have been granted the day off work? She was dreading seeing Mrs Bartram without Mark being there. Her heart sunk as she heard a knock at the door.

Selina stood back as Mrs Bartram waltzed straight through into the hall. She waited as Selina closed the door, then she announced sharply, "You're through the panel, you've passed!"

"Really?" Selina cried as they made their way into the lounge. "We've done it, have we?" She felt herself blush; did she sound stupid?

Mrs Bartram sat her thin frame into an armchair. "Yes, you've been approved as adoptive parents. You are now on the waiting list for a child."

Selina practically fell into the other chair. "I can't believe it." Then she realised she could relax. The wait was nearly over, and they were going to have a child.

Mrs Bartram smiled slightly. "As you know, another panel of professional people meet regularly to match our children with the information they have on our approved parents."

"All these professional panels!"

"I know, but once they find a suitable child, I'll be back to tell you. It might take a while; they have to find a child that's a match for you and Mark." Mrs Bartram's threadlike eyebrows raised as she stared through her narrow spectacles at Selina. "However, once they've agreed to a match, the placement could be quick. Are you both ready for that?"

"Yes, we're more than ready. It's all this waiting that's been hard for us." Selina could feel her heart hammering against her ribs as her mind kept repeating the words, *we're going to have a child!* Her excitement took hold, and she stood up. "The child's room is ready. No, *our* child's room is ready. Oh, doesn't that sound amazing?" She walked towards the stairs. "Mark's painted the room cream. It seemed the safest thing to do as we don't know the sex of the child we'd be having. Can I show you?"

Selina was conscious she was skipping up the stairs, she was so desperate to show Mrs Bartram their hard work.

Mrs Bartram slowly climbed behind her. When Selina reached the top of the stairs, she turned and waited for her.

"This is my favourite room in the house," she said as she opened the bedroom door. Waiting for Mrs Bartram to enter, she added, "Brian and Sandra gave us some of their children's old furniture. The small bed and this large wardrobe are from them, but we bought the little shelves and the drawers ourselves." Frowning, she added, "Mark isn't much of a handyman, his arm plays up if he tries to do too much, but Brian was great with helping to fit the furniture into the room. It wasn't easy because of those two windows." She pointed to the one at the side, looking out towards the church and the other one at the front, looking over the street.

Mrs Bartram nodded approvingly. "Well, it all seems ideal."

Selina opened the wardrobe. "We've been busy buying second-hand clothes," she explained. She waved her arm at the many children's clothes hanging in the cupboard. "We've collected both boys' and girls' things." Mrs Bartram had told them to be prepared for either sex. "Look, I've put the girls' things at the front of the wardrobe and the boys at the back." She stared at her collection. "But our Sandra's been great, there's a lot of second-hand stuff from her Stanley and Minnie." She touched the garments; she was proud they had outfits for every age and occasion. "I've arranged the two sections in order of size, starting with the smallest at the front, and the larger sizes at the back." She took out Minnie's old romper suit. "I do love the idea of a baby," she sighed. "But I guess an older child would probably be easier."

"So, would you and Mark still prefer a baby?" Mrs Bartram's voice was softer than usual.

"A baby would be wonderful, but we've accepted the child could be any age, especially if it's an orphan from the war." Selina's eyes focused on Mrs Bartram. "We'll be delighted with whatever happens." Mrs Bartram fell silent. Selina turned to put the clothes away, her head spinning with plans for her future child. If they had a girl, she'd teach her daughter to be understanding, but also outgoing like Mark. She wanted her daughter to be a woman who could manage in this 'new world' that was taking shape all around them. But if they had a boy, she'd teach him to respect others and be strong like Mark. She shut the wardrobe door. How lucky they were to be getting a child of their own. "Mark's going to be relieved we're through the panel," she said to Mrs Bartram. "He said it would be okay, but I knew he was worried." She showed Mrs Bartram to the stairs. "I can't believe we're finally going to be a family. I feel as if I've woken from a nightmare and seen just how wonderful life really is."

"Let's hope you don't have to wait too long," Mrs Bartram replied with a smile.

CHAPTER 9

24th August 1946

Catherine squeezed Gran's hand as the wedding car moved slowly through the town. Her long fingers touched Gran's engagement ring, and somehow, Catherine felt its love flowing into her own hand. It was right she'd asked Gran to give her away. She turned to check that the bridesmaid's car was still behind them. She could see Angeline pointing at the white cliffs, but she guessed Tia wasn't interested. Catherine twisted back, feeling sorry that Tia's grandmother wouldn't be at the wedding. It upset her that Ada and David still didn't approve. Staring out of the window she felt nauseous as she recalled the awful night they'd told David they were getting married. Poor Joe had tried so hard to be gentle; he'd even asked David to be his best man. She shivered at the memory of David's shouting; he'd said he wasn't thrilled at the idea of supporting Joe to marry her. Her stomach rolled. But David was correct when he said she was "a bossy young girl who was single-minded and stubborn," she was proud of her determined nature. And just because she was nothing like Hannah, that didn't give David the right to say she wasn't able to be a caring mother to Tia. She hated the fact that David was consumed with the idea that she was different to Joe's first wife. Shrugging her shoulders, she surmised that David would never approve of her, and she wasn't sure she would ever be fond of him either.

"Your wedding dress looks beautiful," Gran announced as Catherine got out of the car.

"It's very tight," Catherine grumbled as she pushed down the cream bodice and adjusted the lace on her sweetheart neckline. "And this A-Line skirt is challenging to manage."

"Stop moaning," said Gran, before stretching up to realign one of the little cream flowers pinned into the braid of Catherine's heart-shaped headdress.

"Sorry, Gran," Catherine said guiltily. She appreciated that material was difficult to come by, and Win had paid a fortune for these dreadful wedding garments. She glanced at Gran. She did look splendid in her pink satin jacket and skirt, made from the same material as the bridesmaid's dresses. Her gran's large Gainsborough style hat, together with the broad padded shoulders in her suit, seemed to add to her gentility. As Catherine stared into her bouquet of pink roses sprayed with Stephanotis, she concluded that her gran was enjoying this moment, and that's what mattered.

Angeline walked over with Tia and puffed out Catherine's veil. "There, that's better, the veil now looks like a waterfall gliding down your back."

The rain had stopped, and the sun was peeping out from behind the clouds. As Catherine stood for the photos, she thought about the people already inside the registry office. At the front would be Joe's parents, Jack and Daphne, who had arrived from Ireland. On her side of the room would be Sam, Anna, and Phyllis. She smiled. Joe would be looking handsome in his full-dress army uniform. Next to him would be David. She guessed his army uniform wouldn't make him look handsome – nothing could. She shuddered as she thought about David's womanising. What did women see in him? Then again, he was rich, single and high-ranking in the army, perhaps that was the attraction. She remembered when Joe had told her that David's role in the war hadn't been a pleasant one. She sighed, she couldn't cast the first stone, she'd been merciless when she'd needed to be. Even though she didn't like David, she approved of Joe being close to his brother. She thought it was lovely that they were still working together, but she was intrigued by these post-war investigations.

The photos were over, and they strode towards the building. Catherine felt content, she had her gran by her side and her bridesmaids behind her. But as she stood at the entrance, her thoughts turned to her dad. He would have liked Joe, they were very similar. She wondered what her mother would have said and then with sudden vigour, she turned and gave Gran a hug.

Gran whispered, "They're here, you know. I saw a white feather lying in the grass as we had our photos taken."

Throwing back her French pleat, Catherine gave a loud laugh, and she squeezed Gran's hand. "You can read my thoughts so well." She wondered if Joe would ever understand her as Gran did. She had a feeling he would; he'd already shown potential. Catherine played with her mum's pearl choker while staring at the people sitting on the chairs lining the way towards the registrar. She turned around to see Tia holding onto Angeline's hand. Her little body looked rigid, and her face white. Catherine winked at Tia, while Angeline whispered something in Tia's ear. Then the music started.

Catherine turned to look forward again, and Gran glanced at her.

"It's time, my dear."

"Yes, Gran, it is!"

Everyone stood up as, arm-in-arm with her gran, she walked towards the rows of chairs. She could see Joe standing at the front, looking striking in his uniform. For a moment, she stopped. Walking towards Joe, wearing a smart dark-blue linen jacket and skirt that matched the colour of Joe's uniform, was Ada! Her hair was washed and set with tight curls, completely transforming her appearance. Joe hadn't told her Ada was coming to the wedding! Perhaps he hadn't known. Win pressed her arm, and they continued to advance. Her eyes fixed on Joe; her excitement was unbearable. She wanted to run to him, but she knew she couldn't. Catherine looked at David, who was standing by his chair in the front row, why hadn't he moved, he hadn't even turned to acknowledge her entrance? Ada was now standing beside Joe. Suddenly Catherine realised Ada was Joe's best man! This was a massive thing for Ada to do; it meant she was supporting Joe in his marriage to her! It felt extraordinary but somehow also completely right. She glowed inside as she remembered Joe's words, "It's always important to do what is right." She whispered to Gran, "Did you know about this?"

"It's been planned for weeks now." Gran dipped her head as she acknowledged a guest, then carried on. "Joe's been driving me over to Ada's to discuss things. The woman's just hurting inside, I've tried to guide her." They'd reached the front now so Catherine couldn't ask any more questions. Gran gave her a quick kiss before disappearing to her seat.

"I'm sorry dear," whispered Ada. "Can we start again?"

Catherine bent her head and replied quietly, "We certainly can, and thank you for this." She looked at Joe, who stood beside her. He winked at her and turned back to the front. Catherine gave her bouquet to Angeline, then watched as Angeline took Tia's little hand and walked her to their seats. Her gaze fell on David, she guessed he'd probably been thrilled not to be Joe's best man, but his beliefs about her weren't significant anymore.

After the meal, Catherine turned to Angeline. "I can't believe the restaurant managed to get this much food with post-war rationing. I only wish I could eat it, my stomach's been very unsettled lately."

"It's just wedding nerves, it's perfectly normal." Angeline leant forward and spoke softly, "Saul's heard that the restaurant might be for sale. If it's true, we're going to try to buy it. He'll be the head chef, and I'll run the front of house. It'll be a brilliant opportunity for us."

"That's wonderful news!" Catherine exclaimed. "I can see you as a great businesswoman."

"We'll see." As if the place was already hers, Angeline gazed cheerfully around the room.

Catherine nodded in the direction of Gran. "Look at Gran chatting to Ada. They do seem to be friends."

"They have so much in common, don't they? Your gran's great when it comes to helping others." Angeline turned to watch Tia, who was eating yet another cake. "I'm glad Tia hasn't made a fuss about sleeping at mine tonight."

"Tia said she didn't mind staying with the boys for one night."

"She's quite happy to play their boy games." Angeline turned to Saul, who was telling Thomas off for pushing Tia over. "Thomas is such a rough and tumble two-year-old. George is a lot more sensitive."

"Catherine," David said abruptly, looming in front of them. "Once Ada's finished saying goodbye to Win, I'm going to give her a lift home, she's very tired."

"Thank you, David. I appreciate it," Catherine replied.

"I'm not doing this for you," David retorted. "I'm doing it for Hannah, she would have wanted us to look after her mother."

"You're a very caring man," Angeline said, stroking his stocky arm.

"Family's important to me." He glared at Catherine. "I'll always protect them from being hurt." He bowed his head and walked off towards Ada.

Angeline patted Catherine on the back. "See, David thinks you're family now."

Catherine went to explain, but then she stopped. The reception was nearly over, David wasn't going to spoil her day now.

*

Catherine gasped as she stood at the window of the hotel bedroom. "Oh Joe, look at the magnificent view over the sea." Then she twirled around. "This split-level room is incredible." She ran to the bar, "Gin and tonic?"

Joe nodded, and Catherine opened the cabinet and twisted the top of the tonic water. "I'm glad we're not having a proper honeymoon. I've waited long enough. I

69

just want to move in with you and Tia." She handed him his drink. "I still don't see why David was cross about us letting the nanny go. I guess he doesn't like the fact that I'm now in charge." She went to take a sip of her drink, then stopped. "I still feel queasy all the time, and it's getting worse, not better."

Joe put down his glass and studied her. "I think it's time you saw a doctor."

"I admit, I am getting worried." She put down her drink and moved towards the stairs. "I'll race you upstairs," then giggling, she pushed her way past him.

CHAPTER 10

26ᵗʰ March 1948

Selina stood looking out from her lounge window at the rooftops below. They looked like a river meandering down to the estuary at the bottom. A loud knock abruptly brought her back to reality. Mark had left for work, so it had to be her mum, no one else would call this early on a Friday morning. Thinking something was amiss, she rushed to the front door.

"What's happened?" she said as she stood back to let the well-tailored Mrs Bartram through the door. "You're back so soon." Selina could hear the panic in her own voice, but she couldn't help it. "What's wrong? Mark isn't here. I can't …"

"Everything's alright," Mrs Bartram reassured her. "But we'd better sit down, I have something to tell you." Selina led her through to the lounge, and she felt her legs shake as she sat slowly in a chair.

"Does Mark need to be here?" she asked.

"No," Mrs Bartram replied as she sat down. "I'm here to inform you that the adoption panel met yesterday." Mrs Bartram gave her a grin. "There's a new baby girl that's come up for adoption, and they've matched her with you and Mark."

"What?" Selina shouted, then she put her hands to her mouth.

"She was only born on the 21st March, so I need to know your thoughts about taking on a newborn."

"How amazing ... a baby ... of our own!" Selina knew she sounded incoherent. "Oh, dear, did the mother die in childbirth then?"

"No. But I can't tell you any information I'm afraid. I take it Mark will be alright with this news. I mean about it being a newborn?"

"He'll be over the moon. We thought we'd get a child from the war, we never expected ... I can't wait to tell him."

"That's good. I did tell the panel you'd be fine with a newborn baby, but there's a problem because—"

"I can't believe we've been matched with a child already, let alone a baby!" interrupted Selina. "Will you thank the panel for me?"

"They're just doing their job," Mrs Bartram said abruptly. "The problem is there's an outbreak of measles at the orphanage, so the baby's still with the mother, but there's huge pressure for things to move quickly. The mother has been told to drop the child at the orphanage tomorrow morning. We want you to pick the baby up at midday."

Selina stared at her. "Tomorrow?"

"Yes. Midday tomorrow," Mrs Bartram stated firmly, then she added, "You'll need to go and buy some baby equipment. Can you sort it all today?"

Selina's body felt numb, she couldn't move.

"Selina?" Mrs Bartram said sternly.

"Yes … I'll get Mum to help me. I can't believe this is happening!"

"We need to act fast. I'll go back to the office and let the orphanage know that you can go tomorrow." Mrs Bartram took out a piece of paper from her handbag. "This is the address of the orphanage, and I've written the details down for you. Take a blanket to wrap the child in and Mrs Morrey, the manager, will meet you there. And remember, your collection time is twelve o'clock. Is that alright with you?"

Selina's mind was racing. "It's Saturday tomorrow, Mark will be able to come with me." She wanted to kiss Mrs Bartram, but instead, she raised her arms in the air and felt the relief pouring through her body. "At last, we're going to be parents!"

"Not quite yet." Mrs Bartram got up from her chair. "Remember we have to apply for that court order … and it could be six months before that happens. Selina, are you listening to me?"

Selina nodded, though her attention was elsewhere, she had things to sort and people to tell.

"I'll be in touch next week to see how you're getting on," Mrs Bartram said as they walked towards the hallway.

Having shown Mrs Bartram out, Selina grabbed her coat and bag. Then she ran to the sideboard and collected an envelope from the drawer. She charged out and ran down the road. Entering her mum's house with her key, she shouted at the top of her voice, "Mum, where are you? I need you."

Eileen appeared from the kitchen with a cup of tea in her hand.

"Mum, we're going to have a newborn baby girl," she blurted out, "and it's all happening tomorrow!"

Her mum's cup fell from her hand and tea flew in the air as the cup smashed onto the floor, but Eileen didn't seem to notice. "Are you serious? A baby? And I'm going to be a grandmother!"

"Yes, well, I hope so." Selina giggled as she bounced around. Then she took her mum's hands and started dancing around the floor with her. "It's a girl," they both sang at the top of their voices.

"Mum, you're going to have to help me, we need to go shopping now!"

Selina took the envelope from her bag. "We received this note yesterday, and I've read it ten times over. You know Mark wrote to his parents and told them we'd been approved and that we were waiting for a child to be matched with us?" Her mum nodded. "This is their reply, and it has money enclosed! Look, Mark's mother has written '*It's to buy things for your new child.*' I never expected them to show an interest, it's a huge breakthrough." She took out the money. "But I didn't imagine I'd be spending it quite so soon."

"Come on then, I'll get my coat," her mum cried. "We have a lot to do."

*

After a few hours, Selina's arms were aching. "I'd no idea we had to buy all this," she said as she held the basket containing the bottles, feeding equipment, powdered milk, nappies, safety pins, powders, blankets and bedding. "We'd better spend the rest of our money on outfits," she added. "I haven't got any newborn things in the wardrobe!" She moved towards the clothes section of the department store and reached for a tiny, newborn suit.

"This is gorgeous," she grinned, "but it's all costing a fortune; we've nearly spent every penny we have."

Her mum laughed. "That's what happens when you have a baby!"

CHAPTER 11

27th August - 30th August

1946

Catherine sat quietly, staring out at the hot day through the car window. She noticed the town planners had been busy, there were lots of new buildings appearing on the old bomb sites. Joe parked at Doctor Bryant's new purpose-built surgery, which Catherine thought looked far too modern for a private clinic. However, once inside, the clean and airy coolness offered welcome respite from the heat of the day.

"Doctor Bryant will be with you shortly," the young receptionist informed them.

Catherine perched on one of the cushioned chairs, but as she looked at Joe, she wondered if he'd really managed to get a cancellation slot. She surmised he'd probably told the receptionist she was an emergency case. Doctor James Bryant appeared through the door, and she immediately thought that he hadn't changed; somehow he'd always seemed middle-aged to her. He was a tall man, bald with a small amount of silver hair framing the bottom of his head.

He had a jovial, elongated face, and his bright eyes gleamed with delight.

"Hello, Catherine, it's lovely to see you again. My goodness, you are a young woman now. Where has the time gone? Win told me you were getting married. So, Catherine … Mrs Lawrence, when was the big day?"

"It was on Saturday," she stated proudly. Touching Joe's arm, she added, "But I'm glad the weather wasn't this hot."

Doctor Bryant laughed and shook Joe's hand. "Congratulations, it's nice to meet you, Mr Lawrence. Shall we go into my surgery?" Doctor Bryant sat down at his desk and gestured for them to sit. Catherine instantly felt at ease; as a child, Doctor Bryant had always looked after her well, and he was such a gentleman. "Well now, Catherine, tell me what's the matter."

She pushed back her French pleat. "As you know, my grandfather and my mother both died from heart attacks. Charles was forty-eight, and Cynthia was only twenty-six." Doctor Bryant nodded in agreement. "The thing is, my mother vomited a lot before she died. I don't know if the sickness was a symptom of her heart condition or not, but I've been sick a great deal lately." Her eyes fixed on his. "I'm worried I've inherited her heart condition."

Doctor Bryant looked thoughtful. "There is indeed a belief that heart attacks may have a hereditary connection to them, but we don't know enough about it yet." He scratched his head, "Let me examine you, and we'll see what we find. We'll also take a blood test, that should tell us a bit more."

At the end of the consultation, Doctor Bryant explained, "It'll take a while before we have the blood results. I'll be in touch as soon as I know anything." As they were leaving, he clasped her hand gently. "Please don't worry, my dear."

As Joe drove home, Catherine once again noticed how hard the constructors were working to restore the bomb-damaged sites of Dover. She felt sad for those who had died, but now she thought she might be dying too. She knew Joe couldn't bear to lose another wife, and then there was Tia … Why had she let herself get involved with this family?

"He thinks I'm ill, doesn't he?" Catherine murmured.

"No, he's just checking everything," Joe said, but his voice didn't sound very convincing. It was only a few days later when Catherine put down the phone and stood frozen to the spot. All she could think of was how relieved she felt that Tia was at Gran's. She ambled into the sitting room and sat down.

"Doctor Bryant's visiting us on his way home from his evening surgery, he says he has some news."

"I'm sure it won't be anything sinister," Joe said without looking up.

Catherine sat down, placing the daily paper on her lap. She stared at it, and after a while, she could tell Joe wasn't turning the pages of his book either. She finally heard the bell pierce through the house, and Joe went to answer it. The sitting room door was open, and as she stood up, Doctor Bryant rushed in.

"It seems, my dear Catherine, that you're feeling ill because you're pregnant!" he said, cutting straight to the point.

"No! I can't be," she exclaimed. "We've always been careful. Besides, I've had a few periods … But they were very light and some time ago."

The doctor gazed at her. "Occasionally, that can happen. But your blood results show that you're definitely pregnant."

She looked at Joe. "Our first night … It was the only time we weren't careful. Joe, do you think …?"

"Yes, I do," he said excitedly. "We've been so consumed by your past; we didn't think about the future."

"I must admit I was sure you were pregnant," Doctor Bryant said. "But I couldn't say anything until I had the proof. It was the fact that you'd only just got married that bothered me." He shrugged his shoulders. "But these things happen."

"But I … I don't want children," Catherine stammered.

"My tests show you're a perfectly healthy individual. There are no indications of any heart issues. I'm quite sure you'll be fine having this baby." Doctor Bryant was beaming. "Right, I'm off now. I'll leave you to your evening. I'll see myself out."

Catherine flung herself into a chair and looked up at Joe. "I never wanted this. I just hope …"

"You must stop worrying," Joe consoled her. "The doctor says you're fine." He touched her stomach, and she placed her hand on top of his.

"My stomach feels as if a butterfly is moving around in it, do you think it could be the baby?"

Joe rubbed his hand around her stomach. "Yes, I think it could. This child's a gift I never expected, it's incredible." He stood upright. "Let's go and tell Tia and Win, then when we get back, we'll phone my parents, and David, of course."

She felt her stomach move again and touching it once more, she groaned, "Gran won't approve, I fell pregnant before we were married."

*

"Gran," Catherine said as soon as they arrived at Win's house. "I have some news."

"I'll go and find Tia," Joe said excitedly.

Catherine took Gran's hand. "I've just been told that I'm pregnant. And I'm probably a few months gone."

Gran threw her arms around her. "This is marvellous news, I did wonder ..."

"You don't mind? You know I must have conceived before ..."

"I know, dear. I never did believe you slept in the spare room when you stayed at Joe's! But you're married now, and that's what matters." Then with a wink she added, "But we'll need to explain to Ada that being pregnant wasn't the reason you got married!"

"She won't believe us."

"Yes, she will, and what's more, I think Ada will be pleased. She's often mentioned she didn't want Tia to be an only child." Her eyes twinkled. "I've been working on her, she's stopped blaming the world for her loss and is looking forward to the future now. She calls me her new stepmum, so I've started calling her my stepdaughter. I'm glad because I wanted her to be there for you, Catherine."

"Pardon!"

"Joe's parents are in Ireland and Ada's only in Deal. So, I'm hoping that one day she'll be a stepmum to you." Gran chuckled. "Don't look like that, dear." Once again, she hugged her tenderly.

Joe walked in, holding hands with what looked like an angry Tia.

"I'm not coming home yet. I'm staying the night with Great-Grandma Win," Tia protested as she stood and folded her arms.

"Yes, I know," Catherine said. "We've just come to tell you something." She knelt beside her. "Your Daddy and I thought it would be nice for you to have a little brother or sister and—"

Tia's eyes lit up. "Oh, yes, please! Can I have a sister?"

"Well, I do have a baby in my tummy, but we won't know if it's a boy or a girl until it's born." Tia inspected her tummy then looked up at her as if questioning what she meant. "Babies grow in ladies' tummies, but they take time, so in about five months you'll know if you have a sister or a brother," Catherine explained.

Tia started leaping up and down, then she ran around the room singing, "I'm going to have a sister. I'm going to have a sister."

Catherine stood up and sighed wearily. "I give up, Joe. She'll understand in time." Then touching her stomach, she whispered, "We'll have to tell David now, and we know what he's going to say!"

"Don't you worry about him and his silly ideas," Joe said, linking his arm in hers.

"Joe," Gran said, "when you see David, would you invite him to come and have tea with me. We're all family now, and I think it's time we got to know each other better."

Joe nodded. "That's lovely of you." As he turned to check on Tia, Catherine went to speak, but she stopped as Gran gave her a meaningful wink.

CHAPTER 12

26th March 1948

"Mum, can you put the kettle on?" Selina asked as they entered the lounge. "Mark will be home soon. It does feel strange that he still doesn't know." She collapsed, exhausted, in the chair. "Look at the floor, our bags are everywhere."

"We've had quite a day!" her mum replied. "I can't wait till—"

Mark's key rattled in the lock, and they heard the door open. "I'm home," he called.

"We've just got in, we're in here," Selina called from the lounge, her excitement increasing. "You'll need to come and sit down. I have … I have something to tell you."

"What's with all these bags? What's going on?" Mark asked as he entered the room.

"Mrs Bartram called this morning," Selina replied. "Mark, there's a baby … a girl … a newborn. She's ours … just waiting for us."

Mark leaned against the wall to steady himself. "A girl – did you say a baby?"

Selina jumped up and guided him to his chair. She was crying now, and as she looked across at her mum, she could see she was crying too.

Eileen blurted out, "Apparently, you're to collect your daughter tomorrow. Here's the address."

Nodding, in agreement with her mum's words, Selina pointed to the note. "Read it, love."

He took the note and gazed at it, then he looked at her, and she saw moisture in his eyes. She watched as a tear trickled down his scar and ran down to his mouth. He wiped it away quickly.

"It's all here," he said, emotion oozing from his voice. "The address of the orphanage, the date and appointment time. It's happening then ... we're going to have our own child!"

Selina sat on his lap, and while kissing his tears away, she whispered, "Mark, you're going to be the proud father of a newborn baby girl. She was born on the 21st March. A life born on the first full day of spring." Her eyes fell on his. "And she's the start of our new life too. Can you believe it; we're going to be parents. We're going to have a baby!"

"What's the story behind it?" Mark asked, still seeming dazed.

"Mrs Bartram wouldn't say."

"Well, I guess it doesn't matter to us, does it?" Mark's face returned to normal. "Tell me what needs doing then," he said excitedly.

Selina laughed, "You can help us to unpack these bags."

Mark returned from emptying a bag upstairs, and Selina looked to her mum. "It feels funny, we assumed we'd never need my old cot, but now we do!"

"I know, I'm thrilled to be using it again," her mum replied as she emptied the last bag of goodies. "I do love these new baby bottles."

"I'll walk Eileen home, and then I'll bring the cot back with me," Mark said.

"Don't worry, love," her mum said as she went to get her coat. "I'll watch over him while he climbs in the loft." She turned to Mark. "But you'll need to make sure you find all the parts to the cot. Cyril dismantled it when he put it up there for me."

"The bits slot together easily," Selina assured Mark. "We'll assemble it when you get back. But be careful with your arm, the parts are heavy."

"Honestly, love, I'll be fine."

When Mark arrived home, Selina could tell his arm was hurting, but he didn't moan, and he went straight back to her mum's to collect the mattress and final little bits for the cot. Selina set about cleaning the bars. As she worked, she dreamed about the baby; would she have hair? Would she cry a lot? What would her name be? She stopped and wiped away a tear. Her daughter was out there somewhere – waiting for her!

Mark returned from his second trip, and she started washing down the cot mattress. Then she helped Mark to move the single child's bed out of the way. "I'll assemble the cot, love, while you wash the baby clothes," Mark said quietly.

"They're already in soak. I'll go and hang them to dry by the coal fire," she replied as she ran downstairs. She grasped that Mark needed her out of the way while he tried to fit the cot parts together; he wasn't the best at these things, especially with his bad arm.

"Mark, you've done a brilliant job," she cried as she ran back upstairs.

"Why, the surprise? Did you think I wouldn't do it properly!" he chuckled, standing back to rub his arm.

She was too busy to answer him. "Can you get the teddy bear that Brian and Sandra gave us when we were approved for adoption," she asked while she unfolded the new sheets and blankets. Then she sorted out the baby's essential toiletries on the dressing table beside the cot. She stood back and observed the pale looking Mark placing the teddy bear on the shelf. "It's done," she beamed at him. "The room's transformed from a child's bedroom to a nursery. We're ready for her now."

"Yes, we are," Mark said as he grabbed Selina into a hug. Kissing her forehead, he added, "It's our big day tomorrow; we're going to meet our child for the first time."

"I'm worn out. The sheer speed of all this has left me completely drained," she sighed as she pulled away from his embrace.

"Me too."

"At least we'll sleep tonight."

But she couldn't sleep, and she gathered Mark couldn't either. At 2 am, she got up and made them both a cup of tea. At 3 am, she finally turned the light off once more. But still, she knew as they both lay there, the anticipation was unbearable. Their lives were about to change, they were on the brink of being a family. She smiled to herself, how could anyone sleep through this much excitement?

CHAPTER 13

4th February - 5th February

1947

Catherine screamed again, hoping Joe could hear her, he needed to know the pain she was going through. Why on earth would anyone want to give birth? The nurse had added to her annoyance by telling her that Joe was eating sandwiches with his brother in the waiting area. Catherine wanted Joe to be pacing up and down, suffering in the same way she was, this was not a picnic for her! She screamed even louder; she would make sure he was listening to her torture.

"The head's out," cried the nurse, and then the doctor told her to push again. She gave one more scream, and finally, the baby arrived. At first, there was silence, and then it started crying.

"The baby's fine," the doctor declared. "Premature and underweight but breathing."

Eventually, the nurse sat her up and gave her the child wrapped in a blue towel. Catherine didn't like the miniature thing in her arms that had caused her so much pain.

"I'll get your husband now," the nurse said as she opened the door. Before the nurse had time to say any more, Joe fell into the room.

Catherine forced a grin; he did care after all. "Joe, you have a son, he's small but fine," she announced. "He even looks like you, look at all his black hair." She glanced at the tiny creature and then back to Joe. "This is our family now. I don't want any more children."

He peered at the baby, then kissed her with evident pride. "We have the perfect family, a girl and a boy." His blue eyes sparkled at her. "Can we still call him Jack after my father?"

"I think it's a lovely gesture," she replied as she handed the baby to Joe. "Here you go, Jack, this is your dad."

"I can't wait to tell David and Angeline," Joe said as he held his son, "they're both outside."

"Is Angeline here as well?"

"Yes, she managed to bring David and me some sandwiches through all the heavy snow – not that either of us could eat them."

"Oh."

"We were all worried about you. We could hear …"

"I'm sorry, Joe. I shouldn't have … "

"David wanted a nephew," he said, handing Jack back to her. "I'll need to phone Mum and Dad, they'll be thrilled. It's such a shame Mum's ill, she'd loved to have been here." He gently touched the baby. "David's offered to get Ada, and he said they'd collect Tia from Win's on their way home. So, if it's okay with you, I'll let David tell them about our son."

"Gran will be relieved." Jack was getting heavy, so she pushed him further up her arm. "I hope Tia will be alright with a brother." She looked at Joe. "David has been kinder towards me since he became best pals with Gran, but I think he still feels I'm too bossy; he keeps mentioning how gentle Hannah was." She sighed. "At least he doesn't think I'm a calculated young woman anymore." Jack moved, but she didn't look down at him, then he started to cry, so she awkwardly rocked him. "I'm glad we listened to Gran's advice about having Ada to stay. She'll be useful with Tia, and she can help with Jack when we get home."

"Yes, it's a good way for Ada to get involved," Joe agreed. "Only the other day she mentioned she was looking forward to being a granny to the new child, she seems determined to treat both children the same." His eyes shone. "I've always said that underneath that hard façade, lies a good woman." Catherine gave a condescending smile. Joe turned away. "I'll go and tell David and Angeline. I won't be long."

Catherine spoke loudly to grab his attention. "Joe, I don't want to be in hospital for a whole week. I feel alright to come home."

"You must stay darling, it's what the doctors recommend, and with Jack being early, you have no choice."

*

Jack had been crying all night, and as he started to doze Catherine's anger rose, babies were so demanding. She heard a noise and saw Joe, Tia, and Gran, arriving in the ward. Joe stopped at the desk, and she guessed he was asking what sort of night she'd had. She watched as Tia ran to the cot, leant forward and gave the baby a big kiss.

"Tia, are you upset you haven't got a sister?" Catherine asked.

"It's alright, Mummy, I don't mind. Great-Grandma Win has told me that you're going to need me to help you. And I know boys need looking after, Aunty Angeline has to do so much for George and Thomas."

Catherine smiled, her little daughter was very perceptive.

The sound of Gran's stick, gaining momentum on the stone floor made Catherine turn and hold out her arms.

"My darling," Gran exclaimed. "Are you alright?"

"I'm fine, and so is Jack," Catherine said, cuddling Gran to her. Then she picked up the crying baby, who'd been woken by Tia's wet kiss. "Here, he is ... your great-grandson."

"I'm so pleased to meet you, young man." Gran began to smile, then she looked at Catherine. "You do know that Jack is a diminutive from John."

"That's why I agreed to the name," she whispered with a small giggle.

Gran looked back at Jack. "Your Great-Grandfather, Charles John Demore, always wanted a son, and when I meet him again, I'll tell him all about you."

"Don't say that, Gran, you're not going to join him," Catherine said, quite incensed by the idea.

"Sometime I will be reunited with him – and your mother and father." Gran gazed at her. "But you do know how much I love you, don't you?"

Catherine bent across to touch her hand. "I know," she whispered. "You've been a mother to me. I hope I can love Tia and Jack as much as you've loved me."

Gran stared across at Tia, who was now busily chatting away to a nurse. Turning back, she said, "Remember my dear, the word 'mother' is a verb, not just a title. A mother's love is how you feel about your child – and the relationship that you have with those who God entrusts to your care. It isn't just about giving birth; it's the love you give that makes you their mother. I have total faith you will love Tia and Jack as much as I love you."

"Gran, you're right, but then you always are."

Joe appeared and planted a kiss on Catherine's cheek. From the corner of Catherine's eye, she noticed Gran taking off her large ruby ring. Gran started to speak, but her voice seemed different.

"I have something I want to do, something that's been playing on my mind for some time now." She turned to Catherine. "I want you to have my engagement ring, then part of me will always be with you. Even after death, I'll always be by your side. You can look at the ring as a reminder that I'm close by."

"No, Gran, stop talking like this!" Catherine exclaimed. "I don't need your ring to remind me of your love."

"Please, dear, I want to know that you have it." Gran nodded towards Tia. "Then, when the time is right, I want you to give it to Tia, and she can pass it on as a family heirloom. It's quite valuable, you know." Gran placed the ring into Catherine's hand. The heart-shaped ruby must have been of the highest quality as it still shone like new. Catherine's eyes fell on the small inscription inside the band, *C and W forever.*

"Gran, I can't …" she tried to protest, but Gran rolled her slender fingers around the ring.

"It's yours, and I want – I *insist* – that you have it."

Catherine accepted she'd lost the argument. "Alright," she said, reluctantly placing the ring on her finger. It fitted as if it was meant for her. She held up her hand, and it glinted in the sunlight as if it had come alive. Gran sat back in the chair with a look of total satisfaction upon her face. Catherine rested on her pillow. Her family surrounded her; a wonderful family she had never imagined having.

After two hours, the bell rang for the end of visiting. Joe kissed her, then stood back to wait for Gran. Catherine hugged Gran fondly, but this time, she noticed how frail the older woman felt. With all the excitement of the last few weeks, she hadn't noticed the weight loss in her ... until now.

"Gran, are you alright? You seem to have lost weight."

"I'm fine. I'm just old, and my body's getting weary and tired."

"When you get home promise me you'll go straight to bed and get an early night. It's been a stressful time for you."

"I've had a magnificent day," Gran replied, "and I wouldn't have missed it for the world. I'm so proud of you, my dear. You have no idea how much pleasure you've brought into my life. I thank you so much for that."

"You've done the same for me," Catherine replied. As they kissed, she felt Gran's cheeks, so soft and withered; her skin felt thinner than normal. "Please come back to see me tomorrow, I'm worried about you."

CHAPTER 14

27th March 1948

Selina hated the way the archways of trees were blocking the sunlight, they made the long driveway seem very dark. Then, almost like a light at the end of the tunnel, she noticed a large white sixteenth-century manor house looming up before them. The house looked dilapidated. She was aware the army had used it in the war, and she guessed that its previous beauty had been destroyed. There was a sign just above the front door, which had become loose and was swinging in the wind. It read *Checkton Park Orphanage, Canterbury*. Selina felt like a new mother who had just given birth. She too was about to see her baby for the first time, her daughter, how strange that word felt. Her breath was becoming faster, and she could feel her heart galloping in her chest. She grabbed Mark's hand, and he squeezed her fingers tightly, she knew he was thinking the same.

The taxicab drew up at the front of the orphanage. Selina got out of the car holding her large bag of baby things, while Mark paid the driver. The front door of the orphanage opened, and an older lady with a cheery face stood in front of them. Selina flinched, yet another professional person to meet.

"You must be Selina and Mark." The woman stepped towards them and offered her hand to Mark. "I'm Patricia Morrey, but please call me Pat. You're earlier than we expected, was it a reasonable journey for you?"

"Yes, it went very smoothly, thank you," Mark replied.

"Before we go in, I've something to ask you," Pat suddenly sounded tense, and Selina felt her stomach turn. She'd presumed something would go wrong; this amount of happiness couldn't possibly last. She observed Pat's face more carefully, then felt awkward for staring. "There's nothing amiss," Pat assured them, "just a small, unusual request. The mother's stayed and is asking to meet you. This isn't our normal practice; we prefer for there to be no contact at all. However, she's adamant and asks that you give her five minutes of your time."

"Does she want to see if she likes us?" Selina asked cautiously. "If she doesn't, will she change her mind about giving us her child?"

"She doesn't wish to keep the baby," Pat replied. "She claims she wants to discuss something with you."

Selina clutched Mark's arm. "I think I'd like to see her. If nothing else, it will give us an idea of what the baby might look like when she's older." Mark nodded in agreement. Selina knew he would go along with whatever she wanted.

"Follow me." Pat gestured towards the front door. Selina's knees felt weak; all of this was too much for her, but she had to be brave for the sake of the baby. They went up some steps and through the door into the building. The noise of children echoed through the hallway. "Sorry about the racket, it's nearly lunchtime," explained Pat as she pushed passed a crowd of girls. She opened the door to a room on the left, which Selina imagined had probably been the parlour for all the posh families who must have lived there in the past. "Wait here, and I'll go and get the mother." Pat looked anxiously at Selina, who found herself nodding positively. As Pat left, Selina looked around at the room. It was large and spectacular, but it only had two sofas and two well-worn armchairs to sit on. She sat on a sofa while Mark stood looking out of the bay window, staring at the front drive.

"What do you think she'll be like?" she asked softly. He shrugged his shoulders and kept staring ahead. She knew he often went quiet when he couldn't cope. She sat, watching the door in front of her. A few minutes later it abruptly opened, and Pat entered with a woman behind her.

"This is the child's mother," Pat said. "I've suggested you don't exchange names. She's just here to talk to you and then she'll leave." Pat nodded at the woman before leaving the room, shutting the door gently behind her.

The woman was left standing in the middle of the room. Selina wanted to memorise every detail of her appearance, her own daughter might look like this one day. She understood that she needed to remember this moment for the rest of her life as in the future, her child might ask her questions about this woman. Mark walked over and sat beside Selina, taking her hand in his, while the woman perched on the chair opposite.

"You're probably wondering why I've asked to see you." The woman had an unusual tone in her assertive voice. "I need to explain that I don't want any contact with this child, not ever. I have to know you'll make sure that she never sees me again."

Selina needed to check that she understood the woman correctly. "Are you asking us not to allow the child to look for you?" she said, surprised.

The woman glared at her and Selina sunk back into her chair, finding this self-assured woman very daunting. "That's what I'm saying."

"That's fine by us," Mark said.

"We want the child to be our daughter." Selina swallowed hard. "I want to be her mother more than anything, and I don't want that taken away from me. I know that finding you and her calling you mother would be painful for me." Selina then muttered, "So yes, we can promise we won't encourage her to seek you out."

"That's exactly what I wanted to hear. Thank you." The woman stood up from the arm of the chair. "I needed your promise, and I'm pleased I've got it. Giving this child up is the right thing to do. Now that I've met you, I'm sure of it, and I can go away happy." Without saying goodbye, the woman walked to the door, opened it, and left.

Selina stared in amazement as the door closed behind her. Turning to Mark in disbelief, she cried, "That woman's so emotionless and cold. She's pleased to give up her baby, and she's gone away happy! Does she not know how lucky she is to have had a child?" Mark put his arm around her and pulled her towards him. She knew he understood what she was saying.

"She's giving us our daughter; it's us who will be going away happy." He chuckled. "We're the lucky ones."

She gently kissed his lips, she loved how he always said the right things. "You're right, as always. But that woman was vile."

The room fell quiet, and all Selina could hear was the distant rattle of plates and the hub of children's voices. Pat suddenly opened the door and in her arms was a tiny newborn baby, wrapped in a pink blanket. "This is the child," she said as she handed over the baby.

As Selina cradled her adorable daughter for the first time, tears of joy flowed down her face. "Oh, Mark, she's beautiful. She's sleeping so quietly. Oh look, she's got sandy-blonde hair just like mine. I bet that's one of the reasons they matched her with us." She glanced bashfully at Pat. "What's her name?"

"The mother says you can call her whatever you wish."

"Really! That's perfect." Selina smiled. "I want to call her Maria." She looked at Mark, "After her dad." Mark sniffed heavily. Clearly, he was also finding it hard to control his emotions.

Pat looked at them both and smiled. "It might not be a conventional birth, but I do love this part of my job. However, I must make things clear before you leave. You do understand it takes about six months before you can legally adopt Maria. It's part of my role to remind you that until then the mother can change her mind. However, once you've gone to court, Maria will be legally yours, forever." She folded her arms. "To be honest, I don't think the mother will change her mind, but you can never know for sure."

Selina frowned. "It's going to be the longest six months of my life. I hope and pray I'll never have to give Maria back to that woman!" She pulled Maria close to her body as if she was protecting her from harm. "Losing Maria is going to be my greatest fear."

Pat gave her a warm smile. "You're just like any new mother seeing her baby for the first time. I can see you've already formed that strong emotional bond." Pat turned to the door. "I'll go and phone for a taxi to take you all home."

CHAPTER 15

5th February - 10th February

1947

Win walked down the hospital corridor, leaning heavily on Joe's arm. She turned and gave a wink and a little wave to her granddaughter and her great-grandson. She watched as Tia kissed her new baby brother goodbye and hugged Catherine. Tia then ran off down the hospital corridor to join them. Win knew her mobility was slow, but for the first time in her life, she was glad of it, it gave her a few more chances to turn back to look at Catherine. She only stopped turning to look when she felt a tear trickle down her own cheek, then she forced herself to walk faster down the corridor towards the hospital door.

She didn't feel like talking during the car journey, and as Joe escorted her through the snow to her front door, she realised how tired she felt. She waved as Joe and Tia drove off back to Ada, who was still staying to help with Tia. Going into her house, Win closed the door behind her. As she did so, she saw her beloved Charles standing on the stairs, a shadow, but it was clearly him. He was smiling with his arms stretched out towards her.

"It's time, isn't it?" she said, looking at him with affection. The figure nodded then slowly disappeared in front of her. Win turned to look one last time at the front door and the life that she knew she was leaving behind. She could still smell the hospital, and she savoured the time she'd just spent with Catherine. She thought about all the good moments they'd shared together, Catherine was indeed her pride and joy. Sam appeared in the hallway, and Win took a deep breath as she asked him to help her up the stairs. She felt exhausted, she had to get to bed. Halfway up the stairs, she noticed a small white feather lying on the carpet. She knew Charles had visited; he hadn't needed to prove it!

Sam followed her stare. "Anna changed your bedding today. I'm sorry ma'am, those feathers always come out of the pillows." She just gazed at him, then continued up the stairs. Once in the bedroom, she pulled the cord to get Anna to come and help her to undress. She was happy she'd left a will that would enable Anna and Sam to afford a little cottage somewhere and still have enough to enjoy their retirement. They'd been good to her. They were part of her family, and she loved them both. She also had total faith that Catherine would look after them – everything was in order.

She was ready to face death. She had her faith, she believed she'd be with her beloved Charles again, and she couldn't wait to be with her precious Cynthia once more. She had missed them both so much. She wasn't frightened, in fact, she embraced it. Her only sadness was that she was leaving her granddaughter behind. After Charles had died, she'd appreciated his support. His white feathers had always proved he was there, and she was sure she'd be able to help Catherine in the same way. But she was confident Catherine would be fine. She had the love of a good man. Win's job of being a mother to Catherine was done, she'd taught her all she knew. Now Catherine could do the same with her own children – and she was content that she'd lived to meet them both. She also expected that Ada would be there to help, and as for David, she'd discovered he was one of life's protectors, he would support Catherine now. Her granddaughter wouldn't be alone. She was thankful to know all was well with the world she was leaving. She lay on the bed to await Anna. All she wanted to do now was sleep …

*

Catherine sat on the side of the bed, staring at the ward entrance. She couldn't wait to see Joe and Win again. Jack, having had his bottle, was sleeping peacefully beside her. She was glad the hospital said she didn't need to breastfeed, she wasn't going to anyway.

"There you are," she said as she saw Joe coming through the door. "The nurses said the new snowfall last night has blocked the roads again." Joe trudged towards her, looking drained. She looked past him.

"Where's Gran?" Sitting on the bed, Joe put his arms around her. "Joe, what's wrong?" she squeaked as she tried to pull away from his grip.

"Oh, my darling, I've some terrible news."

Her body tensed. "Joe, what is it?" He was holding her closely now, and she could feel him shaking. "I had a telephone call early this morning. I thought it must be the hospital calling about you, but it was Sam phoning from Win's house."

Numbness took over her entire body. "Is Gran ill? What's happened?"

Joe seemed to be in a daze. "I threw on some clothes and crept past Ada and Tia's rooms. As I dashed through the snow towards Win's house, I could see Doctor Bryant's car was already parked outside." She felt his grip tighten.

"Joe ..."

"I wish I didn't have to tell you this, but last night Win passed away peacefully in her sleep. Anna found her at seven this morning. She couldn't wake her, so Sam called for Doctor Bryant, and after consoling Anna, he called me. I've been with Doctor Bryant then when I returned home, I had to tell Ada and Tia."

Catherine sat in silence, her mind trying to process what he'd said, then refusing to accept it as true. "She can't be," she exclaimed, mindful that she sounded ridiculous.

Joe's voice was gentle. "Doctor Bryant told me her heart was worn out. Apparently, he told her a few months ago that her time was short."

Catherine's grief overpowered her, her agony was more than she could bear. She howled so loudly she fathomed everyone in the ward could hear her – and probably those further down the corridor. She gave up trying to control herself, her whole body trembled with heartache. Eventually, she forced herself to stop wailing, but the sobbing wouldn't cease. As a comfort, she touched Gran's ring, nestled so neatly on her finger. Now she understood why Gran had been so strange the last time she came to visit. The ring, the words of love and advice, were her way of saying goodbye. Why hadn't Gran told her the truth?

She would have been by her side, but instead, Gran had died on her own. Suddenly Catherine felt annoyed. Gran had needed her, and she hadn't been there to support her. She would have liked the chance to have repaid her for everything she'd done for her. "I would have cared for Gran," she said crossly. "If only she'd told me."

"Don't you see darling, she didn't want to hurt you?" Joe said. "Imagine if she'd told you, it might have caused you to miscarry. She loved you too much for that." But Catherine wasn't listening, his words weren't sinking in. Joe took her face in his hands. "When you returned from France you didn't want Win to know about your involvement with the French Resistance. You told me it was because you loved her, and you didn't want to cause her pain. Sweetheart, your gran was just doing the same for you." He wiped a tear from her cheek. "You're both strong-willed individuals and would protect each other to the end."

"We would!" she whimpered. "And how are Sam and Anna?"

"Sam's looking very grey and frail. Anna was downstairs in their quarters, but I could hear her crying her heart out."

"They're both so fond of Gran. They've given their lives to helping her … and me. Oh, Joe, I should be there for them."

"It's alright, darling. Sam said Phyllis is on her way."

Catherine had a sudden thought. "Is Doctor Bryant alright? He's known Gran for such a long time."

"He said he was pleased Win had died painlessly at home. He was more concerned about you. It seems he admires the strong relationship between you and your Gran." Joe's expression softened. "He also said that fortunately you have me now, it would have been worse if you had been on your own." Joe took out his hanky to wipe his nose. "He said he'd come and see you tomorrow."

Catherine stared at him. "It was her heart, Joe, just like Grandfather and Mum."

Joe frowned at her. "It wasn't the same as your mum. Win's heart was old." Catherine went to speak, but he quickly interrupted her. "We have to accept that birth and death are the facts of life."

Catherine touched Win's ring. "Birth and death may be the start and finish of life, but I guess what happens in the middle is up to us."

The next day, Catherine decided that she couldn't stay in hospital for a week, she had a funeral to arrange.

"You're not ready to leave," the doctor declared. "But if you discharge yourself, then I must insist the baby remains here; he's too weak to go home yet." Catherine nodded. She wasn't bothered, she had other things on her mind. Nursing Jack was an additional task, and one she didn't need.

Everything had to be right for Win's final day yet to Catherine, nothing about it felt right. Her head was full of cotton wool, she couldn't think straight. Ada was a great help with Tia, and even David and Angeline assisted whenever they could. But Catherine knew she wasn't showing any appreciation, her despair was overwhelming. She discovered Gran's will stated that she wanted to be buried with her husband, Charles. The snow and the frozen ground were an issue, but Catherine was determined Gran's wishes would be carried out. Her grandfather had been laid to rest in his hometown, which was quite a distance from Dover.

"I'm glad, Joe," she declared. "The weather will deter people from travelling to Gravesend. I don't want to have to socialise with anyone!"

*

On the day of the funeral, Catherine stood behind the coffin, amazed at how many of Gran's friends had made it through the snow. She nodded to the Bridge Club members, especially Gregory's mother. Gran's church brigade had travelled as well, and all of the dignitaries from Dover seemed to be present. Angeline had stayed at home with Tia, but Catherine wished her friend was by her side instead of Ada. Sam, Anna and Phyllis were stood quietly behind her. Catherine looked up and nodded at Doctor Bryant as he walked solemnly into the church. Gran would have been pleased he'd come. Joe and David, once again in their full-dress army uniforms, were pallbearing at the front of the coffin. She could hear the music starting, so she forced herself to walk with the others down the aisle, behind the coffin. She couldn't look, this wasn't happening, it wasn't real. Next, they were placing the coffin on the altar, and she went to sit in the front row with Joe and Ada. Sam and his family sat behind them.

As David squeezed next to Joe, he touched Catherine's arm and whispered, "Are you alright?" She found herself nodding positively, which she thought was strange because she didn't feel alright.

Catherine considered the service to be very personal. The elderly vicar had known Win and Charles from his childhood, and he referred to them both with real affection. She thought that Joe's eulogy was marvellous, Gran would have loved the moving things he'd said. At the graveside, she stood staring down at the frozen earth while touching her gran's ring. She was oblivious to the snow falling on her clothes, while the freezing wind propelled her French pleat around her face. Now, as the coffin lowered, she felt such a heavy loss, the thought of not having Gran around was more oppressive than she'd ever imagined it could be. Her thoughts turned to Doctor Bryant, who'd said she was suffering from post-natal depression. He was wrong, it was simply post-Gran depression. All she could think about was Gran, there seemed no point in life anymore, and the thought of caring for a baby seemed far too daunting to contemplate.

CHAPTER 16

27th March 1948

As they walked down the steps from the front door of the orphanage, Mark noticed a fabulous, new-looking, red Triumph 1800 Roadster car, parked a lot further down the drive. He thought it must be the next couple arriving to collect a child and he assumed the driver was waiting for them to leave before pulling up nearer to the door. It was good to think that lots of children's lives would be changing through adoption. A taxicab was waiting for them, and Mark opened the door, while Selina turned to Pat to thank her once again. He felt proud of his wife; this adoption process had helped her confidence grow. He would remember this part of the day forever, his wife standing there with their new baby asleep in her arms. Then he noticed Maria opening her eyes. She didn't cry, she seemed content. It was as if she already understood she was safe in her mother's arms.

Pat handed a bag to Mark. "This is a small bag of clothes given to me by the mother." He nodded as he shoved it into the back of the taxi along with their much larger bag.

"Are you sure we can keep the pink blanket?" Selina asked politely. "We were told to bring our own. We have one in our bag."

"The pink blanket came with the child, so it's hers," Pat assured her. "Just so you know, Maria has recently had her bottle, so she should be alright for your journey." Pat shook Mark's hand. "Good luck to you all," she said caringly.

This was it, thought Mark, the start of their lives together as a family. He got in the back with Selina, and they waved as the taxi drove on. Mark noticed his wife's eyes were locked on Maria as she cradled her in her arms.

Then, looking up at him, Selina murmured, "She looks like a Maria, doesn't she? The name suits her."

He wasn't religious, but Selina was right; it felt as if the child had been given to them by the mother of God herself. Nothing about any of this seemed strange to him. It was as if it was meant to be. Fate had put them all together. He had a wife and daughter, a family of his own – that is if the next six months went by without any problems.

After an hour or so, Mark noticed the road signs to Gravesend were starting to appear. They were nearly home. Selina was minding Maria intently and he stared out of the window, watching as the world flashed past them. His thoughts turned to the small bag the mother had left. He wondered if he should check its contents. He turned to the back shelf where he'd left the bags. As he reached for the woman's bag, he noticed a red Triumph 1800 Roadster three or four cars behind them. Surely it couldn't be the same one he'd seen earlier. No, it must be another one. He pulled the bag from the shelf.

"What are you doing?" Selina asked.

"I'm just looking inside to see what she's given us."

Selina nodded and focused her gaze back on Maria.

"There's just some nappies, a bottle, some baby powder and a few clothes," Mark continued. Then he saw a sealed envelope tucked away under everything else. He could see some writing on it, and it felt as if something was inside. He looked up to check on Selina. She glanced briefly at him then turned back to Maria. His hands still within the small bag, he moved the envelope so he could read the inscription. *'Please keep this safe and give it to her when she's old enough to understand.'*

He stared at it. Should he tell Selina? He assessed the contented scene of his wife and daughter together. No, he wasn't going to spoil this moment. Maria was hopefully going to be their daughter and whatever was in the envelope could wait. He closed the bag, deciding he'd deal with it later.

As they entered their road, Mark leant towards the driver. "Ours is the house beside the footpath, the one with the purple front door." He recalled how, when they'd first moved in, he'd painted the door Selina's favourite colour. All the terraced houses in the lane looked the same, so the landlord loved the idea of making their home stand out from the rest. The taxi driver nodded and parked outside their house.

"Welcome to your home, Maria," Mark announced as he took the bags and got out of the car. Then he heard his mum-in-law's voice boom from behind him.

"Did it go alright? Have I got a granddaughter?" Eileen cried as she pulled open the car door. Then she squealed with excitement. "She's gorgeous!"

From inside the car, Selina laughed. "Oh, Mum, you're so funny. You can't see her properly from there."

"Let me have her, please." Eileen sounded desperate. "I want to hold her in my arms and tell her I'm her nana."

Mark watched his wife as she proudly handed the baby across. More than anything, he hoped this tiny creature would give his mum-in-law a purpose to her widowed life. Mark watched Eileen caressing her granddaughter in her arms, and it brought a lump to his throat.

Eileen looked up from the baby. "She's wonderful," she exclaimed, "and she has sandy-blonde hair!" Then, looking down again, she murmured, "We're going to have such fun together, my little love."

"Mum, they said we could choose her name, so we can call her Maria after all," announced Selina, as she climbed out of the car.

"This child is meant to be ours," Eileen said, her voice cracking with emotion. "How I wish Harold were here to see this."

"Me too," Mark echoed.

"Perhaps Dad is here," Selina said, waving her arms in the open air.

Eileen was now kissing Maria's little hands, and Mark found himself in awe of how Maria didn't seem to mind. She seemed such a happy little baby or was it just that she knew she was loved?

He whispered, "You know, Mum, I have a feeling Maria will be spoilt with love."

Eileen cuddled Maria into her chest. "You and I, my little treasure, are going to be the best of friends."

"Mum, remember we have to wait for about six months before we'll know for sure that this will be your grandchild," Selina said anxiously. "But my God, I hope she's going to be!"

Leaving the two women cooing, Mark bent down to pay the driver. He was glad they'd saved so hard for today; the total bill was a lot more than he'd imagined. As he stood up, he noticed a red Triumph 1800 Roadster car parked further down the street. His body stiffened – it must be the same car. He felt a swift need to protect his family, so as fast as he could, he ushered them inside. Once they were in, he dropped the bags and turned to go and talk to the person in the red car, but as he looked down the street, he saw it driving off and turning the corner. It had gone. But what was it doing following them home? Perhaps the orphanage had to check that the child reached its new home safely? He sighed, how he hoped the next few months would go quickly, he didn't like this uncertainty. He wanted Maria to be legally their child, and then all of this would stop. He tried to calm himself down. He supposed six months of uncertainty would be a small price to pay for what would be a lifetime of happiness. He turned and went back into the house, securing the front door behind him. He was entering his new life, and he wasn't going to frighten Selina and Eileen by mentioning that car. As he went into the lounge, he saw Eileen cuddling Maria, while Selina was standing over her. The two women didn't even notice he was there.

"Now Selina, I think it's time to feed this little one," Eileen said. "Then I'll teach you how to change her nappy." The two women giggled before disappearing off to the kitchen.

Taking the bags, Mark went upstairs to Maria's new bedroom. As he unpacked, he saw the envelope lying at the bottom of the small bag. He wondered what to do with it. He didn't want to open it, the envelope wasn't for him. He'd wait and give it to Maria when the time was right.

Then he remembered the loose floorboard between the wardrobe and the door frame. Brian was going to fix it, but they'd run out of time. For safekeeping, he bent down and put the envelope under the floorboard. He'd tell Selina about it another time. He wasn't going to cause his wife any pain or upset, not today.

He stood looking out of the side window. He loved their quiet and peaceful street … except on Sundays when the church car park brought in too many people, he grinned. He felt utterly content; nothing could ever make him happier than he was at this very moment in time. He could hear Maria crying, and he imagined the first nappy change wasn't going well. But he was sure it wouldn't be long before Selina was an expert mother, and it helped that Eileen would be there to teach her. He had a beautiful wife, and with a bit of luck, they would soon be a proper family. He thought back to the meeting with Maria's mother. He didn't like her, she seemed so hard. He hoped little Maria wouldn't be like that. No, he decided, they wouldn't let her. Maria would have their love to guide her. She'd have the influence of Selina's caring and thoughtful nature, and he'd offer support and protection. How could any child not respond to that? He couldn't help but smugly think that perhaps the adoption would be Maria's salvation. They'd saved her from a life with a woman who didn't care. There would be nothing they wouldn't do for this much-wanted child, and he hoped that nothing would go wrong with their future. He picked up the empty bags and closed the door behind him.

CHAPTER 17

28ᵗʰ June 1947

Catherine hated talking to the solicitor, who was organising Gran's probate; it made it all seem so final. As she put down the phone, she thought about the issue of emptying Gran's house. She had no idea what to do with all those treasured possessions. Tears burned her eyes. She remembered selling her father's things when he died, but Gran's belongings felt so much harder to let go of. She walked into the kitchen, concluding that the misery of closing Gran's life was never-ending. Her heart was breaking, she missed her so much. She groaned as she heard Jack crying.

"Happy birthday, darling," Joe said as he cradled Jack in one arm and handed her an envelope with the other. "I've bought two theatre tickets for you and Angeline to go and enjoy a girls' night out." She grinned. Joe always told her what her present was before she opened it. "It will do you good," he said. "You need to relax, and Angeline will help with that." Joe kissed the baby. "David's agreed to come over to help me with Jack and Tia." He laughed. "It's going to be our boys' night in."

"That's sweet of you, Joe, but—"

"I won't take no for an answer," Joe interrupted. "You'll enjoy the play, it's 'The Foundling,' by a French writer called W. Lestocq. I've seen it before, it's excellent."

"But I can't be bothered to go out."

"Listen to me, darling, this play's part of the community's attempt to raise money to restore the Hippodrome to its former glory. Everyone was heartbroken when it got destroyed in one of the last shell attacks on Dover. The theatre helped to keep morale strong during the war, it would be lovely to rebuild it again, don't you think?"

"It would. I loved that theatre." She looked at the ticket. "Oh, the play's tonight! It's in the Town Hall, so, at least I won't have to drive."

After the play, Catherine sat with Angeline in the little café attached to the Town Hall. "I really enjoyed that," she said. "And Joe was right, unwinding with you has lifted my mood."

"That was our plan," replied Angeline. "But I suppose we'd better get going. The men will be wondering where we are."

Catherine stood up and linked arms with her friend. "*Allons.* It's not far to your house, we can walk quickly." As they walked arm-in-arm, the clear summer night, bright stars and warmth from her friend made Catherine feel alive again.

"At last," Saul said as he greeted them at Angeline's front door. "I was getting worried about you both. Hang on a minute, Catherine, I'll get my keys and drive you home."

"No, thanks," Catherine answered. "I want to take in the fresh air." She kissed Angeline on the cheek. "Thank you for a lovely evening. For the first time in ages, I've enjoyed myself." Waving, she strode off happily down the road.

"Wait," cried Angeline.

"*Non,* I want to walk," Catherine shouted as she kept up a brisk pace.

Catherine soon approached the long alley that was the shortcut through the cliff. She knew the main road was lit, but it would take her longer that way. It was very dark in the alley, but she stayed close to the chalk wall, feeling her way through as it curled towards her house. When she was about a quarter of the way down, she noticed a figure coming towards her. She quickened her step to move past.

"Well, if it ain't me little French, Catherine Leblanc."

She looked up. The man had sandy-blonde hair, and his face looked severely burnt on one side.

"You don't know who I am, do you?" the man said gruffly." It's me, Gregory Jones."

She shuddered. Then she felt sorry for Gregory. He'd had a strong-looking face at school, the war had been brutal. She stood straight and tried to control her astonishment.

"Hello, Gregory. How are you? I saw your mother recently."

He was swaying from side to side, clearly drunk. "I told people you were dead," he said. "You always acted as if I was dead. Ignoring me, like I was beneath you." His voice sounded bitter. "Why didn't you ever reply to me love letters?" She didn't know what to say, so he persisted with his questioning. "Why didn't you want me? I liked you so much in those days." Gregory's voice grew loud. "I was obsessed with you, I tried so hard, followed you everywhere. I used to watch you when you were in your bedroom. You never closed the curtains. I even saw you undress once—"

"Stop it, Gregory, that's enough!" she interrupted angrily. "I need to get back to my husband." She went to walk past him. Gregory was breathing heavily, and she could smell the liquor on his breath. He stretched out his arm to block her way.

"Not so fast, we've things to discuss. I hate you for treating me like dirt!"

"I didn't mean to upset you, I just wasn't interested … in that respect," she replied, as she tried to push his arm away.

"Oh, so you weren't interested, ha! Well, I've got you now, haven't I?" With that, he grabbed her and lashed out with his other arm, slapping her across the face. She screamed, knowing it was more from outrage than fear. "I wouldn't scream if I were you, or I'll hurt you more," he scoffed.

She tried to break free of his grip. She wasn't going to put up with any terror tactics. He lashed out again, hitting her in the chest. Then he thrust out his foot, and she stumbled but regained her footing. He turned and punched her several times in the stomach.

"That'll teach you to hurt me," he roared. "You needed a good lesson. No one treats me like I don't exist." His rage seemed uncontrollable. Thrashing out again, he struck her around the head, sending her flying backwards. There was an almighty crack as her head hit the chalk wall of the alley. She slid to the floor, feeling herself falling into a semi-conscious state.

"Fallen at my feet 'ave you?" Gregory kicked her viciously as she lay helpless on the ground. Then he grabbed her and stood her up, pushing her against the chalk wall. He put his hand across her mouth. She could smell his revolting skin as his hot, filthy body pressed into her. He fumbled and pulled up her skirt. She bit his hand as hard as she could, and for a second he let go.

"Please don't," she pleaded. "I've recently had a baby."

But he wasn't listening or didn't care. The hand went back across her month with extra force, and she couldn't move. He fumbled with his trousers and then in her dazed state, she felt the penetrating pain as he entered her, thrusting with vigour into her body. She knew he was enjoying his vengeance, embedding the torture with all his power and strength.

"Now I have you," he snarled with satisfaction. His vindictiveness seemed to be making his fury even worse. The agony was intense, and she thought she was going to pass out. Then it occurred to her that she had no idea what he might do next. She had to stay in control. It was only minutes, minutes that felt like hours, and then she felt his juices pouring down her legs. He stopped and pulled away. Would he kill her now?

Catherine heard a noise from the other end of the alley. It sounded like someone walking towards them. Gregory turned, seeming unsure what to do next. He waited for a second then ran off in the other direction. She could hear the footsteps getting closer. Then a man's voice spoke through the darkness.

"Hello, is someone there?" She was sure it was Joe's voice, and her relief was overwhelming. She slithered down the chalk wall and once again felt the alley floor. Then there was blackness ...

When she came to, Joe was placing her on her bed, and David was by his side. "Catherine, speak to me. Are you alright?" Joe said quickly. "I need to take you to hospital. I'll go and phone the police."

"I'm fine, Joe. I just need a cup of tea," she replied, exhausted.

David offered to make one and disappeared downstairs.

"Joe, please don't make me go to hospital and I don't want the police involved. I couldn't bear for people to know what's happened." She grabbed his hand. "Please, I beg you not to tell anyone. I don't want the looks, the gossip and the stigma that'll come with it. I don't even want to tell Angeline. I want to forget it ever happened. That's what the women in France did in the war, and now I'm a respectable wife I want to remain one."

Joe looked stunned. "I thought this was a mugging. What did he do to you? Catherine, what's happened?"

She tried not to cry, but she couldn't stop and, sobbing her heart out, she told him everything ...

"That man has defiled my wife, he has abused ..." Joe spluttered after Catherine recounted the horrific events.

Now Catherine felt that shame was taking over from her physical pain. How could Joe love her after this?

He studied her face then he turned pale. "It's not your fault; the man is evil. Good God, if I hadn't got to you when I did, he might have killed you. My darling, I couldn't bear to lose you now. I couldn't cope without you. Thank goodness Angeline phoned to say you were walking home. When you didn't arrive, I ..." he bent down and gently kissed her lips. Then standing up, he said, "Right, I'm going to phone Doctor Bryant to come and check you over, you must be in terrible pain. As for the police, you should report him. We'll discuss it properly once I've phoned the doctor. I'll be back in a minute. Lie still and rest, everything's going to be alright now."

"Joe, can you forgive me?" she pleaded as he walked towards the door.

"It's him I can't forgive. I can't bear to see you hurt like this."

She listened as he ran down the stairs and she heard him asking the operator to put him through to Doctor Bryant. Then she drifted back into a semi-conscious state. When her awareness returned, she could hear him talking to David in the kitchen. His voice sounded stern.

"David, we're not at war anymore." His voice dropped, and she could only catch the odd word. "We need to think … clear … won't … again." Then she heard his footsteps back on the stairs.

"Doctor Bryant's on his way," he said soothingly, as he placed her tea carefully on the bedside table.

"Have you told David … everything?"

Joe seemed hesitant. "Yes, but he's promised not to tell anyone. He also said he'd sort some work business for me so that I can stay at home for a while."

Catherine's pain was excruciating, and she couldn't summon up the energy to question him anymore, she was hurting everywhere. She could feel the swelling coming out on her face, her head was still bleeding, and her stomach felt as if it had been run over by a tractor. As for elsewhere – it felt as if she'd been ripped apart. She rested on her pillow, glad Joe would be at home, she needed him. The next thing she heard was David escorting Doctor Bryant up the stairs.

After Doctor Bryant had examined her, he folded her clothes and handed her a nighty to put on. Then he shouted downstairs for Joe. As he was putting his equipment in his bag, Joe appeared in the room.

"Your wife has no major damage, just a lot of bruising and injuries that will heal with time," the doctor said to Joe. "However, I want her to go to hospital, they can keep a closer eye on her there."

"*Non,* I'm not going anywhere," shrieked Catherine. "I don't want people fussing over me. I'm staying here, where I can get some rest. You'll look after me, won't you, Joe."

Doctor Bryant looked uneasy. "You may need medical assistance."

"Well, Doctor, you can give me medical assistance here." Catherine saw the doctor raise an eyebrow as he looked across at Joe. Her eyes met Joe's, and she threw him one of her determined looks. "I'm not going to hospital."

Doctor Bryant looked defeated. "Hmm, well, in that case, I insist on visiting you daily. We'll defer the hospital – for now, but if—"

"I'll be fine," Catherine said, and she laid back, satisfied that she'd won. "I do appreciate your concern, Doctor Bryant, and thank you for agreeing to look after me at home."

Joe took her hand. "But we have to tell the police. You can't let this man get away with this."

She sat up again. "*Non,* Joe, I've told you, I'm not doing that." She looked from one man to the other. "I forbid either of you to involve the police. The shame and embarrassment it would cause to me, and you, Joe, it's unthinkable. I'll not put us through it."

"Catherine," Doctor Bryant interjected. "You must do as your husband tells you."

"I won't do any such thing! I'll not have people talking and sniggering behind my back. I'm going to hold my head up high and pretend nothing's happened." Doctor Bryant looked shocked, and he mopped his brow. She stared at them both and realised that she'd switched off her emotions in order to turn on her ability to cope. The unemotional Catherine from the war had returned. "Please, both of you, now that my wounds are dressed and my painkillers are working, it's time for me to be left to sleep." She lay down, clutching her swollen stomach and crying out in agony. Doctor Bryant bowed his head and collected his bag while Joe opened the bedroom door to escort him out.

After the doctor had left, she could hear David's voice downstairs. "No one should be allowed to get away with this."

"David, come into the sitting room," she heard Joe say. Then the door closed, and the voices became muffled. She tried to turn over to sleep, the drugs were making her drowsy. On the chair by her bedside, she noticed her clothes piled on top of her coat. As she looked, she saw a small white feather had attached itself to the wool on her collar. No, it couldn't be! Leaves and dirt were all over her clothes, she was certain the feather meant nothing, it was just from when she'd slid down onto the alley floor.

CHAPTER 18

23rd September 1948

Selina focused on Mark as he paced up and down the room. Her fingers started to twitch, and her stomach churned as she looked across at Mrs Bartram. She wondered what she'd written in her report, these professional people still made her feel so inadequate. Maria stirred and Selina turned to check she was still asleep on her mum's lap. How she hated the fact that Mrs Bartram had insisted 'The child must be present at court in case there are any issues.' Selina knew what that meant; the judge might take Maria away from them. Losing Maria was the worst outcome imaginable, her most frightening demon, a terror she couldn't face.

"Can I have Maria for a moment?" Selina whispered nervously to her mum. She took Maria in her arms. Her child was at peace, and it was the best feeling in the world. She decided that no matter who the professional was, she had to fight for her child, she would always protect 'her baby'.

"We're ready for you," the county court usher said as he entered the waiting room. He had a cold and unfeeling voice, and Selina shivered as she had a flashback to the maternity doctor who'd spoken to her in that same tone. Now things felt uncertain again. She kissed Maria and handed her back to her mum. Mrs Bartram stood up, and with determination in her heart, Selina moved towards Mark.

"Good luck, love," her mum said, looking worried. Selina nodded, then pushing her skirt down, so its hem was below her knees, she walked hand-in-hand with Mark.

The courtroom was massive, with an enormous table in the middle, but her eyes fell on the judge, who was sitting at the top of the table, looking very formidable in his wig. Her breathing quickened as her grip on Mark's hand tightened. Another court officer was sitting beside the judge, who was busily passing across paperwork.

"Please sit down," ordered the court usher as he glared at them and pointed to the chairs at the side of the judge. "Mrs Bartram, you are to sit over there, please." He pointed to a chair on the other side.

Once seated, the judge looked sternly at Mark from beneath his wig. "For the record, please state both of your names and your address."

Mark stood up and answered, his voice shaking as he spoke. Selina thought he was terrific, and she gave him an approving grin when he sat down again.

The judge then turned to Mrs Bartram. "Please state the case for this adoption."

Mrs Bartram stood up and stated that her clients were upright citizens. Then she read from her notes. Selina was amazed as Mrs Bartram recounted to the judge every meeting they'd ever had. What a professional woman she was. Mrs Bartram then closed her report, put her spectacles on the desk, and finished with the words that made Selina want to cry.

"I conclude by saying that I strongly recommend this couple be allowed to legally adopt this child. In my professional opinion," Mrs Bartram smiled across at them, "I cannot fault them."

The judge didn't respond to her words. "Has the mother contested the case at all?" he asked sombrely. It felt like Selina's biggest fear had hit. Had the mother said anything? Did she want her baby back? Mrs Bartram hadn't mentioned anything about this. She held her breath as she waited.

"No, my lord, the mother hasn't contested, she still wishes for the adoption to go ahead. The mother wants to give up all rights to this child." Mrs Bartram then sat down, and there was silence. Selina felt her normal breathing rhythm returning, though her heart felt as if it would take longer to recover. She watched as the judge asked the court officer if all the paperwork was in order, then they checked through loads of forms for what seemed like ages.

"Please stand," said the judge as he inspected them both. As they stood, Selina leant heavily on Mark, she was too frightened to move.

The judge stared at Mark. "Mr Tozer, do you have anything to say?"

Mark seemed hesitant, and Selina could sense his nerves. Then to her amazement, she found herself speaking.

"We would be proud to be this child's parents," she stated quietly. Mark looked at her, admiration written on his face. Her voice strengthened. "You see, over the last six months we've grown to love this child. We've bonded with her and she with us. We're already a family. I've become her mother, so, please, please, my lord, please don't take that away from any of us." She was quaking now, and she stopped, unable to utter another word.

The judge stared at her, then he spoke loudly, "I hereby grant the adoption order. From this day forth, the child in question will be legally adopted by Mr and Mrs Tozer. Parental responsibility for this child will now be vested in these applicants." He turned back to Selina. "Congratulations. For the record and her registration, can you give me the name you wish to call your new daughter?"

With total relief, Selina announced, "Maria Tozer. Thank you, my lord, for giving her to us."

"Actually, I think I'm giving you to the child," the judge said to her. "I can see how nervous you are, yet you still spoke up. In this formal situation, I have not seen many young women do that." His voice softened, "I do believe I am giving an ardent mother to this child." Looking down, he started to sign his paperwork.

"My lord?" Mark said. "Please, can we call her Maria Selina Tozer?" The judge viewed him for a while then nodded.

Selina gazed at Mark, and squeezing his hand, whispered, "Trust you to make it all so perfect."

The court usher who had first led them in stood up and indicated they could go. "But can you stay Mrs Bartram," he said. "We need you to assist with the paperwork."

Selina felt Mark press her hand as they went to move. "Maria is ours," he said with delight.

While the judge was still writing, Mrs Bartram dashed round the table towards them. Her voice was full of genuine happiness. "I'm thrilled." Her smile seemed warmer than ever. "My job is over, and I have to say, it feels right."

"Thank you for all your help, Mrs Bartram." Mark shook her hand with vigour. "Your report was great, I never expected …"

"Don't be silly, I just told the truth," she said with a look of satisfaction on her face. "I was only worried because this judge is known to be a difficult man, he likes to be sure. So believe me, we've all done well. I wish all three of you the very best of luck." Turning to Mark, she added, "Now as you leave, don't forget you'll need to pay the court fees of 15 shillings and 6 pence."

Mark laughed. "Maria's worth every penny." Then, clasping Selina's hand tightly, he led her towards the door.

Once in the corridor, Selina fell into his arms and cried, "You and I, are a mum and dad."

He kissed her passionately. "Yes. We've done it. We're finally parents," he said with relief oozing from his voice.

Kissing him again, Selina uttered, "We'd better go and tell Mum. She'll be panicking by now."

As they entered the waiting room, Selina could hear Maria crying. Her mum was standing by the window, rocking the baby in her arms.

"Well?" her anxious voice echoed above Maria's screaming. "How did it go?"

"She's ours, Mum," Selina exclaimed, holding them both close. "Maria Selina Tozer is officially your granddaughter."

"Selina, love, our dreams have come true; we have our family." She rocked the crying Maria. "How I wish my Harold were here to meet her."

"Me too, Mum," Selina said as she took Maria into her arms. "Hello, my own little daughter, this is our first official mother-daughter hug." Instantly, Maria stopped crying. Selina looked up at Mark, and said softly, "The stress is over. I think Maria knows I'm her mother forever. Even her full name reflects both of us, now surely your parents and other people can never say we aren't her real parents?"

Mark didn't answer.

CHAPTER 19

29th September 1947 - 27th March 1948

Catherine picked up her cup of tea from the kitchen table, but as she took a sip, it felt like drips of guilt sliding down her throat. How she wished everyone hadn't been so sympathetic about her 'falling down the stairs'. She'd hated having to lie, and she didn't deserve their support. The rape had made her feel like damaged goods, and if people ever found out the truth, the disgrace would be unbearable. She took another sip. At least Joe had been patient, they hadn't been intimate for such a long time now. Another mouthful of tea went down her throat. And how could David know for sure that she would never bump into Gregory again?

She looked up as Angeline returned from the playroom. "Tia and Thomas are having a great time," Angeline said.

"Good," replied Catherine, knowing that meant she could now leave. "Here's the extra key I had cut for you."

"Thanks. Now, when I take the children with me to collect George from school, we can come back here and wait for you."

"You're a star. You know where Jack's things are." Catherine hunched her shoulders as she heard Jack screaming again. "Angeline, you're much better with this baby stage than I am."

"Motherhood doesn't always come naturally. You managed to learn with Tia, I'm sure you can do it again."

"It's baby tolerance that's too hard for me," Catherine said as she tossed back her plait. "But I don't feel too well at the moment, so that's affecting my patience too."

"You're just run down, it's normal with a new baby. You go out and enjoy your time on your own. I bet you'll feel more refreshed when you come back."

Hours later, Catherine stood at the sitting room door, her hand felt clammy against the cool metal of the handle. She swallowed before pushing it open. Joe glanced up from his book.

"At last. Where have you been? I got home from work to find Angeline and her boys here. She told me you'd gone shopping?"

Catherine closed the door behind her and stood with her back to it. "I have to tell you something."

Joe stared at her. "Are you alright you look –"

"I'm pregnant. Doctor Bryant confirmed it this afternoon."

The book slipped from his hands and his brow furrowed. "But you can't be, we haven't—"

"It's Gregory's … and I want an abortion."

He sank back into the chair. "I need to think."

"There's nothing to think about. I can't, this ..." she glanced down at her stomach, slapped it with the open palm of her hand ... "this thing inside me has to go."

He gazed up at her, his blue eyes glistening. "This is terrible. Haven't we been through enough already?"

"You're not the father, and I don't want this child." She folded her arms across her chest and squeezed her eyes tight shut. "I want rid of this and all it stands for."

"Abortion's illegal, and it's against my religion." His eyes turned distant. "I won't allow you to have one." Then he muttered, "Besides, many women have died having abortions."

"We can afford to have it done properly."

"No, and that's final." His eyes focused on her. "I'll bring the child up as my own, everyone will assume it's mine, anyway." He grinned as if a revelation had smacked him. "Of course, I can love the child; it's your flesh and blood after all." He wiped his forehead with his hand. "You know how much I love every part of you. This baby is part of you, even if it's not part of me."

"How could you do this to me?" she cried. "I want an abortion!" He turned away. "Joe, I wouldn't be able to look at the child without seeing Gregory's face. I couldn't possibly love and nurture his baby. I hate it."

Joe glared at her. "I'm not discussing it. I won't agree to an illegal act of killing an innocent life. What's happened to you isn't the baby's fault."

Catherine scowled in disbelief. "You can't love me. Otherwise, you'd give me what I want!" She turned and flew out of the door, slamming it behind her, before storming up the stairs.

The next morning Doctor Bryant was in their sitting room. "I've come to see you and Joe today because I've given things a lot of thought."

"Please, Doctor Bryant," Catherine cried. "You must understand that my mental health will be affected if I'm made to bring up his child."

"I do sympathise." Doctor Bryant sat upright. "But I cannot condone your wish for an abortion." He leant forward and took her hand in his. "But there is another option." He looked across at Joe. "Once the baby's born, it could be placed for adoption."

"That's not a bad idea," Catherine said, glancing at Joe.

"No," declared Joe. "I want to keep this baby. It's Jack's half-sibling." He stared at Catherine. "And it'll have half your genes too. I'll love it as my own."

"Joe, if you don't agree, then you'll be wrecking my life," Catherine snapped. "I can't constantly be reminded of what happened. I'm not going to give in to this. It's the only way I can be happy again."

Doctor Bryant was still focused on Joe. "I can make all the arrangements for the process to be prepared," he said with an understanding tone. Catherine could see Joe was thinking it through, and for once, she waited.

Eventually, Joe turned to her. "To give up a child who's part of the woman I love is a painful thought." She saw his eyes were welling up. "But the most important thing to me is your happiness. I have no choice; I have to compromise with you, don't I?"

"Yes, you do!" Catherine said. "It's what I want, and you have to do this for me." She then whispered, "But I still refuse to tell anyone about the rape, so the adoption has to be our secret." She took a deep sigh and stood up. "No-one must know the truth." She looked from Joe to

Doctor Bryant. "I think after the birth we should say the baby died."

"What?" Joe cried.

"I insist on it, Joe. I won't have anyone knowing about all of this." She focused on Doctor Bryant. "Thank you, I know you have helped me, and I'm grateful." She shook his hand. "I'll leave all the organising to you." Then, without turning to Joe, she left the room.

*

The months had dragged, and all Catherine wanted was for this pregnancy to be over. Now David and Joe had added to her frustration.

"I can't stop long, I've left Saul with the boys," Angeline said as she entered the kitchen and put the food shopping on the table. "I've just passed David in the hallway, he looked rather annoyed."

"We've all just argued," Catherine replied. "David can't understand me, and Joe's just stomped upstairs to get the children ready for bed."

"Is the row because you're still not enthusiastic about the new baby? You shouldn't be getting upset when you're so close to your due date." Angeline cast Catherine an understanding nod. "I'll make us some tea."

Catherine forced a half-smile. It felt hard having to cope with everyone's excitement about the pregnancy. Even Tia was convinced that at last, she was going to have her sister. "I can't get motivated about anything," Catherine said as she looked at the shopping. "I'm struggling with Gran's house finally being sold. It feels like my home has gone." She looked up. "Is the pot of tea ready now?" she asked indifferently.

After Angeline had gone, Catherine laid in her bath and thought about David's rage. Why had Joe told David about the adoption? And why did Joe always need his brother's support? She washed off the soap, remembering David's bellows that a new-born baby should be looked after, not abandoned to some terrible orphanage and discarded like some unwanted object. She should at least wait for the adoption to be made. He'd shouted at Joe, saying that he couldn't understand why Joe was giving in to her demands. If Joe wanted to keep the child, then he should make his wife obey him. Catherine sank further into the water. She didn't regret yelling back at David that he'd never been in love, so he wouldn't know that love meant compromises. She took a breath. That man might be clever, but he knew nothing about life. She rose and got out from her bath, her anger increasing as she put the towel around her and dried her wet body. She touched her stomach. The baby felt like a cancer growing within her. She couldn't wait for Gregory's genes to disappear from inside her body.

Without any warning, she felt a sharp pain, and her waters flooded the bathroom floor. The pain came again, severe this time. Her nighty was on the floor, so she grabbed it and put it over her head. Then she unlocked the door and hollered for Joe. In an instant, she heard him running up the stairs.

When he saw her sitting on the cold, wet bathroom floor, his face turned sallow. "I'll get Doctor Bryant." With that, he ran downstairs again. She could hear him on the telephone, first to the operator and then the doctor. He put down the phone, and she heard the same thing again, but this time, he was asking for Angeline. Her contractions were getting stronger and stronger.

"Joe," she yelled. She heard the telephone go down, and then he was back in the room. The contractions were becoming excruciating; the pain of the baby's head pushing down felt intense. She tried hard to remember everything that had happened with Jack's birth. It wasn't easy giving instructions to Joe while at the same time giving birth.

"Where's Doctor Bryant? she roared as another contraction hit.

As if in answer to her screams, Angeline appeared through the bathroom door. "Let me through," she said breathlessly, pushing Joe aside. Catherine shrieked as she felt the baby's head force out of her body.

"One more push, Catherine," Angeline said calmly. Catherine obeyed, and finally, she felt the baby leave her body. "It's a girl," yelled Angeline. The doorbell went, and Joe rushed down to let Doctor Bryant into the house.

Catherine heard them racing up the stairs and then Joe shouted, "Tia, go back to your room. I'll be there in a minute to explain what's happening." There was silence, and Catherine breathed deeply, thankful that Tia had obeyed. By the time the doctor got to the bathroom, the baby was crying.

Angeline looked relieved and stepped back. "I'll leave you to it. I'll go and tell Tia, and then I'll let myself out. I need to get back, Saul has to go into work."

After Doctor Bryant had finished his tasks, Catherine looked up to see Joe holding the baby in his arms. She comprehended that by not allowing the abortion, Joe had saved this child's life, but now he had to realise that he could never be a part of it. She didn't want the baby, and he'd lost the battle to keep it.

"I have a sister!" came a huge yell from Tia's bedroom. Joe laughed while Catherine turned away.

"Look, Catherine, she's gorgeous, just like her mother," Joe said as he brought the baby to her.

She twisted to look, then glanced away again. "She has sandy-blonde hair," she whispered.

"Yes, isn't she stunning?"

"No."

"Let's call her Angeline," Joe announced.

"She's not to have a name," Catherine growled.

"We have to give her a legal name."

Catherine ignored him and stared across at Doctor Bryant. "Will you organise things to move as quickly as possible, please?" He bowed his head and said he would telephone the orphanage in the morning. Joe turned away. She knew he'd tried hard to make her change her mind, but he needed to realise that she was his priority; they owed nothing to some offspring of a rapist. It would have been so much easier if she'd had that abortion. How on earth was she going to explain the baby's pretend death to Tia? At that moment, she hated Joe. He'd made it impossible for her to protect Tia from the misery of losing this baby.

A few days later, Catherine put down the receiver and turned to Joe, who was holding the baby in his arms. "The orphanage said I can now take the baby. They have a couple who are a match for the child, and they can collect her straight away. We've agreed on eleven tomorrow, and the couple are due to arrive soon after I've gone." He didn't speak. "It's been too long, Joe. I allowed this wait because of the measles outbreak, but Tia's been getting far too attached to the baby, and I hate the way you and Tia call it 'baby Angeline,' you know she wasn't to have a name." Then the doorbell rang and without looking at her, he turned to answer it.

"David's arrived with Ada, they've come to meet the new baby," Joe said as he passed the child to Ada.

"She's beautiful," Ada announced. "Have you decided on a name yet? Oh, look, she's fair-haired, she's very different to Jack."

No one spoke. Breaking the tension, Catherine said with a wearied voice, "No, we haven't decided on a name." she sighed. "Ada, I'm exhausted, the doctor says I need to rest. Do you think you could have Tia and Jack, just for the next few days?"

"I'd love to have them, and to be honest dear, you do look awful."

Joe glared at Catherine. He'd obviously deduced that Tia and Jack would be out of the way while she did what she had to do.

Ada handed the newborn to David. "Here you go, Uncle David, you can have a cuddle now."

Catherine watched as David cradled the tiny creature in his beefy arms.

"I bet Win would have loved her new great-granddaughter," David said as he looked up at her.

Catherine stared at the floor. The man knew nothing. He didn't know Gran like she did. Gran would have approved of her adoption plans.

David lifted the baby to his lips, and Catherine vaguely heard him whisper, "You've got caring parents." Catherine's eyes met David's. A look of embarrassment greeted her, and she realised David probably hadn't wanted her to hear him. Was he mocking her and Joe? She turned away; she really didn't care.

The next morning, Joe announced, "I'm off to see David. I want to see his new sports car, it's a red Triumph 1800 Roadster." Catherine didn't know what a Triumph

1800 Roadster was, but she nodded, pretending she understood. She guessed Joe didn't want to see her driving off with what he called his daughter. She appreciated David would look after his brother, and he'd give support. Joe wrapped the baby in Tia's old, pink baby blanket, kissed her tenderly and placed her back in the carrycot. He put the small bag of baby essentials that he'd packed by the front door, took one last look, grabbed his coat and walked out of the house.

Catherine waited until Joe had gone then she shoved the baby and its belongings into the car. As she twisted to check that the carrycot was placed safely, she noticed a small white feather on Tia's old blanket. For a moment, her body became taut, but then again that feather had probably been attached to the pink blanket for years. She put the key in the ignition. As she drove towards Canterbury, the memory of Gran's words started echoing around in her head. "A mother's love isn't just based on giving birth; it's the love you give that makes you a mother." She smiled as she looked at her gran's heirloom ring shining on her finger. It felt so full of love. She knew she could never love this child and therefore she couldn't be a mother to it. She loved Tia and Jack, and she could be a good mother to them. But what if the baby tried to find her later in life? The truth would come out, and that thought terrified her. How could she make sure Tia and Jack would never find out what she'd done? As she drove, she thought long and hard. She made her plans, she knew what she had to do. She would speak to the new mother and …

*

136

The deed was done, and she was on her way home, content that it was all over. The child, with the pain it had brought, was gone for good. She admitted to herself that she liked the new parents, but most of all, she was relieved she had their support. However, it was probably best not to mention the meeting to Joe. She guessed he wouldn't approve of her demands. But now she could return to her legitimate children and her respectable family. Her life was moving on, and she felt happy once more. As she drove, she prophesied that David was her problem. She hated having to rely on him not to say anything. As she thought about her brother-in-law, her palms turned clammy. She was returning to her beautiful life with the family she loved, and no one, not even David, was ever going to take that away from her – she'd make sure of it

.

PART TWO

Separate Families.

CHAPTER 20

6th July 1952

Catherine stared at her grandfather's football photo above her fireplace and admitted to herself that it gave her sitting room a positive feel. Suddenly, someone on the radio started talking about infant deaths from unknown causes. Catherine stood up and turned off the radio, but it was too late, Angeline was talking about the past. In Catherine's head, she could hear Win's voice telling her the baby's 'sudden death' was the right thing to say to people. The truth could never escape, freedom from her painful lies wasn't an option open to her. She noticed Angeline had stopped speaking, and she turned to see her friend was waiting for an answer.

"How many times have I told you?" snapped Catherine. "The child died from my family's hereditary heart condition. The doctor said it was a miracle the child was born alive in the first place." She threw her friend a half-smile, then looked away as she admitted to herself that she wasn't lying. If she'd had an abortion, the child wouldn't have lived at all.

"I wish you'd allowed me to come to the cremation," Angeline said. "I feel I wasn't there for you."

"You were very supportive, and you know Joe and I wanted to say our goodbyes alone. It was a bad time for us."

"I'm sorry to rake it all up again," Angeline said with sympathy. Catherine couldn't bring herself to reply. Then Angeline changed the subject. "I do think your new hairstyle gives you a much softer look. It's very modern. I like it."

"I feel less weighed down with my hair short. I wanted a new me, and Joe likes it. Even David said it makes me look sophisticated."

Angeline reached for a biscuit. "You and David seem to be getting on."

Catherine felt awkward. David had helped them so much since … She pushed up her new curls. "He still comes round most evenings. Jack loves it when David sits with his legs dangling from the side of his chair. Jack stands on his feet, and David lifts him up and down, making him scream with laughter."

Angeline sipped her tea. "I remember him doing that with Tia when she was younger."

"Tia loves her Uncle David. She always asks him to read her bedtime stories. She says Daddy tries to hurry things along by missing out some of the words." She twiddled her hair and added, "David still doesn't like me, but it's a comfort that he and the children are so close."

"It's all in your head. I'm sure he does like you," Angeline said, grabbing another biscuit. "You always judge people without real cause." Catherine didn't bother to answer. She couldn't explain the truth. "Look at the time," Angeline cried as she jumped up from her chair. "I'd better get back for the boys. Saul has an afternoon function at the restaurant today."

A car pulled up on the drive. "It sounds like Joe and the children are home," Catherine said. "I need to sort lunch."

"Bye then," Angeline called as she hurried to the front door.

"Hello, Mummy," Tia said as she came bounding into the kitchen, her pigtails flying like two planes about to land.

"How was church?" Catherine asked as she started the sandwiches.

"As boring as ever. Jack cried all the way through the service. I felt sorry for him."

"Tia, out of Mummy's way," instructed Joe as he walked into the kitchen and stole a biscuit. "Hello, darling," he said, and she felt his lips peck her cheek. He glanced down at Tia. "I'm going back to Uncle David and Jack in the dining room, are you coming?"

"No. I'm staying here to help Mummy."

Catherine chuckled, "You can stay and talk to me if you want." Then she pointed teasingly to the door. "But Joe, out, please!" Joe pretended to run out of the kitchen, saying he was going to the safety of the men in the other room.

Tia stood, watching her make the sandwiches. "Mummy, why don't you ever wear your ring, the one that Great-Grandma Win gave you?"

Catherine felt the hairs on her skin stand on end, how had Tia noticed? "It was stolen when I went to the beach with Aunty Angeline. I left my ring on my towel, but when I returned from swimming, the ring was gone."

"Oh, no, how sad." Tia put her arms around Catherine. "That's horrible." Pulling away, she added, "Will Daddy buy you another one? I'll ask him to."

"The ring can't be replaced. It was very expensive, and it was special because it was Gran's ring."

"I think you're brave. I'd be heartbroken. I hate to lose things."

Catherine sighed. Her lies felt harrowing, but she had to be careful, she couldn't risk being found out, she had too much to lose. How she wished she could completely blank that baby from her mind. She hated it when other people talked about it, at least Joe had agreed they wouldn't mention the child again. She'd told him they needed to concentrate on their own family and that was what she had to do. She turned to Tia. "Here you go, you can help take the sandwiches into the dining room."

After lunch, the phone rang, and Joe went to answer it. Catherine's gaze fell on David. She wished he could be friendlier; he never spoke if Joe wasn't in the room.

Tia suddenly yelled, "Mummy, Jack's heading to the playroom. You need to go and check on him."

"Don't worry, Tia, he's safe in the playroom."

"He isn't old enough to be on his own," Tia bellowed. "He might do something dangerous. I don't want him to die like our sister Angeline did."

Catherine froze. "Tia, Jack's fine."

But Tia didn't hear; she was already running towards Jack. "I'll go and watch him."

David looked up from his paper. "Tia is overprotective towards Jack. You should tell her the baby didn't die."

"She's too young to understand," Catherine replied. Then shuddered.

"Can't you see you're making things worse for her?" His large nostrils flared as if they were about to explode with smoke. "You're doing this all wrong," he shouted.

"And a perfect person like you would know what's best!" she barked sarcastically.

"Is everything alright?" Joe asked as he entered the room.

"Yes, fine," snapped David, flipping his paper as he spoke.

"In that case, David, can I have a quiet word in my study?" Then, turning to Catherine, Joe added, "I've just been given some information about a job David and I are doing together." His voice sounded stern, and he was looking uptight, so she guessed it must be a serious work problem.

"Is it the doctor's information?" David muttered as they both walked out of the room.

"Ada will be here soon," Catherine called after them. "She's caught the bus over. We're taking the children to the beach while you two play golf." Catherine smiled to herself, Gran had been right, Ada had turned into a wonderful person, and she was a good granny to the children. Then her thoughts turned to Joe's parents. It was a shame Daphne's mobility wasn't good, Jack and Tia should see more of their Irish grandparents. She'd talk to Joe about visiting Ireland soon.

Catherine watched as Ada wheeled Jack's pushchair in the soft afternoon sun. Ada was aiming carefully down the windy path to the beach, while Tia held on tightly to the handle.

Ada said quietly, "Jack's too old for a pushchair. He doesn't seem to want to grow up, he's so insecure. I do worry about him."

"I know, he seems to love being looked after."

"That's my job," Tia said with glee.

Catherine laughed, "You're such a loving person."

"I want to be like you," Tia grinned, then she swiftly turned to Ada. "Or am I more like my other mummy?"

"Well," Ada swallowed, "I think you're a combination of all your parents." She smiled at Catherine. "You've picked up the mannerisms and strong-mindedness of Catherine, which is a good thing in life." Then she looked down at Tia. "However, you do look like Daddy with your dark hair and beautiful complexion, but your eyes and short, round frame are from my Hannah." She studied Tia for a while. "You have Hannah's observant and inquiring mind, as well as her thoughtfulness. You understand and care about people, and that's a quality that not many people have."

As Ada continued to push Jack, Tia asked more questions about Hannah. Catherine realised that Tia seemed fascinated with her and Ada's united ancestry. She could see a special affiliation forming between Granny Ada and her grandchild. She grinned. It was just like the partnership between her and Win. A lull fell in the conversation so, thinking about Gran, Catherine said to Ada, "I'm going to visit Sam and Anna tomorrow."

"Are they happy in Eastry?"

"They love it there. It was the right decision for them to move nearer to their daughter. Phyllis has decorated their cottage beautifully."

"It's lovely that Win gave them the money for the cottage."

"It's such a relief. Sam would never have accepted it from me. I miss that wise old woman so much."

"Don't you think it's time you visited Win's grave?"

"I know I should, but it still hurts."

"It's been five years now, and time does heal. You're stronger now. You should go."

They returned from the beach to find the men were back from golf.

"The pot's still hot," shouted Joe from the kitchen.

"I'll go and bath the children first," announced Ada. "I'd like to have some time with them before I leave. You go and have a drink, dear."

"Thanks, Ada," Catherine said, turning towards the kitchen. She poured herself a cup of tea and sat down next to the men. "Ada's persuaded me to visit Gran's grave," she said excitedly. "So, I've decided I'll plant some flowers and make the grave look beautiful for Gran."

Joe smiled. "That's wonderful news, darling."

"You should leave the grave alone," David snorted.

"That's rubbish, David," said Joe. "It's all part of the healing process. I think it's excellent that at last Catherine's able to visit the grave. This is a real step forward."

David glared at him. "No, it isn't. It's a huge step backwards. Catherine needs to move on and forget the past."

"I want to tell Gran all about Tia and Jack and what they've been up to, so I am moving on with the future."

"But Win's spirit isn't there," David snapped. "I can't comprehend why you need to go and talk to an inanimate stone!" His voice sounded fierce. "Win will be with you wherever you are." His burly finger pushed up his glasses, making his thick eyebrows enlarge into bushes. "It's a long drive just to look at a grave, it's unhealthy. You shouldn't go, it's not good for you to visit Gravesend."

Catherine felt her irritation growing. "You always think you know best, but it's my choice."

Joe put his arm around her. "David, I don't know why you're getting so angry. It's irrelevant whether you believe Win's there or not, if it helps Catherine, then it's a good thing."

"You're mad," David scoffed. "It's pointless." Then he stared angrily at the table.

CHAPTER 21

7ᵗʰ July 1952

"I'm glad we met today," Selina said as they left the park.

"Me too," replied Annette as she fought to hold onto her wayward son. "Come here, William," Annette yelled as he rigged free and ran off. "Will starts school this year. I hope he behaves better with the teacher than he does with me. Is your daughter starting school this year?"

"No. She's only four."

"Will's five in a few weeks. Gosh, he's a whole school year older than Maria. She's tall for her age. Is her father tall?"

"Yes," Selina replied truthfully, although she knew that wasn't what Annette meant.

"Sorry Mummy," Will shouted, his beech-brown hair ruffled. "I just wanted to get Maria's ball back." His freckly face contorted. "I'd kicked it into the bushes over there."

"Oh, alright then," his mum said as she took the ball and gave it back to Maria.

Selina watched as Maria bounced her new ball along the street. She'd just learnt how to bounce the ball, and she seemed so pleased with herself.

"It must be lovely to have a daughter," Annette said as they walked down the road. "I'd like a girl next time. She looks so much like you, she has your beautiful light green eyes, and your sandy-blonde hair too."

Selina felt a lump in her throat, and she didn't know what to say.

"It's my ball, leave it alone," yelled Maria as Will kicked it away from her.

Relieved by the interruption, Selina called out, "Maria, you must play nicely with William." She turned back to Annette. "I'm sorry Maria doesn't seem to understand that she has to share." Then, out of the corner of her eye, Selina noticed William snatch the ball and drop it.

"Don't worry, all children go through that stage," said Annette.

Selina nodded, then she saw the ball spin off the pavement and into the road. Maria sprinted after it. "No, Maria, STOP! Leave the ball!" screamed Selina.

There was a loud, screeching noise. Then as if in slow motion, and with a thunderous bang, she watched a car hit a tree on the opposite side of the lane. Maria was standing still in the middle of the road, not seeming to understand what had happened. She was staring at the ball that was squashed flat in the middle of the road. Selina ran and grabbed her daughter into her arms, pulling her to the pavement. She found herself collapsing on the path, with Maria falling on her lap. She couldn't stop herself from shaking, and her heart was pounding. Her grip around Maria was tight, but she appreciated that her daughter didn't understand why. Maria started to howl, but she guessed it was only because her ball was broken. Annette was talking, but Selina couldn't hear what she was saying above Maria's loud sobbing. Then Annette turned and roared at William, but again she couldn't catch what she was saying. Out of nowhere, a large man appeared. He was standing looking down at her, his posture imposing and his face red with anger. Both she and Annette fell silent. Maria also seemed scared and stopped crying.

"The child shouldn't have been running in the road like that," the man shouted. "This lane is narrow and full of bends. Drivers can't see around corners you know! Why didn't you keep a closer eye on her?"

Selina looked up in a daze. "Don't you think I know how stupid I've been? You've no idea how precious my daughter is to me." With that, she kissed Maria repeatedly. "Are you alright, love? Do you hurt anywhere?"

"I'm OK, Mummy. Why did the car hit the tree?"

The man glared at Maria, and with a posh accent, he announced, "That's my car, and I hit the tree to avoid hitting you, young lady."

Maria stared for a while and then said, "Oh, I'm sorry, Mister. I'm sorry, Mummy." She put her head into Selina's chest and started to cry again. "I didn't mean to break the man's car. Is he going to hurt us?"

The huge man bent down next to them on the pavement. "I'm not going to hurt you," his voice sounded throaty. He looked at Selina. "She is alright, isn't she?"

Selina was still in a daze and unsure what to say, all she could do was hold onto Maria as firmly as she could. "I nearly lost my baby ... how could I have taken my eyes off her ... I never take my eyes off her, never?! Oh, my love, I could have lost you." She kissed Maria endlessly, not wanting to let her go.

"Sorry, Mummy. I didn't mean to upset you."

Annette looked down the street. "We need to get you home, Selina, which one's your house?"

The man stood up and stretched out his strong arm to help Selina stand. "I'm sorry, I shouted. I was rather shaken myself." She took his large hand while keeping her other hand attached firmly to Maria. The man continued, "This lady's right, I think you're in shock, we need to get you and your daughter home."

"What about your car?" Selina said, looking at the abandoned red car across the road. It looked terrible with its front caved in and the windscreen all broken. It almost seemed as if it was about to climb the tree.

The man used his thumb and forefinger to push up his thick-set glasses. "Once I've taken you home, I'll get someone to tow it away."

Waving her arm towards her house, she said, "We live there; it's the one with the purple door." She saw the man's face drop, he turned and stared at Maria, his eyes growing larger through his lenses. She guessed he was still worried about her. "I'm sorry," she said. "I'm not thinking straight. I should thank you for swerving and not hitting my daughter. If you hadn't …" Her voice quivered, "I'm sorry about your car. Will it cost a lot to repair?"

"I didn't hurt your daughter and believe me, that's all that counts. What a shock this has been." The man pushed back his thick black hair and looked across at his sad-looking car. "To be honest, I wanted to change my car, anyway." She felt slight relief. He didn't seem to be concerned, which was something.

"We like purple," Maria interrupted. "Will your new car be purple?"

The man peered at her. "I don't think purple is quite my colour," he said in a silly voice, and they all laughed.

As they walked towards her house, Selina held onto Maria. She was grateful for Annette's arm, which was around her waist. Annette was holding William with her other arm, but it didn't look like he was going to run off again. The man walked in silence, but Selina could hear his loud footsteps behind them. When Selina unlocked their front door, Annette insisted on making her a sweet cup of tea.

Selina turned to the man. "There's a phone box at the end of our road. Once you've phoned a garage, you could come back and wait at ours, we'll have a pot of tea ready." The man looked at Maria and then nodded. Selina watched him as he walked off towards the shining red telephone box which had just been installed. She remembered Mark saying those boxes were ugly. He'd said that telephones weren't a necessity, they were a waste of money, and he couldn't understand why they were springing up on every road.

William and Maria ran straight off to play in the yard, leaving Selina and Annette to talk. She drank her tea while also looking constantly through the window, waving and laughing at Maria in the yard. When the man came back, she noticed that he kept blushing every time he spoke. He was probably feeling awkward about the whole situation. She stood up and called the children indoors for more drinks then, returning to her seat, she noticed the man's eyes fasten on her.

Once again turning a little red-faced, he asked, "You have a fine house, have you lived here long?"

"We moved in before we had Maria. We love it here."

"I see." The man turned to Maria, and with a huge smile, he said, "Well, young lady, you certainly have a lot of toys."

Maria looked up from her overflowing toy box. "My name is Maria, not young lady. What's your name?"

The man smiled again. "I think Maria is a very pretty name. My name is David, which isn't a pretty name at all."

"I like David," interrupted William. "It's better than Will, which I get called."

"Will is a fine name," retorted his mother.

Maria ran up to the man and took his hand. "Are we friends now?"

"Of course, we are," he said with another smile.

"Then, you can see my toys."

"I'm afraid I do have to go soon. The mechanic will be here to help with my car."

Maria pouted her lips. "I don't want you to go." Selina knew her daughter loved having attention, and David was giving her lots of smiles.

"Next time I'm in the area maybe I'll pop in and see you, how about that?"

"Yes please," Maria said as she squeezed David's hand. "You will come back, won't you?" She gave him one of her adorable grins, which displayed her slight dimple.

Serena noticed that David looked slightly unnerved. She guessed he didn't really want to return. Picking Maria up, David said, "You must be careful and stay on the pavement at all times. Promise me you won't run into the road again, and please don't play ball in the street."

"I promise. Anyway, my big ball is broken. Now I'll never learn to kick a ball like Will."

"And I promise I'll never try to kill her again!" mumbled William.

"Will, it wasn't your fault Maria ran into the road," David said sternly. "You mustn't blame yourself. Girls will always do what they want to do, you can't stop them! However, it would be good if you could keep an eye on this little princess; she seems quite headstrong." With that,

Selina thought David seemed to wince, but then he winked at Maria and put her back down on the floor.

"I promise I'll look after her," Will, replied in a very grown-up voice.

Selina grinned, David probably had children of his own, he was very good with them.

After David had left, Will and Maria went back into the yard and played with a small ball from Maria's toy box. Selina glanced out of the window. Maria was bouncing the ball to Will, and he was returning it to her. Maria was sharing! This boy was a good influence. Selina was determined that she'd make sure Maria learned to share, her daughter's self-centred ways needed sorting, and as her mother, it was her job to guide her.

CHAPTER 22

7th July - 1st August 1952

David watched his car being towed away by the truck then, feeling uncomfortable about the day's events, he slowly climbed into his waiting taxi. He didn't speak to the driver except for giving him his home address, his thoughts were running back to the past. As he closed his eyes, he felt thankful he hadn't told Joe exactly where the child lived. Then his eyes flew open. It wasn't right to tell him now either!

David sat back in the taxi, remembering how his political contacts had made it easy for him to get the reports for the adoption process. He'd wanted to choose the right parents for Catherine's child, but he'd never anticipated that the man who'd saved his life would be on the list! He recalled visiting Mark in the army hospital, he'd realised then that the lad's accent was from Kent, but he never expected to hear of him again. The adoption report had shown they were the best parents for Catherine's child, but he was also glad he'd been able to repay his debt to the lad. He pushed up his glasses. He needed to concentrate on the matter in hand, he had to find a way of dealing with the danger that had taken him back to Gravesend. It hadn't worried him before, Catherine hadn't been interested in returning, but now...

He sat upright as he thought about Maria. If the child had stayed with Catherine, she'd have been raised as his niece. Catherine had taken that role of uncle away from him. He huffed. Joe was weak, he hadn't protected the child that he claimed to have loved. He gazed out of the window. He was nearly home. Dover High Street was empty, the shops were closed, and even the seaside holidaymakers had disappeared for the night. The taxi stopped at the traffic lights, and David stared at the department store beside him. The display in the middle of the window involved a small brown leather football, lying next to a child's miniature wooden goal post. He remembered Maria wanting to kick a big ball like Will could. She was such a gutsy little girl, very like Catherine in lots of ways. Should he revisit his step-niece? Mark probably wouldn't recognise him. David thought about his upcoming work meeting in Rochester. He could drop into Gravesend again. Perhaps by getting to know the family, he could find a solution to his problem.

*

David pulled up outside Maria's house then realised his car looked conspicuous in such a poor street. The terrace houses were run down, and the lane itself was full of potholes. He felt guilty for having money when others didn't. As David got out of his car, he heard a man shout,

"Are you lost, mate?"

David turned to see a tall, strapping, young man marching towards him. He recognised him instantly.

Mark's scar looked awful, but thankfully, his left arm seemed to hang normally. "No, I'm calling on this house here," he said as he waved at the purple door.

Mark was next to him now. "That's my house," he said. "Is it me you want?" His face had turned red. "My name's Mark Tozer."

David kept up his act. "Oh, you must be Maria's father. I nearly ran over your little girl the other week. I've been in the area on business, and I just thought I'd pop around to see how she was?"

Mark stared at him. "It can't be you, Sir, can it? After all these years. Do you remember me? Corporal Tozer, from—"

"Oh, my goodness, so, it is!" David gave Mark a warm handshake. "Of course, I remember you. I have never forgotten what you did for me. Pushing me away from those falling rocks saved my life."

"Well, I can't thank you enough for swerving to miss our daughter, and I'm sorry our Maria ran out on you like that, Sir."

"Call me, David, and I'm just grateful I didn't hit her."

"Me too! Come in," Mark said, putting his key into the lock. "Selina! Maria! I'm home and guess who I've brought to see you." Turning to David, he asked, "Can Selina get you a drink, Sir?"

"A cup of tea would be perfect," David replied, realising his voice sounded a little edgy.

"Oh, David, what a lovely surprise, and I see you've met Mark," Selina said as she appeared through the kitchen door.

"Love, I can't believe it, but this is the General I pushed away from those falling rocks."

"What?" Selina turned and glared at David as if he was the enemy.

"Hello," David said with a hoarse voice. "Um, I didn't know your husband was Mark Tozer, it's a small world! Um, anyway, I wanted to make sure Maria was alright, and I … I've brought her some sweets and a little gift." David was aware he sounded awkward, but he felt as if Selina's eyes were boring into his soul. "When I saw the gift in the shop, I just had to buy it for her." This all felt wrong. He shouldn't have come.

Mark looked uncomfortable. "It's very good of you to give our Maria gifts, Sir. But I realise your car must have cost you a fortune to repair. Do we need to pay for the repairs?"

"No," David replied sharply, "certainly not. My car was a write-off, so the insurance paid. Besides, I was about to change my car and ..." Mark went to speak, but David didn't stop, "I'd already decided on the Jaguar, not that I told the sales chap that. I've just driven the Jag for its longest run yet; it's a great drive." He smiled at the staring Selina, who didn't respond.

"I'd never seen a Jaguar close up before. It looks magnificent," Mark said with admiration in his voice.

"I'll show you the car, we could even go for a spin." David didn't know why he offered this, he just felt guilt-ridden. He was the imposter here.

"That'll be great!" Mark turned to Selina. "You don't mind if we go out, do you love?"

Her cat-like green eyes ignited on David. "You won't know that Mark's injuries were severe. He took the brunt of the rockfall. If he'd moved away sooner—"

"Stop it, love," Mark interrupted.

Selina's piercing eyes still didn't leave David's. He nodded. Of course, this woman blamed him for her husband's injuries, he did too! David had often questioned why he didn't react faster when they first heard the roar.

Mark took his wife's arm. "Selina, love, I would have saved any man who had been standing there, it's not David's fault."

She nodded at Mark. "You're a good man."

"Where is Maria?" David inquired, wanting to change the subject.

"She's at my friend Annette's house, you remember, William's mum?" He nodded. "It was William's birthday party today. When I went to collect Maria, she refused to come home, she wanted to play with William's new toys. Annette said Maria could stay for a while, so I'm going back later." David frowned as he imagined Maria in charge of Williams's new toys. She had Catherine's stubborn personality! He felt himself blush; this deceit felt unbearable.

"I'll leave my gift as a surprise for when she gets home," David said as he moved towards the door. He handed Selina the sweets then muttered to forget the cup of tea.

When David and Mark returned from their drive, Selina had already collected Maria from William's house.

Maria ran straight to David. "This ball is the best present I've ever had," she announced as she stroked her football. "It's much better than any of the birthday presents Will got, and I'm going to tell him so."

Selina gasped. "Maria, you mustn't boast. And we're waiting for you to say thank you to David, please."

"Thank you," Maria muttered as she started kicking the ball around in the lounge, knocking things over as she went.

Selina raised her voice, "Stop that, Maria. I've told you, this is an outside toy. The ball's too big for in here."

David watched as Maria fell into a sulk and looked at the floor. She reminded him of Jack when he couldn't get his own way. He felt himself redden. This wasn't the time or place to compare Maria to her half-brother. "Your mummy's right. How about your daddy and I set up your new goal in the yard?"

"Oh yes, you can teach me how to shoot," Maria yelped as she ran off with the ball in her hand.

Mark turned to David. "After we're done, why don't you join me brother and me in the pub? We always have a drink on a Friday night. I'd like to buy you a pint for saving my daughter."

"Mmm, well …"

"That's a yes, then," Mark said as he opened the back door. He shouted to Maria, "We can only play for a while. David and I have to go and meet Uncle Brian soon."

David loved the quaint little pub, with its dried hops draped over the low timber beams. It felt as if he was back in another time, in a world where alcohol solved all your problems.

"So, Brian, where were you based in the war?" David asked as he gulped from his third pint.

Mark snorted. "He was busy doing crosswords while I was holding the fort in Gibraltar." David turned and stared at Brian.

Brian whispered, "Mark, you know I hate the fact you got injured in those tunnels, while I got lucky being transferred to intelligence." He sipped his beer. "I might have had a desk job, but it was important, there are things I can't tell you about."

David leant across the table to Brian. "I can guess where you were based, we owe so much to your section."

"What section and what did he do?" asked Mark as he ate another crisp.

"Nothing," murmured Brian.

David knew both men had given a lot to the war effort, but he also knew he had to change the subject. "So, what do you think of the new plans for the Welfare State? I believe it's right that everyone should have the same entitlements."

Mark raised his glass of beer. "You're spot on there."

"I'd like to make the world a better place for everybody," David said as he took off his spectacles. "But how do you make it better for people who won't listen?" He cleaned his glasses and placed them back on his face. "I'm a bit of a know-all, I tell people what I think, which doesn't always make me very popular!" He groaned as he looked at his watch, "It's getting late, I'd better get going, I have a long drive back."

"Will you join us in the pub next week?" Mark asked as David reached for his jacket.

David gave one of his awkward smiles. Mark had every reason to hate him, but instead, he'd accepted him. What's more, David liked the fellow. "I believe I will. It's refreshing to talk to people who believe in the same things as I do."

As David walked back to his car in Church Lane, he berated himself for getting involved with Mark. But why shouldn't he be allowed to make friends with the man who saved his life? He respected Mark; he was a real salt of the earth type of chap. His thoughts turned to Maria, and he realised he was in the middle of two families. Should he tell either of them the truth? No, it was best to leave the two families as separate entities, there was no point in upsetting either of them. Catherine's proposed visits to the graveyard weren't that worrying either, the two families didn't know each other, they weren't aware of their connection. David opened his car door and stood looking across at the church with its vast churchyard sloping away. Then he stared up at the bright stars and found himself thinking of Win. She would want him to make sure her great-granddaughter was alright. Besides, Maria was his step-niece, if Joe couldn't be there for her, then he could. He was the one who had chosen this life for Maria. He got into his car. He liked Mark, and he would join him in the pub next week that way, he could keep an eye on things. It was his job to protect everyone from finding out the truth.

CHAPTER 23

18th June 1953 – 18th October 1954

Talking in French, Catherine snapped, *"Hurry up, Jack. You need to get ready for your doctor's appointment."*

"Maman, don't you think speaking in French is more fun than in English?"

"I think it's great that you can speak in both languages." Her voice softened, "But, Tia can't understand French, and she's starting to feel left out. So, Daddy and I think it's best if from now on, we don't talk in French when Tia is around. Then she won't get upset."

"I don't want Tia upset." Jack's breathing deepened, and he coughed loudly.

"The sooner we get your chest sorted out, the better. Then you can go back to school."

"I hate school. Everyone calls me names. But at least there's Tia to look after me at playtimes."

"But you know she goes to secondary school next year," Catherine said as she tied his shoelace. "She won't always be there for you. Do you play with anyone else at school?"

Jack shrugged his shoulders. "No. I work hard, though, don't I, Maman?"

She nodded and smiled at him, knowing that he only studied hard because it meant he didn't have to socialise.

"It's just another chest infection," Doctor Bryant said as he put down his stethoscope. "I'm sure he'll grow out of them soon." While he wrote the prescription, he added, "I'm retiring in a few months, but there's a very agreeable doctor taking over the practice."

"Oh, no! You've been with my family for so long," wailed Catherine as she took the prescription from him. "What will we do without you? You know I can't thank you enough for all you've done for me."

"Before I leave, I might be able to find out some information about the child."

"What child?" asked Jack, looking enquiringly at her.

"Just someone the doctor and I knew once," Catherine said as she felt a sweep of apprehension.

"I won't be able to find out much, just where she went to, but at least you would know something. Would you like me to?"

That evening as Catherine tucked Tia into bed, her mind mulled over the day's events. As she looked up at the portrait, now above Tia's bed, she found herself gazing into Hannah's azure eyes. What would she have done about the existence of another child? She grinned, it almost felt as if they were friends.

"Mummy, I'm worried about Jack." Tia's face tightened. "The children at school call him odd. He's really unhappy. Can you help him?"

"Don't you worry about your brother. I'll talk to Daddy. Night-night, darling." Catherine kissed Tia and turned off the light.

As Catherine walked downstairs, she could hear Joe on the phone. He was speaking uncharacteristically quietly, so she strained to hear what he was whispering, "We've done it then. Thanks, David, for everything."

"What was that about?" she asked as he put down the receiver.

"Er, David's finally finished a job we've been working on. We're rather pleased with the outcome," Joe said, with a smug smile on his face. "It's chilly in this hall, let's go and sit by the coal fire," he added as he leapt towards the sitting room door.

Once seated, Joe picked up his book, but she could see the smile was still on his face. She judged this was a good moment to approach him.

"Joe, Jack isn't enjoying school." Joe continued staring at his book, but she carried on. "The children see him as different. He's so awkward around others, he reminds me of David in so many ways."

"He does take after his uncle," Joe muttered, without looking up.

"I'm sure the support Jack needs would be better in an all-boys' school. I'm wondering if we should look at sending him to the Citadel School now, rather than later."

Joe put down his book and shifted his position in his chair. "I thought we agreed we would send both children to the independent schools when they're eleven. It's expensive ..."

"I realise how extortionate the school fees are. But Jack's got his Uncle David's intelligence, I bet he'll pass their scholarship exam. Then we won't have to pay for him."

Joe leaned back in his chair. "Alright, it's worth a try."

*

The September term came around quickly. It was Jack's first day at the Citadel School for Boys, yet as Catherine stood with Jack in the playground, her memories about the place made her shiver. She tried to be logical, it wasn't the school's fault Gregory Jones had gone there, but then again, the fact her grandfather had died while refereeing on one of the school's football pitches had never allowed her to warm to the cold red stone building.

"I am glad you got that scholarship, Jack," Catherine said, as Jack's hand tightly held onto hers. He was looking up at her with his blue eyes and black hair shining in the morning sunlight. She realised Jack might have David's antisocial ways, but he looked so much like Joe, she loved him dearly. "I do hope you like this school. It's small and just boys, so there is nothing to be frightened of." A lad came up to them and started talking, she felt Jack let go of her hand, and before she knew it, the two boys were running around the playground together. Tia would be pleased; she was the only sister Jack needed!

*

"I'm a failure," exclaimed Tia some months later, throwing the envelope against the rose bowl.

Catherine reached for a hanky and handed it to her. "It doesn't matter that you didn't pass your Eleven Plus, you're still going to the Citadel School for Girls, just as we planned. And you're not a failure."

"I'm not good at anything, and I can't even pass a stupid exam," Tia said as she ran off up the stairs.

Catherine followed, but as she got halfway, she heard Tia's bedroom door slam and the lock turn. Catherine walked briskly and tapped on the door. "Please, Tia, let me in. We need to talk."

"I'm not talking to you. I don't want to talk to anyone."

"Tia, you're still going to the Citadel School, we never expected you to get a scholarship."

"I don't want to go to that stupid girls' school. I want to go to the Secondary Mod, where all my friends are going."

"Tia, we've discussed this …"

"Go away."

*

It was mid-October when Tia ran into the kitchen after returning from school. "I've got another invite for tea with a girl in my new class." She looked in the cupboard for a biscuit. "I'm sure it's because you befriended all the mothers."

"That's good," Catherine said as she took the packet from Tia and handed her one biscuit. "I just wanted to help you settle in," she added. It was only then that she remembered how Gran had invited all the children for tea when she'd first started at the school. There was also that French nanny employed to help her to learn English. She giggled; Gran had done the same for her as she was doing for Tia!

Tia spoke with a mouthful of biscuit. "The fact that you and your mum went to my school impresses everyone. People are starting to treat me as if I'm royalty."

"The staff were lovely when I was there. Mrs Roberts was my favourite. I can't believe she's still there."

"Mrs Roberts told me off yesterday."

"Why?"

"I pushed a girl who was being nasty to Isabel's sister. I explained to Mrs Roberts that I was sorting out Joanne's bullies." Tia went quiet. "I don't see why I got into trouble for protecting Isabel's sister." She glanced at Catherine. "I do think about my sister Angeline, sometimes. Do you, Mummy?"

Catherine's body went numb. "Sometimes."

Tia looked away. "Mrs Roberts said I should have told her about the bullying. Then Mrs Roberts laughed and said you used to protect your friends too."

Catherine couldn't help but grin. "Anyway, do you think those extra maths lessons in the summer helped you at all?"

"Yes, they did, and I've made up my mind not to fail any more exams. I'm going to study hard. I know Jack's brilliant at French, so I plan to find a subject I can be good at." With a beam, she added, "Just like you, Mum, when I decide to do something I do it!"

"That's my girl," Catherine said as she pulled her close to her chest.

CHAPTER 24

22nd August - 7th September

1953

Maria was sitting on David's feet, while he swung her up and down from the side of his chair, causing her ponytail to flip through the air.

"David's a decent bloke considering he's so posh and all that," Mark whispered.

"It's great that you and David are such good friends now." Selina looked into Mark's eyes. "Even I don't hate him anymore. If David hadn't acted so quickly, God knows what would have happened to our Maria that day. And he's so good with her."

"It's a hot Saturday," announced David, "so why don't we all go for a trip in my Jaguar? I'll take you to the new ice cream parlour on Deal seafront. It's a bit of a drive, but they make the best ice cream in Kent." He turned to Mark, "And I insist on paying the bill."

"No, you won't," Mark replied.

Selina interrupted. "Can we be back by teatime, only Annette is bringing Will round later?"

"Yes, we'll be back well before then," replied David. "Come on, I want to teach Maria how to skim pebbles into the sea."

Selina sat in the back of the car listening to the men chattering, while Maria fell asleep in her arms. She noticed David glance in the mirror. "Maria looks like a little sleeping princess," he said softly.

Maria stirred as she heard her name. "Are we nearly there yet, Uncle David?" she asked with her eyes still shut. Selina went to speak, and then stopped herself; it didn't matter that David wasn't family; he acted like an uncle.

As they went down yet another narrow side-street, Selina muttered, "David, you seem to know these roads well."

"My brother's ex-mother-in-law lives here, but she's staying in Dover at the moment," David replied. He turned a corner quickly, and they were on the seafront.

"I can see the sea," shouted Maria.

*

Eileen sat Maria on her lap. "It's Monday, so I think we'll bake cakes today."

"Oh, yes, please, Nana, and can I lick the mixing bowl afterwards?"

"Honestly, love. I think you like the mixture better than the cakes." Eileen cuddled her granddaughter in her arms.

"Nana, you smell of lavender, you make me feel safe. You won't leave like Grandad Harold did, will you?"

"Grandad didn't have a choice, but he didn't want to go."

"I like your stories about Grandad Harold. Can you tell me another one?"

"I'll go and get the shopping now," Selina intervened, "and when I get back, I'll make us all some bread and dripping for lunch."

As Selina walked to the shops, she thought about her dad; it was lovely that Maria was so interested. She admitted to herself that she was thankful Maria didn't really know Mark's parents, they hardly ever saw them. But at least Brian and Sandra both doted on Maria, she grimaced, she'd promised to visit them this afternoon. She understood that young Stanley was getting fed up with Maria; there was a definite clash of personalities there. Selina waited at the corner of the road as a car turned left beside her. Deep in thought, she settled on telling Maria to play nicely with her cousins. As Selina turned back to the car, she caught sight of the driver. It was only a second or two, but she was sure the red-headed woman was … The woman's hair was short, and she looked older than she remembered. The woman drove off without noticing her and Selina walked on. Her head said no, it couldn't be, but her heart said yes it was. Selina determined that it couldn't have been … And anyway, that woman wasn't part of their lives, and she never would be.

*

The August afternoon heat felt sticky and humid. "Have you got Maria's uniform yet?" asked Sandra as they stood and watched the three children playing in the garden.

"I'm going to get it tomorrow," Selina replied. "But thanks again for the school clothes you've given us."

"Every little helps."

"I want some sweets," Stanley cried to his mum.

Selina noticed Maria's face as she turned smugly towards Stanley. "I have loads at my house. My Uncle David always gives me posh sweets."

"You're spoilt."

"Mummy, Stanley's horrible to me."

Stanley pulled a face. "She's not your real—"

"Stop it, Stan," yelled Sandra, smacking him sharply across his leg. He screamed, turned and ran off into the house, howling as he went.

Sandra put her arms around Maria. "Sometimes Stan can be like Grandad Tozer, they can both be nasty. It's in their make-up." Maria scowled at Sandra, then went back to play with Minnie. Selina's heart stopped. Her deepest fear had returned; Stanley didn't see them as Maria's real parents, just as others wouldn't. She looked away. There was no point in telling anyone about the adoption, people would never understand. It had been hard telling Maria she'd come from another mummy's tummy, but the worst bit had been explaining that the woman had chosen to give her away. Selina fathomed that the red-headed woman would always be a threat to her own role as Maria's mother. She had been wrong earlier, that woman was never going to go away!

The next day was emotionally exhausting, it reminded Selina of the day she and her mum had gone shopping for Maria's baby things.

"Daddy," Maria announced as Selina collapsed in a chair. "You should see my new school uniform. Mummy said I looked grown-up, she and Nana even cried in the shop."

"Can I see what you've bought?" Mark asked.

"Come on, Mummy, let's put them on again. I wish Nana hadn't gone home." Maria turned and ran up to her bedroom. Selina understood how much her daughter loved to show off so, seizing the bags, she followed closely behind.

Selina felt proud as Maria pranced up and down the lounge like a model, turning and swinging her hair as she went.

"My little princess looks lovely," Mark grinned. "You're growing up so quickly," he added fondly.

"Do you think my other mummy would like me in my school uniform."

A knife pierced through Selina's soul. "Of course, she would, love."

*

The 7th September had come around all too quickly, and Selina's heart pounded as she and her mum walked Maria to the school gates. Selina held on tightly to Maria's little hand, while her other hand was threaded through her mother's arm. When they all entered the playground, Will ran towards them and shouted,

"Don't worry, Mrs Tozer, I promise I'll look after Maria." Selina couldn't help but smile at the small boy.

"I trust you, William." Tears were welling in her eyes. "I can't be with Maria today, so I'm putting all my faith in you."

She watched as her mum bent down to Maria. "Now, don't be scared love, Granddad Harold will be watching over you." Selina knew that statement usually calmed Maria down, but today it didn't make her daughter smile.

CHAPTER 25

7ᵗʰ September 1953

Maria looked up at her mummy and saw the tears in her eyes, then she saw her nana was holding onto her mummy's arm. For the first time, Maria understood.

"Nana, will you look after Mummy as I'm not there today, so I'm putting my faith in you?" Everyone burst out laughing, and her mummy was smiling at her. Maria felt pleased with herself. She was aware everyone said she was a strong-willed child, and now for the sake of everyone else, she knew she had to be strong-minded. She pushed back one of her sandy-blonde plaits and glared across at Will. "Shall we go into school?" She said, hoping he'd understand the urgency in her voice.

Clasping her hand, he declared, "Maria will be fine, Mrs Tozer."

"You'll be here to pick me up later, won't you, Mummy?" Maria asked in a brave voice.

"I'll be here early, waiting for you. I want you to promise to tell me about everything that happens today."

"I promise," Maria replied as she stood as straight as she could.

With that, Will led her forwards, but her heart was breaking. She was walking away, and she didn't know how she was going to cope without her family. Other children around were screaming and crying, but she was determined to appear fearless. She wasn't going to make her family upset. As she walked to the school door, she turned to wave, and she smiled and pretended she was alright. But as soon as they were inside the school, she burst into tears.

"Will, don't leave me. I don't want to be on my own, and I don't want to go to this horrible school."

Will took her in his arms and hugged her. "I'll take you to your classroom. I'll wait for you at playtime. I'll sit with you at lunchtime, and I'll wait for you at afternoon play. Then, when it's all over, I'll walk out of school with you, and we'll find your mummy again." She frowned at him. She didn't understand, but she guessed he meant he would be around. Will found her classroom and ushered her through the door.

"See you later," he said, and off he went to his own room.

She thought the classroom looked large and scary, with lots of desks and chairs everywhere. As she entered, the teacher came up to her. "What's your name?" she asked as she glared at her.

"Maria Selina Tozer," she responded quietly.

"I'm Mrs Morris," the woman said, ticking some list she had in her hand. Then she led Maria to a table where three other girls were sitting. "Sit here, Maria, and we'll start when everyone else has arrived."

Maria sat and looked at the other girls. The two girls opposite her were very pretty and were chatting to each other about their dolls. She gazed at the girl who sat quietly next to her. She had blonde hair, cut short in a boy's style.

Maria noticed the girl's eyes were fixed on the table, and she guessed she was as scared as she was. "I'm Maria Tozer, what's your name?" she asked her quietly.

"I'm Janice Troop." Then there was silence.

Not wanting to give up, Maria tried again. Tilting her head towards the other two girls, she asked, "Do you like dolls?"

Janice stared at her and then said, "Nope, I like football."

"Me too," Maria retorted. They looked at each other and giggled.

"I have two little sisters and a dog called Kira," Janice told her. "What do you have?"

"I don't have sisters," Maria explained. She decided not to mention that her mummy couldn't have babies. Instead, she added, "I've always wanted a dog, but my parents say we can't afford one." She guessed Janice's parents had loads of money. Mrs Morris started to speak, and they were told to stop talking and listen to her.

Playtime came around, and Will was by her side.

"This is Janice," Maria explained. "She has a dog."

"What sort of dog do you have?" Will asked with interest.

Janice thought for a while and then replied, "A spaniel." Will nodded and seemed to understand what she meant. Maria thought he was clever. She realised that she couldn't imagine life without Will, it felt like he was her older brother. The three of them stood and talked for the whole of their playtime. At lunchtime, Will was there again. He showed her and Janice how to get their lunch, and he sat with them while they all ate. They played tag in the lunch break and again in the afternoon playtime.

Then, as school finished, Will appeared by the door.

"We need to find your mummy," he said to Maria.

Maria nodded, remembering that her mummy would have missed her. She wanted to tell her about how good school had been, but most of all she needed to tell her about her new friend Janice. Will took her hand and walked out into the playground with her. A sea of women confronted her eyes. Panic hit, where was her mummy? She started to cry. Had her mummy deserted her?

Will shouted and pulled her across the playground. "There she is, she and your nana are talking to my mum."

All of a sudden, her mummy turned, knelt, and stretched out her arms towards Maria. While still crying, Maria ran as fast as she could, flying into her arms.

"I thought you weren't here! I thought you'd left me," Maria squawked.

Her mummy picked her up and cuddled her close. "Don't be silly, love. I've been waiting all day for this moment," and then she kissed her constantly. "How was school?" Maria didn't answer; she just held on firmly, scared that she might lose her mummy. She didn't want to be left alone. She knew the woman whose tummy she'd come from hadn't wanted her, so one day her own mummy might not want her either.

CHAPTER 26

6th July - 7th July 1956

"There are a lot more cars and lorries entering France than there used to be," Catherine informed Joe as they moved off the dock. She reached for the map in the glove compartment. "It's a long way to Caen," she said as she watched Joe nod in agreement, his focus being entirely on the road ahead. She could tell he was concentrating hard, it had been a long time since he'd driven on the wrong side of the road! "We'll stop in Deauville just so we can all stretch our legs," Catherine announced. Then she turned to the children. "I can't wait to show you where I lived during the war." She turned back and looked at Joe. "I think I'm going to enjoy being back in France, after all."

"I'm looking forward to this family holiday. Next week's presentation in Caen is actually a bit of a nuisance!" chuckled Joe, without moving his eyes from the road.

Catherine was delighted they were driving through Douvres la Delivrande to reach their hotel in Caen. She was enjoying the view as Joe slowly drove through her old town. Then he swung the car to the left and pulled in at the car park next to the Petit Café. "You don't need to stop; we can visit Douvres tomorrow," she said as she turned to look at him.

He studied his watch. "Sorry, darling, I can't wait until we reach Caen. I'm parched. Let's get out everyone. I'll buy you all a French cake."

"Yes, please," shouted Tia and Jack from the back seat. Catherine saw she had to concede, and the four of them piled out of the car and marched towards the café.

"This café is where I worked during the war," Catherine said with a heavy heart. "It hasn't changed much." Joe nodded and opened the café door, signalling for her to go through first.

As she entered the room, there was a sudden fanfare of clapping and cheering. Everyone was shouting, *"Surprise – nous t'aimons Catherine Leblanc."*

People were standing on tables, the chairs were all full, and children were sitting on the floor. Someone put a crown of flowers on her head. She glanced at Joe, who had a smug smile on his face. Then she looked at Tia and Jack, who looked petrified. They didn't seem to have any idea about what was going on.

"Catherine, my darling," Joe announced above the noise of the room, "I still have my contacts, so it was easy for me to get hold of your friends from the resistance movement. These people know what you did for them, and they wanted this chance to say thank you."

She felt someone's arms going around her neck and then she was greeted with kisses on her cheeks. As she pulled away, she looked into the tearful eyes of an old-looking Claude. *It's so good to see you, my dear Catherine,"* he said in French. *"Look, the whole village loves you."* Catherine felt her heart give way as she looked into the crowd. Then men and women from the resistance group came up to her crying, and in no time, she too found herself crying in their arms. She realised how much her resistance friends meant to her. Together as a team, they'd risked their lives, what stronger attachment could there be? She'd been so scared of her memories, and now she knew she should have visited before.

"Mum," said Tia. "Jack says the French people are saying that you saved lives."

Catherine heaved a sigh. "Not all the operations went well … they were hard times."

"I can't believe you blew up train tracks and bridges," Tia's eyes were ablaze. "You're so brave. You helped win the war."

"We were just a small part of a much larger picture."

"I've heard the tales about the landings on the beaches," continued Tia. "It's incredible."

"It was all worth it in the end. I don't think the British realise the impact that freedom has had on the French." She glanced across the room. "Look, Claude's introducing your dad as one of their Special Operation Executives."

"You were both amazing!"

Catherine laughed. "We all had our part to play, that's all."

"You should all have medals." Tia's face became alight. "For the first time, I can see that history is interesting. It's not stories, it's real life."

"It's life and death," Catherine whispered. "While we're here, I'll take you to the cemeteries, so we can pay our respects to those who died."

"You must go to see the new museums," Claude said, as he appeared by her side. "They have some large photos of our escapades, along with lots of photos from the D-Day landings."

"How wonderful. I would love to see that. I'll take the children; they need to understand that history holds many lessons we should learn from." Catherine looked across at Jack. He was talking to Claude's grandson while helping himself to another plate of food. Smiling, she thought, at last, he was socialising well, even if he seemed more interested in the food than the stories being told.

Tia pulled at her sleeve. "Mum, can you translate what you and that man just said? I want to know everything."

Catherine smiled, then found herself getting cross with Jack for not being as excited or amazed as Tia was. But he was only nine. She assumed he'd understand one day, and somehow, she knew Tia would make sure he did!

The next day, Catherine could see they were all exhausted, so she decided they would go to the beach. The museums and cemeteries could wait for another day. While Joe and the children went into the sea, Catherine spread out a rug and sat herself down to watch. She knew Tia desperately wanted to learn to swim, while Jack just enjoyed splashing around. Tia looked so strong and muscular; it was no wonder she was naturally good at every sport she tried. Joe had been a good rugby player at school, and she knew he wanted Jack to learn the sport. She looked across at Jack. He certainly looked like a Lawrence with his dark hair, olive skin and piercing blue eyes, but he also had her long thin, spindly body, which she acknowledged wasn't that of a typical macho rugby player's physique. He was also scared of life. Rugby would be far too robust and powerful for him.

"Of course," she said aloud, "I know what would be good for Jack." She leant back, her elbows disappearing into the hot sand. All was peaceful, even the birds were quiet. Apart from the laughter from the children, there was nothing else to hear. Tia was swimming but seemed to be splashing her arms around, and Joe was trying to show her how to move them properly. She chuckled. How could Joe teach swimming when he couldn't swim well himself? Then, she sat upright. Jack seemed to have lost his footing in the water. The seabed must have taken a dip, and Jack was suddenly out of his depth. Joe and Tia were much further out to sea. She shouted, but they didn't hear her. She could see Jack was splashing and going under the water. He couldn't get back on his feet, and he couldn't swim. She ran as fast as she could into the sea, her clothes were slowing her down, but somehow, she found the strength to move speedily through the water. She got to Jack just as he went under again. Pulling him up, she dragged him out of the sea as fast as she could. Once on the beach, she laid him on his side, and he spluttered and coughed up water from his lungs. Jack's tiny frame looked fragile as he lay there helplessly on the sand, saltwater pouring from his mouth.

Joe and Tia were soon by her side, and Tia was screaming, "Oh no, not again … don't die on me!"

Jack rolled over, then slowly sat up. Joe patted him on the back. "Are you alright, son?" Jack nodded, but he didn't try to speak. Joe looked at Catherine. "I can't believe you moved so rapidly. By the time I turned around, you had Jack under your arm and were heading for the beach. What happened?"

Jack stuttered something about the sand disappearing under his feet, and Catherine told him not to talk just yet.

Tia blubbered, "Mum … you saved him!"

"Jack would have found his feet eventually," Catherine replied.

Joe cast her a knowing look and said, "Everything's alright, Tia, Jack's fine."

Tia knelt on the floor and hugged her brother, sobbing all over his chest.

Jack grumpily pushed her away. "I'm OK. Honestly, you women do panic!"

Catherine felt her body shake with relief as she quietly pondered on the frailty of life. Then, unexpectedly, she realised that she didn't even know if her other child was still alive. Gregory's face appeared in her mind's eye. No, she couldn't allow herself to think about that man's child. Tia and Jack's lives were important to her, nothing else mattered.

Later that evening, as they were having supper in the hotel restaurant, Catherine relaxed in her chair as the day's anxieties seemed to fall away. She watched as Tia, having been convinced by her father that Jack hadn't been in danger, was now in deep conversation with Joe about tomorrow's museum trip. Jack stood up and walked behind her chair. He put his arm around her neck and leant forward to kiss her tenderly on the cheek.

Whispering in French, he said, "Thank you, Maman for saving my life today."

For once she felt relieved that he was talking in French in front of Tia. She murmured, "Jack, it was the most frightening experience of my life. Please don't ever put me through that again."

"Today frightened me too. I'm going to do something to get sturdier and tougher." He looked across at Tia. "I hope my new passion for getting stronger is as powerful as …" in English he continued loudly "…Tia's passion for boring history."

Catherine laughed. *"I think this holiday has influenced all of us."* Then she said in English. "In a few days, your dad's self-esteem will be boosted when he receives his medal from the new French Prime Minister, like us, *Guy Mollet* was also in the resistance movement. As for me, I've realised my fears have gone about this place, which means I can now keep in touch with my friends here." She looked across the table. "And Tia's found a subject she likes; history could be the making of her." Turning back to Jack, she added quietly in French, *"And Jack, I've a brilliant idea about how you can improve your fitness …"*

CHAPTER 27

6th July - 2nd August 1956

Selina pushed back Maria's sweaty hair, then wiped her daughter's red-hot forehead with a cold flannel. She heard the front door open and, glancing at the clock, she realised Mark and David were back early from the pub. Running to the landing, she bellowed for Mark, and within an instant, she saw him charging up the stairs.

"Maria went to bed feeling unwell and then woke with a rash, a high temperature and sickness," Selina explained.

Mark's face turned white when he saw Maria, then he ran back to the landing yelling for David, who came chasing up the stairs.

"Oh God," David said with alarm. "We need to get Maria to the hospital. I'll drive, it'll be faster." He quickly started folding Maria up in a blanket. The shock of David's reaction and the panic on Mark's face soon reduced Selina to a shaking wreck. Her daughter was really ill.

David drove fast. He seemed to be concentrating, but Selina could feel his tension as he raced through the traffic. When they got to the hospital, doctors appeared so quickly Selina couldn't hear herself think.

"Are you the mother?" asked one of the doctors.

"Yes. What's wrong with Maria?"

"We think it's scarlet fever. She's very poorly."

Selina looked at Mark, and he clearly didn't know what to say, so she fell into his arms and wept bitterly.

"We're going to take her to an isolation room," the doctor added as he gently touched Selina's arm. "We will give your daughter all the medication we can."

She looked up at Mark for reassurance, but he still said nothing. For the first time in her life, she had to cope on her own. She had to pull herself together, she had her daughter to support, and her own crying wasn't helping.

Selina rooted herself firmly by Maria's bedside, determined she'd be there in case her daughter needed her. "Maria's shivering, yet she feels so hot," Selina said to the nurse who was rinsing a towel under the cold tap.

"The fever is severe."

"What can I do?"

"Have this cold, wet towel and damp her down as often as you can. We need to keep her cool," the nurse's tone sounded full of concern. "She's had her medication now, so we'll see how she goes."

*

Selina felt exhausted, she hadn't slept, and the nurses kept putting thermometers into Maria's mouth, while the doctors were continually pushing needles into her arm. Maria kept coming to, but to Selina's amazement, her daughter never complained.

"Selina," whispered David as he entered the room. "How is she today?"

"She's sleeping quietly, but I think she's looking a little less red. What do you think?" She turned back to look at Maria.

"Umm, maybe," David muttered as he sat down next to her. She could sense he was staring at her, so she turned to look at him. His face looked serious. "Selina, I've something I need to ask you." He pushed up his glasses as he looked down at the floor. "This isn't easy, but it's just with Maria being this ill. I was wondering if … if I could phone my brother. He's in France at the moment, but the thing is his wife …" There was a moan from the bed and David stopped as he turned to check on Maria.

"Mummy," squeaked Maria as she opened her eyes.

"Oh, my love, I'm here," Selina said comfortingly, and she leant forward and kissed her daughter's forehead. She halted, then she kissed her again. She was right, Maria did feel less hot than before. "David, can you shout for the nurse?" Selina said without looking at him. "I think Maria's temperature's gone down a little."

Maria muttered something about a sore throat and itchy skin, but David had gone.

"Now then, young lady," the nurse said as she appeared. "Stop talking while I just put this thermometer under your tongue." Selina and David held their breath. The nurse looked at the thermometer. "Your temperature's actually down quite a lot," she said and gave Selina a huge smile. Then she turned back to Maria. "Your mum hasn't left your side. She even insisted on staying here overnight. It's unheard of – the hospital doesn't usually allow it." She shook the thermometer. "But because you're in isolation and so poorly the doctor agreed that your mum could sleep in the chair next to you." The nurse muttered under her breath, "I hope this doesn't

186

catch on." Then she spoke up again. "If a mother's love can make you better – well, it certainly did." She squeezed Selina's hand. "I'll go and tell the doctor." She turned and disappeared through the door.

"I'll go and phone Mark's work," announced David.

"Wait, David. What were you going to ask me? Something about your brother's wife?"

"Oh, um, his wife had a fever once … I was going to see if they could offer you any advice. I just wanted to help, that's all," he said as he left the room.

Selina thought David was charming. He was always trying to help. She turned back to Maria. "You've been very ill, my love. We've all been so worried about you. The doctors thought … we might lose you." Selina's voice was quivering. "I've been praying to Grandad Harold to give you the strength to get through this." Maria didn't seem to be paying attention, she was too busy trying to sit up. Selina helped her to sit and puffed up her pillows. Then she encouraged Maria to drink some water. As her daughter lay down again, Selina whispered, "I couldn't imagine my life without you."

"Were you thinking of leaving me then?" squeaked Maria as she stared at her from the bed.

*

It had been a long few weeks, but Maria seemed so much better. Selina hoped the news that the doctor wanted to see them was going to be good news. She sipped her tea, wondering who the other people in the hospital café were visiting. Then her attention was drawn back to David.

"But Mark," he said, "I want to pay for you to have a telephone, and not one of these party lines either. I want to get you a line of your own."

"We don't need a telephone," Mark replied. "They're expensive, unnecessary things. I won't let you pay ..."

David looked at Selina. "They are necessary, especially for emergencies like the one you've just had. I believe everyone should have a telephone. In fact, I think they should have been included as part of the new Welfare State!" David pushed his slipping glasses back towards his eyes. "I think my sister-in-law probably had her life saved because of a telephone call. Believe me, so much would have been different if—"

"Why, what happened to her? You haven't told me—" Mark interjected.

"Please, Mark," Selina interrupted, "David's right, we do need a telephone for Maria's sake. We can pay him back when we can afford it."

"No, you won't." David frowned at her. "This is my idea, so let me do this." He looked at Mark. "Besides, the telephone will make my life simpler. I can phone to check you're in, before driving over to visit."

Selina grabbed Mark's hand and put on her best pleading look. She watched as Mark's usual accepting smile crept over his face.

"Alright, David, you win." Mark turned to her. "We'd better go, love. It's time to see the doctor." He stood up and looked at David. "I doubt we'll be long."

"Maria is ready to be transferred to St Mary's children's convalescence home. She'll stay there for a further two weeks." The doctor focused on Selina. "This home is in Broadstairs, in East Kent. It's a tranquil, peaceful and picturesque little seaside town, the air is ideal for convalescing."

Selina felt herself turn cold. "No, I want Maria to come home with us, where I can take care of her. No one can look after my daughter better than I can, and Maria is to have the best." She stopped, realising her fear of professionals had gone; her daughter had given her fortitude. Her voice softened as she gazed at Mark. "Convalescence homes might be normal procedure, but the last thing Maria needs is to be in a strange place, away from us." She looked back at the doctor, her eyes purposely fixing on his. "I promise you I'll make sure she stays away from other people. Also, we'll have a telephone soon, so we can call for help if we need to." She smiled inwardly. Janice and Will both had telephones, Maria would be so excited to get one. She looked at Mark, and with a stunned look on his face, he nodded in agreement.

"Alright, you can have my permission for Maria to be discharged into your care," the doctor said reluctantly as he scribbled on his pad. "You'll need to pay a shilling for the prescription," he added as he passed her the note. "Then you can take your daughter home today if you wish, but it's imperative that she's watched constantly, and has fresh air occasionally."

Selina nodded in agreement, and she gave a satisfied smile. "Thank you." Turning to Mark, she added, "I'm sure David will take us all home."

That evening, Selina lay on Maria's bedroom floor and tucked the blankets around herself. "I love the fact we're going to be together every night. We can chat before we go to sleep."

"I feel so much better now I'm home," Maria murmured as she snuggled down into her bed. Selina grinned into her pillow. Then after a few minutes, Maria piped up, "Mum, can I have my hair cut like yours?"

"It'll be a shame to chop off your lovely long hair."

"I don't like it this long; it gets in my way." Maria rolled over, looked down at her and said excitedly, "I forgot to tell you my news. Before I was ill, Will said if he passes the eleven plus, he's decided not to go to the boys' grammar, after all. He agrees the three of us should all stay together, and go to the mixed technical school."

Selina sat up. "That's great, love, and I'm glad you and Will are doing so well at school." Then she dropped her voice, "But you do know Janice finds schoolwork difficult, she might not pass her eleven plus and then she won't be able to go to the technical school with you."

Maria sat up. "I'm not having her go to a different school," she said defiantly. Then after a moment, she added, "I'll make her come here after school every day so that I can help her with her schoolwork."

"That's good," Selina said as she nestled down again. "Will's a great lad to want to look after you both."

"He's cross with me. Martin Hollingham has told everyone he likes me, and Will says I shouldn't encourage him."

"Good for Will," Selina said, hoping her daughter would now settle for the night.

"Will hates the attention I'm getting at school. I think he feels left out," Maria continued. "He says his baby brother gets all the attention at home."

"Rob is a gorgeous baby," Selina said as she turned over.

"Mum, am I going to have a brother or sister? Would you adopt again?"

Selina sat up again. "Ages ago, your dad and I agreed that we wanted to give you everything we could, and we need money to be able to do that, so no, we aren't going to adopt for a second time. Besides I don't want to go through that system again!"

"Good. I don't want to lose your attention to some baby," Maria sniffed. "But what do you mean about the system?"

Selina sighed; sleep was clearly going to have to wait! "I think it's time to explain all about your adoption..."

*

"Maria's been home a couple of days now," David's voice echoed through the receiver, "and I have a day off work, so shall I take you both to Deal for some fresh air?"

Selina thought the telephone was remarkable. "That's wonderful, David. You know the doctor said fresh air would help."

Once in the car, David was occupied with making Maria laugh, and Selina couldn't believe how quickly the journey passed. She was soon sitting with her daughter in an empty corner of the beach, listening to the waves lapping onto the pebble-dashed shore. She sat back, enjoying the warmth and the summer sun shining on the drowsy sea. She saw David walking back with the ice creams melting in his hands.

"Thanks, Uncle David," Maria said as she grabbed her strawberry whipped ice cream and huddled into her deck chair.

"Thank you, kind sir," Selina joked as he handed her a vanilla cornet.

David sat on his deck chair next to hers. "You've changed over the last few weeks," he said. "There's a new, more assertive Selina now."

"I do feel as if I've finally grown up." She turned to him. "And I want to thank you for all you've done for us recently, you've been brilliant."

He gave her a big smile. "I'd do anything for you and Mark and my little Maria."

"You're marvellous with Maria. It's a shame you don't have children of your own."

"My niece and nephew keep me occupied," he said while eating a mouthful of ice cream.

"Why haven't you ever married?" she asked boldly.

He stared at the sea. "I've never told anyone this, but I did love a woman once. She was an amazing person, but Hannah fell in love and married my … someone better than me." His gaze softened. "I was always there for her." With a sigh, he added, "But I couldn't protect her from being killed in the war." He glanced down at the ground. "I would have liked children, but none of my relationships have worked. I've just never found the right woman." He ate some more ice cream. "My brother's children are my family."

She squeezed his arm. "You're part of our family, as well. I know you have a niece and nephew, but Uncle David is who you are to Maria too." David grinned as if she'd said something astonishing. She leant back and decided that now she, like Mark, trusted David implicitly.

CHAPTER 28

15th October 1958 – 3rd September 1959

Maria snatched up the telephone as soon as it rang. Usually, her mum answered the telephone, her dad didn't like modern equipment. "Is that you, Janice?" she asked, then not waiting for an answer, she added, "Have you got your results?"

"Yes … and I've passed!"

"Me too! We'll still be together," Maria shouted, jumping up and down like a maniac, while the phone wire bobbed along with her.

When she came off the phone, her mum announced, "Let's go and tell Nana your good news. Look, your dad's already got his coat on." As they walked along the road, her mum whispered, "Maria, you did such a good job helping Janice with her schoolwork, you should go into teaching, it's such a respectable job."

Maria grimaced, knowing she'd only helped Janice for her own selfish reason – she wanted Janice to always be by her side.

"Well?" her nana asked, as they all stood on the doorstep.

"I've passed my eleven plus," Maria shouted at the top of her voice.

"My clever little granddaughter," her nana cried, pulling her into a hug. Maria burrowed into her arms, while her nana's muffled voice said, "Come in everyone. I've made a celebration cake. I was sure we'd need one."

As they went into the kitchen, Maria heard a strange sound coming from the backyard. "What's that noise?" she asked.

Her nana pulled her earlobe forward to listen to the racket. "I don't know," she said as she opened the back door. "You'd better go outside and see." Then a small brown puppy ran straight into the kitchen. Maria squealed as it rushed past her. "Oh, dear," cried Nana. "I bet it's escaped from one of the neighbour's yards. Maria, can you catch the puppy and read the address on its collar?"

Maria ran and grabbed the cute spaniel puppy, which had a purple collar around its neck. She searched for a tag. "Here it is," she said as she read the address. "88 Church Lane, Gravesend." She stopped and read it again. Then looking up, she could see all the grown-ups were beaming. "That's our address?" she said, unsure what was going on.

Her mum winked at her. "Nana's bought you the puppy for passing your exam. Dad and I agreed you could have it. You see, none of us ever doubted you'd pass."

Maria threw her arms around her nana. "Is this true? Thank you … thank you, Nana. I love you." Turning to her mum, she asked, "But can we afford to keep it?"

"Now that I've had my steward's promotion at work, we can afford a lot more things," her dad answered proudly. Maria picked up the puppy. It was the same as Janice's dog, though Janice's dog was a lot older.

"Nana knew you've always wanted a dog like Kira. So, when she saw this little one in the pet shop, we had to say yes," her mum said excitedly. "But you can choose her name," she added as she stroked the dog's head.

Maria thought about it for a while and then answered, "Lucky, because I'm so lucky to have her."

Her dad chuckled. "I've always said it's your mum and me who're the lucky ones because we have you."

Her nana handed her a lovely purple lead that matched the collar. "There you go, Maria. Lucky is all yours."

*

The following week, Maria flinched as her mum's out of tune singing resonated around the bedroom walls.

"I'm putting your new secondary school uniform at the front of your wardrobe and your normal clothes at the back," her mum announced.

Maria nodded, then turned to stare at Lucky, who was lying on her bedspread. As she stroked Lucky's fur, the dog looked up, thumped her tail on the bed and then rolled over for a tummy rub. Maria murmured, "I promise I'll always love you, Lucky. I'm not planning to change now that I'm going to secondary school."

"What did you say, love?" her mum asked as she stopped singing.

Maria's long fingers scraped back her now shoulder-length hair. "Will's changed since he went to the Tec, and I don't want that to happen to me."

"Everyone changes when they become teenagers, but I haven't noticed Will being any different."

195

"He won't join in with our football anymore. He acts like all the other boys. He thinks we're just girls!"

"But he likes you and Janice to watch his football matches."

"Yes, and occasionally he'll ask our advice about a football move. But he gets moody if we say anything in front of anyone else." She stretched. "He'd better turn up tomorrow."

"He always does what you tell him to, that won't ever change!"

Going to secondary school seemed so grown up, and Maria was determined to be precisely that.

"Wow, you look nice," Will said, seeming impressed with her new pristine appearance. Maria huffed as she pushed her mum away from straightening her tie for the fifth time. "I think we'd better go, Mrs Tozer," Will said as he looked at her mum. "I don't want Maria to be late on her first day at secondary school."

"You're a good friend to our Maria," her mum laughed. Then she pushed Maria and Will through the front door.

They walked quietly to school. It was only two streets away, but as Maria strolled by Will's side, she noticed how physically different he was now. He looked older and sturdier. He was good-looking too, with his brown hair combed back from his face and his hazel eyes that smiled at everyone. Then she saw Janice waiting by the school gate, and her thoughts turned back to the task at hand.

"See you later," Maria shouted to Will as Janice grabbed her arm.

"We have to go over there," Janice pointed to a door. "But guess what? The classes are alphabetical, so Tozer and Troop will be in the same class!"

Maria thought the school was massive, and the lessons seemed daunting. Halfway through her first English lesson, the teacher announced, "The school play this year is Romeo and Juliet, which is one of our set books. If anyone's interested, I'm holding auditions in the school hall this lunchtime."

Maria whispered to Janice, "I'm going to have a go at that."

"You can count me out," Janice snorted back.

Maria found acting was fun; she loved being someone else for a while.

At the end of the auditions the drama teacher, Mr Swinnerton, exclaimed, "Maria, you're a natural at this, you're definitely good enough for a small part. I'll see you at our next rehearsal."

Maria was thrilled, this felt amazing. After lunch was Geography, but all Maria could think about was the school play. She made up her mind that next year she'd try for a more significant part. Maria drifted into her final lesson, where the biology teacher was explaining something about blue eyes and brown eyes being hereditary, but Maria was still thinking about her acting. She admired the sixth form girl who had got the part of Juliet, and Maria decided that when she was older, she'd go for a lead role too.

"So, class, please put down the colour of your parents' eyes, and then we can see the hereditary links," the teacher said.

Maria panicked. She hadn't been listening. Were green eyes possible with a brown-eyed father and a green-eyed mother? She couldn't risk it, so she quickly gave her dad green eyes. No one must suspect her parents weren't her birth parents. Her family mustn't be seen as different from everyone else's.

As Maria sauntered home with Will, she realised she was now slightly taller than him. She wondered if it was her height that had made her so self-assured. "I think being confident helped me to get into the school play," she told Will. "I loved the attention I got from being on the stage." She heaved a sigh. "Janice seemed to enjoy dull Geography, and I know you like dreary French." She turned to him. "We're all very different, aren't we? But—"

"Maria," shouted Will as he grabbed her away from the kerb. "You nearly walked in front of that car."

"I was about to stop," she protested as she turned to see the car driving off.

"You didn't see that woman's face," Will said. "She threw me such an angry look."

"In that case, I'm glad I only saw the back of her head." Maria scoffed. "Anyway, she had red hair and mum says all red-headed women are rude."

CHAPTER 29

27th September 1961

David stood at the grave, watching the coffin being lowered. At last, he could see that Gregory Jones was dead. It had taken a long time, but revenge for Catherine's rape felt complete. David believed that society comprised of two types of people – the good ones, and the evil ones – and to him, Gregory fitted firmly into the second category. There weren't many people at the funeral, just a small group of onlookers. He lifted his hat to a young woman he knew in the gathering but ignored the others. An older lady, who looked remarkably like Gregory, stood at the top of the grave, crying bitterly. He assumed she was Gregory's mother. He realised he'd seen her before, briefly at Win's funeral. A teenage boy, who had Gregory's unkempt appearance, was trying to console her, while a middle-aged woman was sobbing beside him. He understood Gregory never married, so he assumed they were possibly Gregory's sister and her son. As he stood and watched the three of them, he wondered how they could have loved this despicable man. The prayers around the grave seemed ridiculous as he reflected on the pain Gregory had caused to his own family. Catherine, Joe and Tia's lives had turned upside down because of this man's actions. He remembered the night of the rape and his conversation with Joe. Well, he'd kept his promise; he'd managed to make sure that Gregory would never be free to rape again. He felt a certain satisfaction at having achieved his goal.

The prayers finished, and he looked up to see the mourners saying their goodbyes to the older woman. He thought it would seem strange if he just walked away, so he joined the end of the queue, pulling up his collar as the afternoon drizzle turned into rain. As he reached her, the woman put up her umbrella.

"Thank you for coming," she acknowledged, but then her eyes bored into his. "Have I seen you before somewhere?" She looked towards the grave. "How did you know my son?"

He felt awkward."We … fought in the war together," he said quickly, glad there was no one else there to hear his lie.

She stared at him. "I remember you, you were at Win's funeral," she said with surprise.

His head dropped. "Catherine, Win's granddaughter, is my sister-in-law," he murmured sombrely. His body went rigid, and his eyes didn't move from the floor. He couldn't look at the woman.

The woman touched his arm, distress showing in her face. She moved closer, offering for him to come under her umbrella. "You know what Greg did, don't you?" she said as he accepted her invitation for cover.

He internally groaned, what was he supposed to say? "Yes," he muttered.

"Greg only told me last week." The woman's face fell. "I was a friend of Win's, we played in the same bridge club." Her eyes turned to the grave. "I knew Catherine as a child. Then I met her at the V.E. Day Anniversary, and again at Win's funeral. Such a lovely girl." She turned back towards him. "Did Greg hurt her, I mean, badly?"

His insides twisted with hatred. He couldn't contain his loathing for Gregory. "He caused her great pain. He was mercilessness and vicious in his attack." There was a stilted silence, then tears started to fill the woman's eyes. He felt no remorse. She needed to know how repulsive her son was. He recognised it wasn't her fault, but he didn't see why he should shield her from the truth. He felt she should know the pain her son had caused to his family. Gregory was evil, he wasn't a loss for people to mourn.

She started searching in her handbag. "I wrote a letter the other day. I knew Catherine was married, but now I know it's to your brother ..." her voice became distant as her hands buried further into her bag. "I believe they live in Win's street, but I don't know which house. I was going to ask the people in Win's old house if they knew." She pulled an envelope from her bag. "Could you give this to Catherine?" Her tone mellowed, "I realise now that all mothers love their children. I need to do this for my son."

He looked away, thinking that not all mothers love their children. After all, Catherine had given Maria away without any love attached. But then he thought of Selina, and the love Maria had ended up receiving. He turned back and took the envelope, bowed his head and said politely, "Yes, I'll give it to her." It then occurred to him that Maria would never see her biological father or know any of his family. He fell silent with his deliberations. This woman didn't know she had a granddaughter.

"What's wrong?" asked the woman.

"Sorry," he said, collecting his thoughts. "I just remembered something, it's nothing important." His logical mind was back in control. Gregory's family had no rights to Maria, she belonged to Mark and Selina. He was Maria's protector; it was for the best Gregory's family didn't know about her.

Gregory's mother continued talking about her son for quite some time. The rain was getting heavier, but he could see the woman needed to talk, and he was more than interested. Eventually, she said she must go, saying her family would be waiting for her in the car park by the church gate. She shook his hand, while once again asking him to pass on the letter. He watched as she progressed down the puddled path with the early autumn leaves sticking to her feet. He turned and hurried through the rain, heading towards his car, which was parked on the roadside some distance away. His shoes squelched on the sodden grass as they sprayed the muddy water onto his already soaked trouser legs. All he could think about was driving to Joe's to tell him the news. He'd promised to pass the letter to Catherine, so he would do that as well. They hadn't spoken about the rape for years now. It was as though it had never happened, yet he sensed that none of them had forgotten it. He put the wet key into the door and quickly got into his dry car. Now that Gregory was dead, it felt like the pain was over. Catherine had a right to know what had happened to Gregory, but then he knew Joe wouldn't approve of this final outcome. Joe would never see what he saw – that it was a real blessing this malevolent man was finally dead.

"Come in quickly," Catherine said. "It's pouring!"

He shivered as he put his oversized, dripping coat onto the rack in the hallway. Then he took off his muddy shoes.

"I've just come from Gregory Jones's funeral," he explained. Before Catherine could reply, he heard Tia sprinting down the bottom steps of the staircase. He halted, unsure what to say next.

Tia ran towards her mum, "I'm off now," she said, putting an arm around her mum. Then looking at David, she added, "Hello, Uncle David," then in a half-interested way, she asked, "And who's Gregory Jones?" Thankfully, Tia didn't wait for his answer. Instead, she proceeded to kiss her mum on the cheek. "I need to catch the bus. Have you any messages for Granny Ada."

"Give her my love and tell her I'll be over on Sunday. What time will you be home for supper?"

"I'll be back about seven-thirty. I'm calling into Aunty Angeline's on my way home. George has some textbooks he says I can have. And don't worry about supper, I'll eat with them. See you later, Mum, and bye, Uncle David."

"Tia, it'll be dusk by then, will you ask—"

"I know, Mum, George will walk me home, and we'll stick to the lit roads." Tia grabbed her coat and umbrella from the rack. "Oh, my coat's wet," she said as she brushed off a white feather that had attached itself. "That's your fault, Uncle David, you put your drenched coat next to mine."

Catherine didn't speak, she just stared down at the feather that lay on the floor. Tia took her purse from the hall table, opened the front door, and ran swiftly through the rain.

"Sorry," David said apologetically. "I didn't think."

Catherine's hands twisted together. "That was a close call. At least, Jack's not in." She turned and called up the stairs, "Joe, David's here, can you come down?" Gesturing towards the kitchen, she muttered, "Joe's upstairs changing out of his work clothes. I'll make us all a pot of tea."

Just as she put the teapot and three cups on the table, Joe appeared at the kitchen door. Catherine moved forwards, tripping over the leg of the table. David caught her arm and guided her to a chair. He turned to Joe.

"It's Gregory Jones." David turned back to check on Catherine, and with his back to Joe, he said, "He's dead."

"Is he?" Joe said with astonishment in his voice. David watched as his brother placed himself down next to Catherine and took her hand. "Are you alright? We haven't spoken of Gregory for so long."

Catherine didn't answer him, she was staring blankly at her cup.

David took a deep breath. "Catherine, I'm sorry if I've upset you."

"I'm not upset, just angry," she said as she looked up at Joe. "Just the sound of his name still turns my stomach. What he did and what we went through makes me so mad." Her hand withdrew from Joe's, and her head collapsed on the table. "I thought the past was over."

Joe scowled at David. "You should have spoken to me about this before you went and told Catherine." His voice grew loud. "There was no need to remind her of this man."

"I know but—"

"I don't want to talk about him any further," snapped Joe.

"But Joe, we need to—"

Joe raised his hand. "No, David. We know the man is dead and that's all we need to know. I think the past must stay in the past where it belongs, don't you?"

Catherine lifted her head; her face was flushed.

Joe stood up, facing David, he announced sharply, "I insist, for Catherine's sake, we will not mention this man again. The topic is now closed."

CHAPTER 30

14th October 1962

Selina understood Maria's new teenage hormones were a storm she had to ride, but when Maria's sails flapped in the wind, the waters felt hard going. She sighed. Her mum kept saying she'd been the same at that age and it would all blow over, but she couldn't remember ever having mood swings like Maria's. She hated the way her daughter's sharp tongue lashed out with sarcastic replies to everything. Selina got up from the table to take the toast from under the grill. She believed she needed to be a calming influence on Maria; she'd let her daughter see that sensitivity was always better than sarcasm.

"Mum, Dad," yelled Maria, as she came charging down the stairs with Lucky close on her heels. "I've found this." She was waving a note in the air. "How dare you not tell me?"

Selina could see the thunderous look on her daughter's face, and the child's body was shaking with rage. "What have you found?" she asked, agitated at her daughter's temper but determined to remain calm. "Sit down, love, and tell us quietly."

Mark put down his Sunday paper, while Maria plonked herself on the chair. "How could you keep this a secret? You said you'd told me everything, and you haven't."

"Maria, please, what are you on about?" asked Selina.

Glaring at her with eyes that pierced her very core, Maria snapped, "I couldn't find the dress I wanted to wear because you put my clothes at the back of my wardrobe. So, I heaved everything out, but a dress got stuck on a loose floorboard between the wardrobe and the door frame." Scowling, she added, "You know which floorboard, don't you!"

Mark shifted uncomfortably in his seat, and they both turned to look at him. He placed his cup on the kitchen table and stared at Maria. Selina guessed he must be as confused as she was.

Maria carried on, "I noticed a piece of white paper sticking out from the wobbly floorboard, so I tugged at it, and it came away. It was an envelope, which said, *'Please keep this safe and give it to her when she's old enough to understand.'* Then Maria bellowed, "When did you think you'd give it to me … when I'm fifty?"

Selina threw Mark a questioning frown, and he turned away. "Anyway, I thought it might be some secret, hidden for hundreds of years. So, I opened it." Maria glared at Selina as if she knew what was in the note. Selina again looked across at Mark, and as he turned round, his face told her that he knew something about all of this. Maria's voice quietened a little. "When I opened the envelope, the most beautiful ring fell into the palm of my hand." Selina glared at Mark, who was looking uncomfortable as he played with the corner of the discarded newspaper lying on the table. Maria's voice grew louder again. "There was a note inside the envelope, and it was for me! Did you think it was clever hiding it from me like that?"

Stunned, Selina stared at Mark, who now reminded her of a little schoolboy.

"I'm sorry, love," he said to her. "I hid it years ago and quite honestly, I'd forgotten about it – until now." He gazed awkwardly at Maria. "When we went to collect you from the orphanage, they gave us a bag from the woman who gave birth to you. It had some clothes and things in." He looked at Selina. "I found that envelope at the bottom of the bag. I didn't open it. I had no idea what was in it, and I didn't mention it to you because I didn't want to upset you." He cleared his throat. "It was our big day, the day of Maria's birth to us, and I wasn't going to spoil it by discussing some letter that would cause us both pain."

Selina nodded, she understood why he hadn't said anything, he always protected her. But she felt hurt he hadn't told her, after all, he'd had plenty of time.

Mark carried on, "When we got back, I put the letter away. I was going to tell you about it – I know I should've told you; I just couldn't face the pain it would bring." He looked as if he wanted to crawl under the chair with shame. "Then, as time went on, I just forgot it was there."

Maria butted in. "If you didn't open it, how did you know it would be painful?"

Selina took her angry daughter's hand into hers and said tenderly, "The pain your dad is talking about is that the letter is a reminder that we aren't your real parents." She sighed deeply. "I wish I'd been the one who gave birth to you. I love you more than my own life and giving birth to you wouldn't make me love you any more than I already do. The torture is that I have to live with the thought that I'm not, and never will be, your real mother." She looked at Maria, who remained silent. "And your dad has to live with the thought that he isn't your real father, either." Maria came and sat on her lap. "The thing is, love," Selina continued, "if people knew about the adoption, they would no longer see us as your real parents, and that also hurts." Selina's arms flew around her daughter, and Maria collapsed into her embrace as if she were a young child again. Selina supposed that being reminded of her real mother was hard for a teenager to handle. She cradled her while Maria started crying and Selina added, "But we are a family, we have a history together."

Selina looked at Mark for support. He was looking intently at his daughter, then he said softly, "I'm your dad and always will be, nothing's ever going to change how I feel about you. Relationships and love are what matters, and us three have tons of that." Selina could see the depth of emotion in his face. She understood how much this conversation was hurting him too.

"The letter is painful," Maria murmured, "but not for the reason you've just explained." Her hand shook as she held out the note. "Read this, Dad. It says the man who fathered me wasn't a very nice man."

Mark gazed at it dubiously.

Maria asked, "Shall I read it out?"

He nodded in agreement.

"I'm writing this note to explain my reasons for giving you up for adoption. This is hard for me to talk about, but I feel you need to know. I found I was pregnant after I'd been raped by someone I knew. I didn't want his child, and what's more, I didn't want to be reminded of him. I enclose a ring that's my family heirloom, it's very special and was given to me with love. I bequeath it to you, in the hope that it will somehow bring you the love that I'm quite unable to give to you myself."

From,
the woman who gave birth to you."

Maria threw down the letter. "Rape wasn't something I'd ever thought about as being my reason for living, but it seems, I really wasn't wanted."

Selina didn't know what to say, and she imagined Mark didn't either. Eventually, she said, "We want you, Maria, you know that." Then she turned to Mark. "But now we can understand why that woman said those things to us when we met her. We misjudged her, didn't we?" Mark looked away. Selina could feel Maria's eyes examining her.

"When you told me about the adoption process," Maria said. "You explained that you'd met her, but you didn't tell me what she looked like. I'd like to know."

Selina didn't want to recall the meeting, but for the sake of her daughter, she had to relive it. "She had long, thick, red hair." She saw her daughter frown. "She was beautiful, like you. She had green eyes, but they were darker than yours, and her face was slightly oval. She was tall and slim like you." Selina felt her face contort, but she had to carry on. "She seemed quite hard-natured, abrupt and scary. There was no softness in her face; she wasn't like you in that way. She also had a slight foreign-sounding accent." She felt herself welling up, she didn't want to remember that woman and all the pain she felt.

"Is that the ring?" Mark asked.

Maria held her hand up to the light so they could see the large, blood-red ruby cut in the shape of a heart. It glistened and shone as if it wanted to talk to them. Selina hated the ring on her daughter's finger. It was an agonising reminder of that other woman's existence. It felt like a dagger going through her own blood-red heart.

Selina said apprehensively. "The ring looks very expensive, and it's still a little big for you. Perhaps you shouldn't wear it just yet. When you're older, it might fit you better."

"You're right, Mum," Maria said as she took off her ring and handed it to her mother.

As Selina touched it, she felt annoyed that this woman was back in their lives. Then, still deep in thought, she turned the ring around and noticed the underside. "Look, Maria, there's an engraving on the gold band; 'C and W forever.'"

Taking the ring back, Maria examined it carefully. Then she shrugged her shoulders. "I don't care, that woman didn't want me. I know about her now, and I don't want to think about her, or that man, ever again." She sighed. "Also, I think that wearing her ring will upset you, Mum, and I don't want to do that either."

"It's very beautiful," Selina said, with bitterness in her heart. "Why don't you put it away in your dressing table drawer? Perhaps you can wear it when you're older?"

Maria scowled at the ring. "This ring and the note, with all the pain they stand for, shall be put where they belong – deep in a drawer never to be opened again." Then she grabbed the letter and ran back upstairs to her room, with Lucky following closely behind.

For once, Selina allowed her daughter's single-minded nature to prevail. She sat back, glad that woman was going in a drawer, never to emerge again. She didn't want her on Maria's finger. The woman was a threat, she couldn't bear the thought of her surfacing again. To lose her daughter back to that woman was a nightmare she didn't want to comprehend. She'd make sure the ring and all it represented would always stay hidden from Maria's life.

CHAPTER 31

7th December 1963

Maria looked around the football field and contemplated how much Lucky would have loved to run on the grass. Yesterday, Kira, Janice's dog, had died, so Maria decided it wasn't appropriate to flaunt Lucky in front of Janice today. She smiled. Her mum had been so pleased with her for showing such consideration. She loved it when her mum approved of her actions, not that she'd tell her mum that! Her thoughts turned back to the game. Why hadn't Will and the boys come out yet? It was very cold. She was pleased she'd brought the hat, scarf and gloves that her nana had knitted in the big freeze last winter. She started jigging up and down, trying to keep warm. It wasn't much fun standing in this sub-zero weather. As she glanced around, she noticed the other supporters were also swaying about in the cold. But then she spotted a small huddle of middle-aged men, who were standing upright and still. She nudged Janice and flicked her head towards the men.

"Do you think that's the scouts for the Kent under-eighteens team?"

Janice stared at the men for far too long, then she turned back and tucked into her sandwiches. "It could be," she agreed.

Maria grabbed a sandwich before Janice could take another. Dropping her voice, she whispered, "I hope Will doesn't get too nervous; you know what he's like."

While chewing, Janice mumbled, "He's stressed about today." She took another bite and with her mouth still full of sandwich she added, "We'd better do a lot of yelling and cheering; he'll need spurring on."

Maria thought for a moment. "How about we shout his name every time he tackles or passes the ball?" She nodded towards the middle-aged men. "It might help those men to notice him."

"With your loud voice, they should hear you," Janice chortled. "I guess it might help. I'm up for it."

The two teams appeared, and in no time the match was underway. Maria found herself becoming worried. Usually, Will would try to shoot whenever he got the ball, but he was passing it to his teammates for them to shoot. Why wasn't he trying to score? Suddenly, a lad from the other team had the ball and scored. Gravesend were losing, one-nil. Maria was yelling so loud that her throat was hurting.

"Come on, Will McIntosh … Good tackle, Will McIntosh … Good pass, Will McIntosh … Shoot, Will." Janice was standing next to her and yelling too, except not quite as passionately as she was, but Maria knew how to project her voice! Then the same boy from the other team scored a second goal. Gravesend were losing by two-nil. She was sure this wasn't looking good for Will. He could play so much better than this. She needed to find a way to stop his nerves from getting the better of him. Standing quietly for a second, she racked her brains for ideas. Janice seemed to have got herself distracted by a large, spotty lad who'd asked if he could have one of their biscuits. Maria found the boy annoying, but Janice was being helpful about the delights of certain types of biscuits.

The whistle went for half-time, and Maria ran over to Will. She wanted to catch him before he went off to his half-time talk. "Why aren't you even trying to score?" she shouted as soon as she was close enough for him to hear.

Will's face distorted. "I'm frightened of missing the goal in front of the Kent coaches. I lose my nerve every time the ball comes near me. I can't do it."

She grabbed his sleeve, heaving him closer to her. "Will, you're a good footballer, go out there and prove it." She could tell he wasn't listening. He looked depressed, and his confidence seemed to have gone. "Right, listen to me." She spoke quickly, knowing she only had seconds before he went off to join the rest of the team. "All your life, you've protected me. Remember the story of when we were small, and Uncle David nearly ran me over, but he squashed my football instead? Now I want you to pretend that the football out there is me! I need to be kicked into that net, to save me from being crushed by the other team. Do you understand, Will? Kick *me* to safety – as if my life depended on it!"

A flash of recognition passed across Will's freckled face, and she could see she'd hit a nerve. "You might not remember that day, but I do!" he laughed. "And I promised to look after you, so I'll kick you into safety without a problem," he added teasingly. Then he ran off to join the others.

In the second half Gravesend were playing at the other end of the field, with the sun out of their eyes. She watched as Will won the ball in midfield and started running with it. Faster and faster he went towards the goal, leaving the others behind. He had a clear shot and in it went.

"Yes!" she yelled, leaping into the air. "William McIntosh you're the best." The group of middle-aged men spun round to see who was screaming. She pointed to Will, "He's a marvellous player." One man grinned at her, then turned back to the game. Oh, how she hoped Will would get picked for the county team.

Biscuit boy, or Nicholas, as she'd now been informed, was back rambling to Janice. Maria found herself becoming incensed that Janice was being too polite, she needed to support Will. She turned away, concentrating on the match. After about ten minutes she saw that Will had the ball again. This time, he was close to the goal and surrounded by the other team. His control of the ball was fantastic. Then he found a gap in the group and volleyed the ball straight through the middle and into the back of the net. At last, it was two-all! Maria was beside herself with excitement. This was the Will she knew; this was the footballing star of the future!

The game was nearly over, several others had tried to score, but nothing had happened. Then during extra time, Will, who was at the side of the field, performed the most dazzling slide tackle. He got the ball and was off again towards the corner flag. She couldn't believe it; this was too good to be true. As he got to the byline, the other team were closing fast. He shot, the ball curled over the keeper and into the roof of the net. From that angle, the ball shouldn't have gone in, but it did! At first, no one seemed to believe it, then everyone started cheering. The whistle went, and the final score was three-two. Gravesend had won!

Maria was screaming while Janice was shouting. The two teams shook hands, and Maria's eyes turned to the scouts. She watched as the middle-aged man who had grinned at her walked over to the referee. There was some talking and then her heart sank as the referee called over the lad who'd scored the first two goals for the other team. As the boy strolled over, she stared sympathetically at poor Will. To her surprise, he started walking towards the referee as well, then she realised he'd been called over too! She observed the two boys, standing in the centre of the pitch, busily talking to the middle-aged man, while the rest of the players went back to the changing room. She stood watching every action and arm movement. Eventually, the middle-aged man shook hands with the lad from the other team, and then with Will. Then he turned to walk back to his colleagues at the side of the pitch. She couldn't wait any longer, she started running as fast as she could towards Will.

As she passed the middle-aged man, he shouted at her, "Hey young lady, slow down, you'll fall over. And by the way, you did well shouting for your friend, but you didn't need to, I'd already noticed him."

She stopped dead in her tracks. "Does that mean he's got through?" she asked with trepidation.

He chuckled. "You'd better go and ask him yourself."

She nodded and ran off towards Will, who was talking to the lad from the other team. As she reached them, she could see they were slapping each other on the back. Although she was breathless and had a very sore throat, she managed to squeak at Will,

"Well, did you get into the team?"

When Will turned and saw her, he flung his arms around her in a big hug. "I've made it to the Kent County trials."

"Not the team then?" she asked, her breath turning into steam as she spoke.

Will laughed. "You have to get to the trials before you can get into the team. But Mr Baldwin said he was impressed and very hopeful that we'd both get in."

She squealed with pleasure. "Oh, Will, that's great," and she hugged him again.

As she pulled away, Will said, "Maria, this is Jack. He's made it to the trials as well."

Maria looked at the tall, lanky boy from the Dover team. She thought he was good-looking with his dark hair and olive skin, and he had the most piercing blue eyes she'd ever seen.

"Hello," she said politely. "Congratulations, you played well, even if it was for the other side."

With an endearing smile, he replied, "You're very supportive of your boyfriend here; he's a fortunate chap." He spoke with a posh accent, just like Uncle David did, and she found herself thinking that all people from Dover must talk like that.

She blushed, and she noticed that Will was blushing too. "No, we're not a couple," she announced assertively. "We've grown up together. Will's the older brother I never had."

With a sigh, Jack said, "I wish you were my sister. She's not as supportive of my football as you are of Will's. She and Dad wanted me to play rugby." He stopped for a moment. "But Mum will be happy. It was her idea that I became involved in football. You see football's on her side of the family. She often says it's in my genes." He grinned as if he'd achieved the biggest goal of his life.

Maria could tell this boy needed supporting, so she tried her best to help. "You're obviously a very natural player."

He looked down at his lanky body. "Well, let's just say all my hard work has paid off. I wish my mother had been here today. She's away visiting friends in France, but she'll be back for the trials."

With that, Will slapped him on the back again. "Shall we go and get changed?"

Jack nodded and turned back to Maria. "See you at the trials then."

"I won't be able to come to any more games this season. My mum's organised some weekend singing lessons for me. I'm trying to get into the school musical." Jack gave her an understanding nod. There was something about him that she took to, she liked him. Scraping back her thick hair, she added, "I'm sure you'll both get into the squad."

Waving as she walked away, she shouted back, "I'll be keeping my fingers crossed for both of you." They hadn't heard her, they were strolling off towards the changing rooms, deep in conversation as they went. She turned to walk towards Janice, who seemed happy enough to be stuck listening to boring Nicholas. Maria looked back at Will and Jack striding towards the changing rooms, their arms over each other's shoulders. She recognised that neither Janice nor Will needed her, and she suddenly felt alone. She stood still in the middle of the football field, and as snowflakes started to fall all around her, she realised that like the weather, the three of them were changing. They were finding their own interests – they were growing up.

PART THREE

Entangled Families.

CHAPTER 32

21st March 1964

"I still think those music lessons cost too much money," Mark said as he appeared from the kitchen.

"I'm glad we did it," Selina replied as she stood at the bottom of the stairs. "Listen to her, she sounds amazing."

"She's spending too long practicing those songs for the show. The timing of the play's all wrong."

"Stop it, love. You have to trust Maria when she says she'll work hard for her O-Levels." She gave Mark a pretend punch in the chest. "She's finished the song now. I missed the end." Then she turned and shouted up the stairs, "Maria, it's present opening time."

"Come on, love," she giggled as she grabbed Mark's sleeve and pulled him back into the kitchen. She understood her daughter loved any chance to be the centre of attention, and birthdays were certainly that. "I'll put Maria's presents on the kitchen table, can you quickly get the milk in?"

Selina arranged the gifts on the table. There was one from her mum, one from Brian and Sandra, one from David and one from Mark's parents, which had arrived in the post. She heard Maria's long legs thumping down the stairs with Lucky's thuds behind her. Excitedly, Selina quickly placed her and Mark's present at the top of the table. Then she felt Maria's arms as they went around her waist. "I need a hug."

"Happy birthday, love," Selina said fondly as she looked up at her daughter's beaming face.

"Can I open them now?" Maria asked as she scanned the table. Selina jumped as the front door banged, and Mark rushed in with the milk from the doorstep.

"Sit down both of you, while I make the tea and toast. Then we'll have the grand opening." To her surprise, the excited Maria obeyed her instructions.

Once they were all seated at the table, Selina started to feel nervous. She hoped their gift would make her daughter happy, but she wasn't entirely sure it would.

Mark asked enthusiastically, "Can Maria open our present first? I can't wait!"

"Really, Mark," Selina exclaimed, "you're just a big kid at heart."

Maria stood up from her chair and leant precariously across the small table. "Which one is yours?"

Selina picked up their small present and handed it to her. "For a long time, Dad and I have been putting money aside from his wage packets. We were going to wait until your eighteenth birthday, but your dad persuaded me that you were sensible enough to have this on your sixteenth."

"Go on, open it, love," Mark said eagerly.

Nervously, Selina stood behind Mark and watched as Maria released the gift from the wrapped jewellery box. As her daughter held up the heart-shaped halo ring, the tiny red stones glistened in the sunlight. Selina explained, "We want you to have this as a symbol of our love for you."

"It's incredible, but you shouldn't have spent all your money on—"

"But there's a reason." Selina reached into her pocket and apprehensively drew out the ruby heirloom ring that Maria had buried in her dressing table drawer. "This is also your ring." Selina tried to control her wavering voice. "That woman's ring is yours, and I think you should wear it – regardless of how I feel about her." She swallowed to push down the lump in her throat. "I admit, the ruby heirloom ring was difficult for me to accept, but I've felt guilty about that, so …" She took the new ring back from her daughter. "Watch this." She gently placed the new halo ring over the top of the ruby heirloom. The new heart halo fitted snugly around the single ruby ring, framing it beautifully with its similar red stones. The two rings nestled together and became one! Selina then placed both rings onto Maria's middle finger. They fitted perfectly. Maria had grown more than Selina had realised. She wondered if the original owner of the ruby ring had similarly shaped fingers to Maria, but she quickly stopped that thought. She sat down and added, "The red heart ruby stone represents your bloodline, and the halo heart that surrounds it represents the love your dad, and I have for you." She chuckled. "The jeweller had such a struggle making the rings fit together. But we think he did a good job." Maria held up her hand to admire both rings, and Selina thought how the two rings really did look like one large, heart-shaped ring. Her daughter's finger looked as though it had a million dollars attached to it. She grinned. For all she knew, it did have! "This was my idea," she added proudly. "This way, you can wear both rings."

"Mum, are you sure? I don't want to upset you." Maria's voice sounded weepy. "It's the most wonderful gift I've ever had. It's magnificent but—"

Mark interrupted. "Maria, I see it like this, the two rings represent my two adorable women. The ruby heart heirloom ring is my pretty Maria, and the dainty halo heart ring is my gorgeous Selina." His voice softened, "Don't you see, your sensitive mother's nurtured that strong personality of yours, she's formed you into the person you are. Jointly, the two rings make a perfect match, one that's only complete when they're put together." He grinned.

"Mark, you're so understanding," Selina said admiringly.

Mark winked at Maria. "I understand, but with you two inseparable girls, I just never need to show it."

Maria got up and kissed them both. "Thank you, you're the best."

Selina rested back in her chair. "Nana helped me to sort the new ring with the jeweller. She also insisted on giving us some money towards it; she said it symbolises her love for you too." Nodding to the other gifts, she added, "That's why her gift is only a small one this year."

"That makes my ring even more special," Maria said as she reached for another present.

Selina felt pleased with herself. That woman's heirloom ring was just an object, it no longer felt like a threat. She breathed deeply, the thought of that woman was a demon she'd never be able to chase away. She appreciated she'd have to stop thinking like this; it wasn't as though that woman was ever going to be a real part of her daughter's life. She stared at the two rings on Maria's finger. The stones were sparking against each other, making the red colour more intense than when either ring was on its own.

Mark was right, the two rings enhanced each other; neither was complete without the other. "Maria," she said as her daughter opened her last gift. "The two rings are very valuable, so I think it's best if you only wear them in the house, for now."

"Alright, in that case, I'll keep them here, in the sideboard drawer," Maria announced as she put the empty jewellery box into the drawer.

"Also," Mark added, "I'd prefer it if you didn't show our ring to Uncle David. He'll think it's a waste of me wages, and I don't want his disapproval."

"You're right, love," Selina agreed. "He wouldn't understand the significance of it all." She turned to Maria. "I don't want David to think we're spoiling you too much."

Maria looked at her rings. "In that case, if I can't wear your ring when Uncle David's here, then I refuse to wear the heirloom ring on its own," she said forcefully. "Your ring is the one that's important to me." Now Selina knew for sure that the adoption wasn't something she would tell anyone about, there was no point. They were a family – just the same as everyone else.

CHAPTER 33

5th April 1964

Maria sat opposite Will and found herself drifting away from his endless talk of football. She looked around the café at the few people dotted around, and she picked up her coffee. How she wished Janice was there to talk to. She missed her when she was away with her family.

Will dropped his voice and leant forwards. "I need to tell you something, Maria. But you must promise never to tell anyone, it's important," he said, his hazel eyes full of fear.

She put down her cup and stared at him. "What's wrong? You're not ill, are you?"

"No, I'm not ill ... though some people would think I am."

She was getting worried now. "Will, what is it? And of course, I promise not to tell a soul." She reached over the table and took his hand.

He whispered into her ear, "I like other men ... in a way I shouldn't." He then looked down at the floor.

"What?" she said, pulling her hand away. "Will, don't be silly, you aren't ... why are you saying this?"

He gazed up at her, then he glanced around to check that no one else could hear him. In a low voice, he said, "Maria, I've known for ages. Do you remember the boy who liked you at junior school – Martin Hollingham?"

She nodded.

"Well, I was jealous because I liked him! That was when I first realised I liked ..." He wiped the sweat from his brow. "I chose not to go to the boys' grammar school because I didn't trust myself." He looked distraught, and there was heartache in his eyes. "I'm different ... it's time I accepted it. I can't tell anyone, you know it's illegal, don't you?" He looked scared and checked around again.

Her thoughts turned to the past. She and Janice had always been Will's 'sisters', in fact, he'd never shown any attention towards any girl. She recalled her recent English lesson about the life of Oscar Wilde. Mr Swinnerton had explained that Oscar Wilde was imprisoned for his practices and that if he'd fled when he'd had the chance, his premature death may well have been avoided. "Will, I promise I'll never tell anyone. You're far too important to me. I know it's against the law, and there's no way I want you to go to prison."

"I haven't done anything wrong." He looked so sad and forlorn. "Maria, my life won't be worth living if anyone found out. You mustn't tell anyone – ever."

Her hand reached out to his again. "I won't. Believe me, I do understand. It's scary to be different. People jump to conclusions and judge you unfairly; they can be vile with their opinions." She squeezed his hand. "I'll keep your secret to myself, and if ever you want to talk, then I'm here to listen. That's what friends are for, and you've always been there for me."

Will appeared pensive, but she could see the pressure had gone from his face. He took his hand away. "I'm glad I've told you my secret," he said, and he gave a small smile. "It feels right, you should know. I should've told you before, you and I have never had secrets from each other."

Now she felt ashamed; she had a secret she'd never told him. He'd confided in her, and she wondered if she should respond in the same way. She thought about her treasured rings still lying in the drawer; they'd helped her to understand so much. She sat quietly for a while, could she trust Will to understand?

"I do have a secret I've never told you." She felt uneasy; this was the first time she'd spoken about it to anyone other than her family. Will looked taken aback, she had to tell him now. "I haven't told anyone that … I'm adopted."

Will stared at her. "But you're so much like your mum, and you have her mannerisms and everything." He looked confused. "I know how close you are to your parents … this is unbelievable. They're not your real parents!"

She glared at him. "How dare you? Mum was right when she said people would say that."

"What have I said wrong?"

"For sixteen years, Mum and Dad have given their lives to loving and protecting me; no one else in the world has done that." Her thoughts returned to the hospital, where her mum hadn't left her side. "My family love me just as much as your family love you; genetic factors aren't everything. I'll not stand for you, or anyone, saying that they aren't my parents. You make them sound as if they're not valid."

"I'm sorry, Maria, I didn't mean to upset you." Will frowned sheepishly. "But do you know who your real mother is?"

"You don't understand," Maria snapped back at him. "My real mother is the one who tucks me in every night." She looked at the floor. "When I was young, I didn't really understand about the adoption. Later on, I didn't talk about it because I didn't want to appear different to everyone else." She ran her long nails through her glossy hair. "But eventually, I understood that I wasn't different because, like most people, I had a family who loved me." She scowled at Will. "My parents are the ones who raised me; they have made me into who I am. The other woman just gave birth to me and then gave me away."

"I do understand," Will said quietly.

Maria felt her body tensing as her brain went into overdrive. "Can't you see, it's a bit like what you're going through. People don't understand when something isn't the norm. Just because my family is different, it doesn't mean it isn't as good." She swallowed to clear her throat. "So, Will, yes, I do understand the importance of protecting our secrets."

Will looked thoughtful, then he took her hand and gazed at her. "Maria, I'm glad you've explained, and I promise you, I'll never tell." Still holding her hand, he whispered, "You're right; love exists in all relationships, and it doesn't make it any less important. Just because you're not related biologically, or just because I don't fancy girls, that doesn't make us any less able to love. The problem is, society tries to dictate who we should love, and who should love us. It's society that's prejudiced." He smiled softly at her. "Who would have thought we both have such important secrets – ones that only the two of us can really understand?"

CHAPTER 34

April - July 1964

Maria stopped abruptly at the door of the school hall. The number of pupils auditioning for the musical was more than usual. She walked in and sat down. The competition was going to be high, and she wanted the lead role, no other part in the play was going to be good enough. Eventually, the room fell quiet, and Mr Swinnerton stood up.

"For those pupils from the music department, I'll just explain that the auditions are always held in alphabetical order. When your name is called out, please come and stand on the stage." He pointed to the stage as if they didn't know where it was. "You'll be given a few lines to act, and then we'll ask you to sing a small part of a song that Mrs Bailey will hand to you."

Maria breathed in deeply, at least she wasn't going to have to sing a whole song. But having to wait was unfair, being a 'Tozer,' meant she was always almost last. Maria was getting bored, but then her attention moved to a boy who was walking towards the stage. His Nordic stature, combined with his likeable roguish face made him appear slightly on the wild side, which she knew fitted the main character of the play. She guessed he must be from the music set because she hadn't seen him before. As he performed the acting part of his audition, she established that he wasn't too bad. Then he started to sing, and his voice was astounding. When he'd finished everyone in the hall stood up and clapped. Well, it was obvious who the leading man was going to be – now she was even more determined to be the leading lady! She heard her name called, and she walked apprehensively towards the stage. This was the time to make her hard work mean something. The acting role was easy, but then the music started for her singing début. She stumbled a little, but she kept her head up and looked out at the audience. Her eyes fell on the boy who'd been so remarkable, he was pushing back his flaxen flyaway hair. He threw her a wink and a playful smile. That was it, her singing took off with passion and determination. As she finished her piece, her heart was beating so fast she was sure people could hear it from the back of the hall. Everyone started clapping and cheering, so she guessed she'd done alright. She turned to see Mr Swinnerton scribbling in his file. Was her singing good enough for the main part, she wondered? As she walked away, she saw the boy winking at her and smiling again. She pretended she hadn't noticed him, but she certainly had!

The next day as Maria approached the school board, her body was shaking. Had she done it? There was a group of pupils already huddled around the sheet. She pushed her way through to the front. It was a long list, and her eyes blurred as she stared at the writing. Taking a deep breath, she blinked and read the first name at the top of the list: '*Calamity Jane – Maria Selina Tozer.*' She squealed with excitement. Then she jumped as a hand touched her shoulder from behind. She spun around to see that it was the flaxen-haired boy.

"So, are you my leading lady?" he asked with a smooth, deep voice that made her body tingle. "I'm Peter. I've got the role of the leading man."

She felt speechless and came over all shy; she wasn't used to feeling like this. She assumed she was smiling stupidly at him. She tried to speak. "Yes, I am ... I'm Maria. Well done by the way ... I knew you'd get the part of Wild Bill Hickok. You must be very pleased."

Peter looked at her and gave her that playful smile again. "I've never been in a show before. I'm nervous. I know I can sing, but my acting isn't brilliant."

She giggled. "I can act, but my singing isn't the best."

Peter held her arm and gently guided her out from the crowd. "If you like I can help you with your singing. Then in return, you could give me advice about my acting."

The idea of being friends with Peter sounded fantastic. "Yes, please ... I mean that would be great if we can work together ... for the good of the show," she added quickly.

Peter had a sparkle in his eye that seemed to dance while he looked at her. She felt herself wishing she could sink deep into his arms. She knew the play so well, and the plot involved a kiss. She felt herself going slightly pink as she imagined kissing Peter. She stared at his heart-shaped lips. Then she panicked, she needed to say something.

"The only problem is, I'm in the fifth form, I have to work on my revision as well."

He looked surprised. "Oh, I thought you were older than that. I'm in the lower sixth, studying music. But I'm sure we'll find some time together to rehearse our parts."

231

"Because I'm tall people always assume I'm older than I am," she said shyly. Then, wistfully, she added, "I'd love to go into acting, but I don't suppose I will. My mum wants me to be a teacher."

"You only have one life, don't ever give up on your dreams," he said with a cheeky grin.

She found herself drifting off again, at this moment in time, her dreams involved him. She tried to stop herself from appearing like a speechless idiot, but she wasn't finding it easy. "I didn't have time to … to read the whole board … did you see when our first rehearsal is?"

Peter was looking intently at her. She wondered if her hair was out of place, or did he think she was ugly? He gave an impish smile. "It's after school tomorrow, and I can't wait to see you again. This play's going to be fun. I just know you, and I are going to be … spectacular."

She raked back her hair with her fingers. "Yes, I agree. Together we're going to be fabulous!" She'd never flirted before, and she found herself feeling flushed again. This was all a new experience for her, but she liked it!

*

A few months later, Maria felt tense as she sat, waiting for Mr Swinnerton to finish preparing the stage props for the dress rehearsal.

"Where's Peter?" asked Will.

"He's still backstage getting changed." She stared into space. "Peter's been great, he's helped me with 'Secret Love,' which is the song I find the hardest to sing."

"You do know there is chemistry between you two," Will replied.

"We're just determined to be the best leading actors the school has ever had," Maria answered as she lifted her hair from her sweating neck.

"Are you feeling a bit hot, Maria?" Will teased before he turned to talk to the boy next to him.

Maria glanced at Janice and whispered, "I don't know how I'm going to cope with everyone watching."

"You need to pretend Peter is someone you don't fancy, that way this first kiss won't bother you."

Maria squeezed Janice's hand. "Thank you for coming to support me."

"I just wish Will hadn't picked this dress rehearsal to watch. I said this wasn't a good time, but—"

"We're ready now," announced Mr Swinnerton. "Maria and Peter, can you come on stage, please."

"Maria, you're truly stunning," Peter gasped, as she walked onto the stage in her ballgown.

"Now Peter," said Mr Swinnerton. "I want you to lean across and touch Maria's cheeks with your hands and then gently kiss her. Maria, I want you to push him away because you don't like him. Then show the audience that you've thought about it and pull him back to kiss him again. Is that alright with both of you?"

Maria nodded and watched as Peter grinned. Then the moment she'd been waiting for happened. Peter held her face, and his mouth came towards her, his lips were so gentle she felt her body burn with pleasure. She forgot she was supposed to imagine someone she didn't fancy, and instead, she disappeared into the moment.

Mr Swinnerton's voice snatched her back to reality. "No, no, no! That's not right, Maria. Remember, you need to push him away. Then you have to pull him back for the long kiss." She looked sheepishly at the teacher and nodded.

Peter whispered in her ear, "I enjoyed that. If we keep getting it wrong, we'll just have to keep doing it again!"

She gave a little nervous chuckle, this was embarrassing. She did the scene again, this time remembering to push Peter away, and then she grabbed him back for the full kiss. She could tell neither of them wanted to stop. All of a sudden, the room filled with whistling from the other members of the cast. Then she heard Will's voice echoing from the back of the hall,

"I told you so Maria."

Mr Swinnerton said with an amused tone, "That's excellent acting, but perhaps you could make it less realistic next time."

Peter whispered, "I wasn't acting."

After the scene, Peter grabbed Maria's hand and dragged her behind the stage. He put his strong arms around her waist and pulled her into his body. Pushing her hair back from her face, he touched her lips with his. "Maria, you must know how I feel about you." He leant forwards and kissed her lips again.

This time she relaxed and enjoyed kissing him back. Then she pulled herself away. "Peter, my parents won't approve of a boyfriend coming onto the scene just yet. Once the play's over, I promised to revise for my exams."

"I don't mind waiting, we can tell people when your exams are over, and then we can start courting properly."

"That sounds good to me."

He gave a cheeky grin. "Maria, just think you really are my secret love."

Giggling, she said playfully, "Well actually, I might just tell Janice about our little secret!"

CHAPTER 35

24th July – 31st July 1964

Selina couldn't sleep, and Mark's snoring was getting louder, so she pushed him onto his side. She turned over onto her back. It was wonderful that the local newspaper had said that Calamity Jane was "the best play the school had ever produced." Then she lay thinking about how happy Maria seemed to be, her teenage moods had almost disappeared. Mark thought it was because Maria's O-Level exams were over, but Selina had seen her daughter's connection with the leading boy in the play. She had to face the fact that Maria was growing up. Turning over, she looked at Mark, who had rolled onto his back again. She knew he hadn't noticed his daughter was becoming a young woman. Starting to feel sleepy, she pulled the blankets and bedspread up to her chin. She'd wait for her daughter to tell her about the boy, but life was definitely about to change.

"Mum, Dad, I have something to tell you."

"It's the first day of the summer holidays, so I guess you want some pocket money," Mark said as he bent down to give the dog a biscuit.

"No," replied Maria. "You remember Peter from the school play?" she said sheepishly. "Well, he has waited until I finished my exams, and now he wants me to be his girlfriend."

"Oh, love, how wonderful," Selina exclaimed as she raised her hand to her face and forced a surprised expression. Then she turned to Mark and saw his face had turned red.

"You're not old enough to go courting," Mark bellowed.

"Honestly, Dad, I am old enough."

Selina touched Mark's arm. "She's becoming a young woman now, you have to let her grow up."

Mark looked back at Maria. "You're not going anywhere with the lad," he said, and then his gaze returned to Selina. She grabbed the moment and put on her usual, pleading smile. He turned back to Maria and added gently, "Not until I've met him and made sure he's suitable for my little princess."

"How about we invite Peter round for supper?" Selina suggested hesitantly. "It would be good for us to meet him properly." She desperately wanted Mark to like the boy, but deep down, she assumed that no one would be good enough for his daughter.

"Okay, you two can sort it," he said indifferently.

It was only one week later when Selina held out her hand as Peter entered the hallway, and Lucky ran to give him a little sniff of friendly interest.

"It's lovely to meet you, Peter. But I'm afraid we have a house full today," Selina explained. "Maria's nana wanted to meet you, and our friend David is also over for dinner. He's been visiting his parents in Ireland, so we haven't seen him in ages." She patted Lucky as the dog darted past her.

"Maria's dad's finishing work early, so he'll be home in a while." She glanced towards the kitchen. "I'll go and make a pot of tea. You take Peter into the lounge, Maria."

Placing the drinks on the small table, Selina watched as her mum handed Peter a rather large piece of her homemade sponge cake.

"I loved you in the school play," Eileen said with a smile. "I thought your singing was superb."

David leant across to get a slice of cake. "Maria is our little princess, so I hope you'll be a Prince Charming to her."

Everyone laughed, but Selina suspected that David's comment wasn't a joke.

"I'm honoured to be the prince in her life," Peter replied as he winked across at Maria.

David chortled his approval, then the conversation moved on to Peter's vast knowledge of music. Selina had to admit she was astonished by Peter's intellectual ability, no wonder Maria liked him. Then she heard Mark arriving home, and the room fell silent.

Peter stood up as Mark entered the lounge. "I'm so pleased to meet you, Mr Tozer. Thank you for inviting me to your home."

"I'm glad you've come," Mark replied politely. Selina thought this was a good start, but they had a whole evening ahead of them yet. She wondered if she should go and check on the dinner. She suspected a roast was over the top for a Wednesday evening, but she wanted to make Peter's visit into a special occasion. Perhaps it was best if she sat tight for a while, just in case Maria needed her.

"So, Peter, what does your father do for a living?" Mark asked as he sat down.

"My dad works as a manager at Chatham Docks."

"I work there too. What's your dad's name? I might know him."

"Percy Moss, but he doesn't work in the yard, he works in the office."

Mark's face lit up. "Percy Moss has been me manager since I started working there. Your father's a good bloke, a real gentleman and a great boss." Mark moved forward in his seat. "I remember, years ago, when your dad brought you and your brother to the docks. One of you made us all laugh by saying you wanted him to buy one of the big boats."

"That was me!" Peter exclaimed. "I love boats."

Selina sat back in her chair. She could see Mark wasn't worried anymore. She listened in disbelief as Mark seemed to push Maria and Peter together, asking when Peter wanted to take Maria to the cinema and enquiring about what films were on now.

Selina stood up, "I'll just go and sort the meal."

After they'd finished eating, Selina asked Maria to help her to collect the plates. As they got up to go to the kitchen, Maria opened the sideboard.

"Look at these, Peter," she announced proudly as she held out her hand with the two rings lying in her palm.

"Wow, they're beautiful," Peter proclaimed.

David gasped, and the colour seemed to drain from his face. "Maria, where did you get that one?" he said, pointing to the big ruby ring. "I mean … it's splendid."

Selina said quietly, "That ring's a family heirloom." Selina's eyes met Maria's, and Maria's gaze fell to the floor.

"Can I have a look at it, Maria?" David asked in a stunned voice. Selina watched as Maria gave him the ruby ring. David adjusted his glasses and stared long and hard at the ring, turning it round in his hand. "It has an inscription inside."

Selina said quickly, "We don't know whose ring it was; it's been passed down over several generations."

"I can tell this is a very expensive ring, Maria." David was staring at Maria as if he was going to say something important. "It is indeed a striking ring." Selina assumed his surprise was due to the ring being valuable. David passed it back to Maria then frowned. "What's the other ring?"

Maria handed David the heart-shaped halo ring, and while he looked at it, she mouthed "sorry," to Selina from across the room. Selina threw Mark a quick look of concern. She was conscious David wouldn't approve, and she hated the idea that he'd be cross with Mark for wasting his money.

"Watch this," Maria said as she took the ring back and placed it over the top of the ruby ring, making the two became one. She put them both on her finger, and the sparkle seemed to fill the room. "Mum and Dad had this halo heart made to frame the ruby ring." Maria looked at David. "It was Mum's idea. She says it represents their love that surrounds me. I know they shouldn't have spent their money, but it means the world to me."

"That's fantastic!" Peter said, his admiration quite obvious.

To Selina's surprise, David's mood seemed to change. Looking at her, he beamed. "What a perfect idea, trust you to think of something so thoughtful. I've always told Mark how incredibly understanding you are." She grinned with pride, thinking he was quite clearly astonished by the whole ring thing. David turned to Maria again. "It's delightful that your parents have done this. I know it must have cost them a fortune, but I can see they wanted to give you a symbol of their love." He spoke with real emotion, and Selina could tell that he meant what he said. She glanced at Mark, and she could see he was delighted that David hadn't judged him badly. She turned back to David, who was staring at her and for a second she thought she saw a flicker of comprehension in his eyes. It was as if he knew the truth behind the ring story. But he couldn't, they'd never told him.

Mark turned to Peter and chortled. "Maria will need a very expensive engagement ring to beat that setup!"

"Dad, that's not funny," retorted Maria.

"It's OK, Maria. I think your father's joking," Peter replied with a wink. Everyone laughed, but Selina had seen the sparkle in Peter's eye. She was happy, her daughter had found a delightful lad, and they did make a lovely couple.

CHAPTER 36

22nd August 1964

"Hurry up, Maria," Janice said, as she straightened her legs across Maria's bed. "You know Will hates waiting for us in the café."

"I'm just looking for my cardigan, it's here somewhere," Maria replied as she picked up some of the clothes piled all over her floor.

"Your mum seems pleased about your O-Level results," Janice declared, as she cuddled Lucky into her chest. "She told me you're on your way to becoming a teacher."

"She's determined I'll go to a teaching college. Oh, here it is," Maria said as she pulled the cardigan from a dress. Then she looked up at Janice. "I bet your mum's pleased with you too."

"She is. Like your mum, she's getting ideas about my future, she thinks I'll be good at town planning, which sounds boring to me!" Janice sat up and dangled her legs over the bed. "I'm just so glad we're going into the sixth form together, and I'm looking forward to concentrating on my Geography, all those other subjects bored me."

"And I can't wait to do English A-Level," Maria said as she put on her cardigan. "Even Will's working harder now that he's in the sixth form. He loves doing languages. In fact, I've never seen him this happy." She pushed Lucky off the bed. "I guess when you're doing subjects you enjoy, school becomes more interesting." Maria put on her cardigan. "We'd better make a move."

Janice jumped off the bed. "We'll be able to join Will and Peter in the sixth form common room."

"I hate the idea of the boys going into upper sixth and leaving school in a year's time." Maria opened the bedroom door. "Peter says he wants to go to an academy to study music, and Will hopes to go to university." Maria turned and frowned. "Peter and I have such a short time left together." With a giggle, she added, "But I'm going to make the most of it."

Once they reached the café, they found Will was already there, so, grabbing their drinks they went to join him.

After a while, Will announced apologetically, "The football season starts next weekend, so this is going to be my last coffee with you both."

"Are you excited about playing in the under-eighteen Kent team?" Maria asked as she sipped her hot drink.

"Too right, I am. I'll be in matches against different counties, so I'll have to travel a lot. I've never been outside of Kent before."

"It'll be wonderful for you, Will," Janice said as she bit into her cake.

"And guess what," he added, "everyone at training has admired my football skills, to the extent that I've been chosen to be the club captain for this season."

Maria shrieked, "Well done, that's marvellous."

"We'll have to come and watch some of your home games," added Janice. "I bet there's some muscular-looking boys in your new team."

Will started reprimanding Janice for not being interested in the lads' football skills so, in boredom, Maria found herself looking around the café. It all seemed very busy, probably because it was raining heavily outside. As she turned back to the others, she felt cosy, the three of them were huddled around the table almost as if they were trying to keep each other warm. Then she noticed Will was looking edgy, so she leant forwards as he started to talk.

"I'm not applying to university yet. I'm thinking of going to France for a while." He became fidgety. "I want the chance to experience the French culture and way of life. I want to travel."

"You can't leave England," barked Janice.

"I'm not leaving, just trying somewhere totally different for a year. My parents are backing me."

Maria could see the resolve in his eyes. She understood this must be important to him, so she tried to put on a brave face. "That's fantastic." She thought for a moment. "But what will you do there? And where will you live?" She turned to Janice. "There's a lot for Will to sort out, it's not going to happen overnight."

"But it's another country," Janice cried.

Maria frowned. "It's not for long, and France is only about twenty-six miles across the channel, so it's possible we could visit."

"It's 20.7 miles at its shortest distance," Janice snorted, and that's from the South Foreland to Cap Gris Nez.

"You and your boring Geography!" laughed Maria. Then she gazed at Will. "I don't know how much the ferry costs, but we could save up. The three of us will always stay in touch and be friends – won't we?"

"We'll always be friends," confirmed Will. "Anyway, to prove our friendship, I've got you both guest tickets for the Football Club Christmas Dance. We're only allowed one guest each, but one of the lads doesn't want to bring anyone, so I asked if I could have his ticket. I want you both to come."

Janice grinned. "That's great news. If your friend hasn't got anyone to bring, he might like me, and if not, there will be other gorgeous footballers to choose from, heaven has come to earth!" Janice then did some sort of dance with her arms.

"You're funny," Maria laughed. Then she reflected on how Janice had fallen for Donald, a boy from her Geography class, but he hadn't shown any interest back. She sighed; Janice deserved a considerate boyfriend like Peter. As Maria sat and pondered, she had to admit she didn't like the idea of having to go to the football dance without Peter. But then in her best motherly type voice, she announced, "It seems I'll have to go with you, Janice, someone has to look after you."

"Maria, I want you there to support me too," Will said with slight irritation in his voice.

"I'll be there for both of you," she said fondly.

Janice started jabbering on to Will about the dance and the boys that would be there. Maria sat back in contemplation. She didn't like the thought of Will going to France. He was her big brother, they'd always been together for as long as she could remember. As she pushed back her hair, she realised he hadn't answered her questions about France, and she wondered why he had changed the subject so quickly. She guessed he wanted to stop Janice from having a go at him, but leaving the country, even for a while, was a huge thing for him to do. But it felt as if Will didn't want to talk about it, so she wouldn't bring the subject up again. Besides, he would probably change his mind, it was a whole year away yet.

CHAPTER 37

.

27th September 1964

"The tea's brewed," Catherine announced as she put the teapot down. "Listen to that rain." She sighed as she poured the tea. "I hope the children will be alright. Tia's in Canterbury and Jack's gone into town."

"Tia's with George, he'll look after her," replied Joe, "and Jack's used to the rain."

She noticed David started playing with his teacup, then he looked up but didn't speak. He usually drank his tea in two mouthfuls, yet today he seemed to be scrutinising it. He caught her eye, and his stare seemed odd, so she quickly moved her gaze away, but she was aware David's eyes didn't move from her.

He coughed nervously. "I need to talk to you, Catherine, and it seems that now might be a good time." Quietly, he added, "The thing is, Joe phoned this morning to cancel our golf because of the weather. So, I chose to spend the morning dealing with my bills." He coughed again. "As I searched my desk drawers, I saw a letter that I'd put aside." He frowned and the furrows in his brow deepened. "I remembered that three years ago, I promised

…" His head fell to one side. "Anyway, I put the envelope in my jacket pocket, ready for when the time was right." Catherine noticed David eyeballing Joe. "I'm sorry, Joe, I need to do this for my own peace of mind. I think it is time to put Gregory Jones's ghost to rest." She felt her skin turn cold. She sensed Joe was about to object, but David quickly turned back to her. "Are you alright with this?" he asked gingerly. She nodded in vague agreement. He turned to Joe. "I need to start at the beginning, and I'm going to explain everything."

"No, David—" Joe began.

But David ignored him and turned back to Catherine. "On the night of the rape, I wanted Gregory Jones killed." She shuddered, David's voice sounded serious. "I don't know if Joe has told you, but I have people who work for me who could have ..." She guessed what he meant, and she bent her head. "But we couldn't involve our work colleagues, we had to deal with Gregory ourselves."

"Please, David, don't," murmured Joe. "Catherine doesn't want to hear about that man."

"It's fine, Joe," interjected Catherine. She needed to know what they'd done. "Go on, David."

"That night, Joe and I talked for ages. We wanted Gregory Jones punished and locked away, but we knew you wouldn't allow the police to be involved. So, I came up with a plan, which Joe agreed to." She watched as her husband bowed his head, as if in shame. David rested his bulky arm on the table. "I wanted to do something to help, dealing with Gregory was my way of supporting you and Joe. Gregory was easy to find, so I paid him a visit. It was only fair he experienced some of the physical brutality he'd given to you." Catherine gasped, but she didn't speak. David looked at Joe, "But I kept my promise, I didn't kill him, I just gave him what he deserved." He turned to her. "I informed him that if he ever came anywhere near you again, I'd finish the job." Shock filled Catherine's frame, and her body turned to ice. She folded her arms around her body, her hands rubbing her muscles as if to keep warm. David didn't seem to notice, he just kept talking. "I visited Gregory regularly to check he was keeping away from you."

Catherine hunched her shoulders. Her memories of this madman were strong.

"Stop it, David," said Joe.

Catherine forced herself back to the present. She had to hear the rest.

"I could see Gregory's mind was unbalanced; he wasn't normal by any means. So, we decided to move on with our plan. Joe found out who Gregory's doctor was, and I made an appointment to see him." David's voice became authoritative. "I explained I was concerned about the mental state of my army friend, Gregory Jones. I asked the doctor to visit because I felt Gregory needed treatment, and I mentioned the idea of admitting him to a lunatic asylum so that he could have some help." He gave a lopsided grin. "I said I needed confidentiality on this, and I think my high rank in the army made him think Gregory's possible illness was the result of a secret war matter." Catherine looked at Joe, and she could see the guilt showing on his face. She straightened her back while David's husky voice continued. "After the doctor visited Gregory, he agreed that his uncontrollable anger did concern him, he was also worried about his savage appearance, which made his hostile behaviour seem even more threatening." David grunted. "He thought Gregory appeared to be exhibiting signs of paranoia. It seems

Gregory believed a man was trying to kill him." He sniggered. "The doctor said the war had unbalanced Gregory. He assessed him as insane and had him admitted to Cedarwood as an inpatient." David sat back in his chair. "The best day of my life was when I phoned Joe and told him we'd achieved our goal. Gregory Jones was locked away, you were safe, and Gregory couldn't attack anyone else either."

Catherine stared from one to the other, in sheer disbelief.

Joe took her hand. "I'm sorry, darling, but we couldn't sit back and do nothing, you do understand, don't you? The man had to be locked away."

She looked into Joe's whirlpool eyes and saw love staring back at her. "Gregory needed help," she admitted, "and a lunatic asylum was the best place for him. Also, I confess, I'm glad the man was locked away." She took her hand away from Joe and pressed David's large arm. Flashing a half-smile at him, she said, "I should thank you for being so protective towards me."

David nodded, then cleared his throat. "But that's not everything." Joe looked baffled as David stared down at the table. "Joe's part in this was over, but I needed to make sure the man stayed locked up." She saw David was now twiddling with the tablecloth and he'd turned slightly red. "There was a nurse who worked at the institution, and for a short while, we became … friendly." He stopped adjusting the tablecloth, and as Joe's eyes rolled upwards, she comprehended the implication. "The nurse advised me that Gregory's temper was wild and ferocious. He would lash out with malice if anything or anyone got in his way. They were treating him with various medical techniques, none of which sounded too pleasant to me:

electroconvulsive therapy, different cocktails of drugs, and he even had the occasional sessions in a straitjacket. It seemed that Gregory's anger wasn't responding to any of the treatments."

Catherine could see Joe was starting to look sorry for the man. Joe was too soft. She turned back to concentrate on David, whose eyes fixed on Joe.

"I met Gregory's mother at his funeral, and she told me she'd visited Gregory on the day he'd died. They'd walked and talked in the garden of Cedarwood. It seems Gregory took that moment to confide in her." David's gaze fell on Catherine. "He told her he'd attacked and raped you." His gaze softened. "Gregory's mother was completely devastated because she was friendly with Win, and she knew you." Then David's voice strengthened again. "Gregory also told her that he'd even thought about strangling you, but he'd been disturbed by someone approaching in the alleyway."

She watched as Joe's fists clenched, and she leant forward and gently touched his hand.

David continued, "Gregory said he recognised that his anger was often out of control. He'd caused many fights before he was admitted. He said his rage about his injury made him hate others, he'd gained pleasure from hurting people. He knew it was wrong, and he was sorry." David's expression changed. "That day in the garden, Gregory's mother thought he was looking for her support and understanding. Instead, she was traumatised by what he'd done to her friend's granddaughter." Catherine looked at the floor as David's voice dropped, "Apparently, Gregory became distraught, saying it wasn't his fault; he couldn't control himself." David's voice grew even quieter. "Gregory's mother blames herself because, in the heat of the moment, she told him she didn't want to see him again. After she'd left, he took down the rope from a washing line and hung himself from a tree. He was found later by a member of staff, and it was too late to save him."

"No! I didn't want to kill him!" Joe screamed in a fury.

Catherine knew Joe would think that. There was no point in arguing with him.

Ignoring Joe, David turned to Catherine. "The mother gave me a letter and made me promise to give it to you. At the time of the funeral, you were too angry, and Joe said … but I did promise her." He reached into his jacket pocket, took out an envelope and placed it into Catherine's hand.

She looked at it pensively, then slowly, her fingers began to unseal the flap, and she took out the letter. She read out loud …

"My Dearest Catherine,

As you know, I was a friend of your gran's. I remember you not only as a young teenager, but also as a beautiful young woman, and this makes things even worse for me to bear. I want to tell you I'm ashamed and hurt by what my son did to you. His behaviour was appalling and repulses me beyond belief. But I want you to know that my son did apologise to me about his cruel actions.

Before the war, Greg could control his self-centred nature, but the war damaged him, both physically and mentally. His injuries and all those terrible war memories made him bitter and aggressive. Please understand that he was ill, he suffered a mental breakdown and, in the end, even the asylum couldn't help him.

A mother loves her children unconditionally. If you are a mother, then I know you'll appreciate this. As Gregory's mother, I can now forgive him. I ask and hope that you can forgive him too.

With my sincere and deepest apologies,

Edna Jones."

Catherine tried to make sense of the information she'd just read. In the silence, she could hear the rain knocking on the window as if it was desperate to enter the room. As she started to process things, she identified with the note.

"His mother loved him. When I think of my darling Jack, I know if he did anything awful, I would support him too." Briefly glancing towards the rain as it washed the glass clean, she murmured, "As a mother myself, and I never expected to say this, but I too can forgive Gregory." Reaching across the table, and taking David's large hand in hers, she said, "You and I are very similar, we both see life as straightforward." She contemplated for a while before speaking again. "Perhaps Joe loves me because I'm like his brother, we're both hardened to the world. I'm pleased you made sure Gregory never had the chance to hurt anyone again." Then, gripping David's hand tighter, she said, "I know you did this for me, and I'm deeply touched." David nodded, and she saw pleasure in his eyes. She felt he'd accepted her at last.

Turning to Joe, she added, "Gregory was ill, Joe. The institution was trying to help him, you did the right thing." Dropping her voice, she said, "It was his choice to take his life. His anger was dangerous, and he knew it. He can't hurt anyone now."

Joe gave her a sorrowful nod as he admitted defeat.

Catherine couldn't believe how relieved she felt now the burden of her hatred towards Gregory had gone. She muttered, "It's strange, all of this makes the child feel more real to me now. Do you ever wonder where she went because …"

Joe glanced across at David and David's eyes fell to the table.

"What is it?" she asked.

Joe answered swiftly, "It's just that you haven't mentioned the child for years."

The kitchen door flew open.

"Hi all," announced Jack as he bounded in. "I've got the football boots I wanted, and they were in the sale." He leant down and kissed his mum. "What's for dinner? I'm starving."

"Honestly," Catherine said. "I haven't even started it yet."

Jack pinched a biscuit. "I'm off to change my wet clothes," he said as he disappeared out of the kitchen.

Catherine stood up, smiling across at David and Joe. "Dinner won't be too long." She turned to prepare the food, singing softly to herself as she went.

"I didn't realise you had such a delightful singing voice, it's entrancing," David said with amazement.

"I've always been good at singing, but my trained voice is down to Gran, she made me have singing lessons when I was younger."

David grinned and stared out of the window. It was then that Catherine noticed the rain had stopped.

At last, Catherine felt free from the bitterness and loathing that had haunted her. As she looked across the dining table at David, she realised he'd released her, she'd learnt to forgive. Then she found herself engrossed as Jack excitedly talked about his new football schedule. Recently, Jack's confidence had grown. He was now a young man who embraced life to the full.

"Jack, I have some news for you," she said excitedly. "Your dad had our offer accepted on that apartment in Normandy."

"I gave in," grunted Joe. "With all your mum's trips back to see her friends, she needed a place of her own.

Though she does have expensive taste!" He gazed at her. "Which we'll have to address somehow."

"So, Jack," Catherine announced. "If you do get into the new university in Caen, the apartment will be somewhere for you to live."

"I'll have my own place!" Jack replied excitedly.

"It's my holiday home too!" Catherine reminded him. "It could take ages to sort all the paperwork, so I'm not planning to go back until the spring. Talking of the spring, has anyone any ideas what to get Ada for her eightieth birthday?"

Tia chirped up, "How about I do Granny Ada's family tree for her? She's always telling me stories about her relatives. I could do some research and present the tree on a chart." She scratched her head. "You and Dad could pay to have it framed and Jack, you'd need to put some money towards it too, then it could be a gift from the whole family."

Catherine looked at Joe, sitting at the top of the table. He turned to her as if to question her response.

"I think it's a great idea," she said. "Ada would love having her family heritage written down, and I'm sure Tia would enjoy the task." She turned to her daughter. "It's your heritage too."

Tia grinned, "I'll ask my History lecturer for advice on how to do it."

Catherine sat back in her chair, and as she did so, she noticed David was also smiling at Tia. She respected the fact that he loved his niece and nephew as if they were his own children. She wondered if he would have loved her other child in the same way. Of course, he would have! David always did what was right. Guilt unexpectedly came over her. She needed to stop thinking about that other child, she didn't want to meet her. All those terrible lies would break Tia and Jack's heart, it would totally spoil the relationship she had with them.

CHAPTER 38

12th December 1964

As Maria brushed her hair, she felt ashamed that she wasn't as animated about the Kent Football Club's Christmas dance as Janice and Will were. Only yesterday, she'd watched Janice trying on a dozen outfits before deciding on the one she wanted to wear. Maria opened her wardrobe and took out her red frock. She stood in front of her dressing table mirror and held the dress against herself. Her hands displaying her red rings, which matched her dress beautifully. She was so glad her parents had agreed she could wear her rings tonight. She put on the dress, and then tied the loose cord around her hips. She deemed the frock wasn't the most becoming, but she didn't care what she looked like, her role tonight was solely to help Janice to find a boyfriend.

"And that, Lucky, is what I plan to do," she said, glancing down at the dog by her feet. A horn blasted from outside. She pulled the curtain back and scraped the ice from the inside of her window. There was a car flashing its lights outside her house. "My lift's here," she said to Lucky as she let the curtain drop. She turned, and with Lucky following, she flew down the stairs, shouting to her parents that Janice's dad had arrived. Lucky's tail wagged as Maria put on her coat. "See you all later," she yelled.

"Bye, love. Have a good time," her mum shouted back. "And wear your hat, scarf and gloves, it's cold out there."

Maria frowned, she wasn't a child anymore, but still, she grabbed her scarf and gloves. There was a knock at the front door, and she opened it slightly, squeezing through the gap so that Lucky couldn't follow.

Janice stood there, looking very fashionable in her tight dress. She'd also put smooth waves in her short-curled bob and added a kiss curl on each cheek.

"I love your hair," Maria said.

"Thanks," replied Janice. "Will's already gone, but he's getting a lift back with us."

"Oh, OK. I guess he'll be with his football mates."

"Isn't this fun?" laughed Janice.

Maria gave a forced giggle as they ran to the car.

The dance was full of young teenagers all leaping to the music that was blaring from the stage. Maria and Janice said hello to Will, who was talking to his friend Jack, then they headed for the dance floor. Maria hoped Jack might show an interest in Janice, but he refused to join them. Maria made Janice dance for ages, but eventually, Janice said she had to sit down for a while.

"Hi, Janice," hollered a boy from behind them.

"Oh, hi, Nicholas," Janice said as she wiped her brow. "How are you?"

Maria whispered to her, "I haven't got any patience with Biscuit Boy! I'll go and get us some cold drinks."

Janice laughed and whispered back. "A drink would be good, and I don't mind poor Nicholas. I don't think he has anyone to talk to."

On her way for the drinks, Maria sauntered over towards Will and Jack. She stopped short as she heard them talking in French. "I didn't realise you both spoke French," she exclaimed.

"Jack's fluent in French," Will replied, "and he's giving me some extra practice for my A-Level exams." He gazed at her awkwardly. "Anyway, I need to improve for when we're in France."

"Oh," she exclaimed as she looked at Jack. "Are you going to France with Will?"

"I'm hoping to go to university out there, and I've persuaded Will to get a work visa and come with me." Jack's posh accent once again reminded her of Uncle David's voice. "My parents are buying a three-bedroom apartment in Normandy, and Will's agreed to be my lodger." Jack's stance seemed insecure, and he looked frightened. He leant closer. "It's perfect because everyone will assume we're just flatmates; it's not an easy world for … people like us."

Maria stared at Jack, then she turned back to Will, the sudden realisation hitting her like a bullet. "It's great that you have each other." She turned to Jack. "I think you'll be good for Will."

Jack's boyish face grinned with pleasure, exposing the cutest dimple. "You don't know how much your acceptance means to me, Maria. For Will's sake, I'm delighted you're alright with this."

Will whispered in her ear, "I wanted you to meet Jack properly. It's important to me that you like him. It's strange, there's something about him that reminds me of you. I feel so at ease when I'm around him."

Maria looked at Jack, who appeared so gentle and unassuming, then she murmured, "I think it's because you've always protected me, and now Jack needs you to do the same for him." With a raised voice, she said, "I need to get back to Janice, but I'm just off to get some drinks. What can I get you both?"

She stood with her back to the drinks table and looked across at Will and Jack. Will was talking incessantly about something, and Jack was eagerly listening while pushing his hand through his thick black hair. Neither of them seemed to be taking any notice of anything else that was going on in the room. She thought about her and Peter; they never noticed when other people were around them either. It suddenly occurred to her – that extra guest ticket must have been Jack's. The two of them must have wanted the other team members to think they were each bringing a girl. She thought again of Oscar Wilde. How she hoped things would be better for her friends. Perhaps with time, the law would change. She frowned. She doubted society would ever understand. She looked across for Janice. She was still talking to Biscuit Boy. Interestingly, though, another lad had joined them. The dance floor was full of bodies, all throwing themselves around to the music. She could smell the salty sweat, and the dampness in the air was making her hair turn frizzy.

Once she'd got the drinks, she balanced the sodas on her tray and walked back towards Will and Jack. After the boys had taken their drinks from her, she turned back towards Janice. It was then she noticed Biscuit Boy was pushing the other lad in the chest and was clearly shouting at him. One of the adults appeared, and with force, Biscuit Boy was taken by the arm. It seemed as if he was getting a telling off. Her eyes fell on Janice, who was rapidly heading towards the Ladies.

Will nodded towards Janice. "Leave your drinks here, you'd better go and check on her."

"I'll let you know what's happened," Maria said as she handed Will the tray, then ran through the crowd towards the toilets.

"What's wrong?" Maria asked as she saw Janice crying bitterly over the sink, make-up smudged all over her face, and her kiss curl's dishevelled.

In a voice that was a little difficult to understand, Janice blubbered, "Nicholas … started to become really … so I told him I wasn't interested, we were just friends. Then he started bellowing at me. A boy called Mervyn came up and asked me if I wanted to shuffle." She wiped her nose with her hand. "I said yes, please. Then Nicholas started shouting and pushing Mervyn around." With a loud snivel, she added, "I tried to stop them, but Nicholas shoved me away. I tripped and fell over." Janice stared down at her arm. "I've scraped my arm, and it's bleeding everywhere." Janice looked up at her. "Nicholas was so spiteful. As I staggered to straighten up, he said he was glad I was hurt. He seemed so considerate when we saw him at the match. It just shows you never know what people are really like."

"That's very true," Maria agreed. "Now, come on, I'll sort you out." She took a clean hankie from her bag and laid it beside the sink. Then she hitched up her sleeves, took off her rings and placed them on the other side of the sink. "Let me see your arm." The water felt warm as she washed Janice's arm under the running tap. "Now, that looks better," Maria announced as she turned off the tap and positioned the folded hankie over the wound. "There, the bleeding's stopped. Is it still painful?"

"It just stings a little." Janice stared at herself in the mirror. "I look terrible." She started to repair her tear-filled eyes just as a woman from the organising team walked in.

"Don't worry, love, the coach has taken his son, Nicholas, home." She frowned. "But a boy is waiting outside for you. He seems very concerned. What shall I tell him?"

Janice grabbed Maria's arm. "It must be that Mervyn. What does he want?"

"I'm sure he's worried about you. Being shoved, hurt and told you deserved it isn't a nice thing to happen to a girl."

Janice grabbed her hand. "Stay with me, Maria, while we go and see him."

Maria nodded. After all, getting Janice an acceptable boyfriend was why she had come to the party. She took her hankie and picked up her bag. "OK, we'd better hurry up before he gives up on you!"

As they pushed their way through the girls queuing for the toilets, Maria saw the boy hovering by the door, and he threw Janice a very handsome, yet concerned, smile.

"I'm sorry you got hurt." He spoke with a soft rural accent that sounded so genuine. "I could see that boy was getting angry with you. I wanted to get you away from him, but I just made things worse."

A little shyly, Janice replied, "It was good of you to help. I was only talking to Nicholas because we'd met once before. I think he assumed we were together, but we're not."

"In that case," the boy held out his hand and gave her a cheeky grin. "Can we have that shuffle now?" Janice turned to Maria with a questioning face.

"You go," Maria said. She nodded towards the dance floor, while gently pushing them both forwards. "I'll be fine."

Maria scanned the crowd and spotted Will and Jack talking across the room. With her head down, she started to push her way over to them. Jack caught her just as she reached the middle of the dance floor. "I can't explain," he said, sounding panicked. "But will you have this dance with me? It's important." She nodded as he slung his arms around her waist, forcing her into a slow dance. Frowning, he quickly whispered, "I've just seen my sister's arrived to pick me up. It'll look good if she sees me dancing with a girl. I hope you don't mind."

"I'm glad to help," she chuckled.

"My sister will be over in no time to quiz you. She's very nosy."

As Maria laughed, she saw a girl tapping Jack on the shoulder. The girl had the same dark hair and skin tone as Jack, but she was much shorter and plumper. She was wearing an expensive-looking coat, with a feather scarf draped around her neck.

"Hi, Jack, I'm here!" She sounded posh too.

Jack stopped dancing and pulled away from Maria. "Oh, hi, sis, you're early, but I'm ready when you are. I'll go and get my coat."

"It's okay. I'll wait over there. You can have a last kiss before we go," his sister said with a pronounced wink. Jack's face turned red.

Maria said hastily, "I was just telling Jack that I have a boyfriend." To enhance the point, she vaguely waved in the direction of Will.

"Oh, poor old Jack," sniggered his sister.

Jack shrugged. "Win some, lose some!" Winking at Maria, he then disappeared to get his coat.

The girl smiled. "I'm sorry for teasing you. My brother's useless with girls!" Then she stared at her. "Do I know you?" Maria shook her head; quite sure she'd never seen the girl before. "There's something about you that feels familiar." The girl's eyes remained fixed on hers. "It's such a shame; Jack needs a girl like you."

Maria giggled as she found herself liking Jack's sister, she seemed to care for him. But before Maria had a chance to speak, Jack jumped over the small rail surrounding the dance floor and landed right by her feet.

"I'm back, Tia. Let's get going."

Waving them goodbye, Maria looked around for Janice. She was still slow dancing with Mervyn. It must be getting late; Janice's dad would be due soon, and he'd told them to be ready on time. She glanced at her watch, and it was then that she saw her rings weren't on her finger. How could she have forgotten to pick them up? She rushed back to the Ladies, and noticed the room was now empty. As she looked across, she could see her mum and dad's ring balanced precariously on the side of the sink, but the ruby ring was missing! She picked up her ring, then searched around for the other one, but it wasn't there. She bent under the sink and checked the floor, but it wasn't there either. She checked every cubicle to see if it had rolled onto the floor. It wasn't anywhere in the room. Could it have fallen down the plughole while she was washing Janice's arm? It must have! Her expensive heirloom ring had gone forever, and it was totally her own fault. That red heart ring represented her natural heritage, and she'd carelessly washed it away. With relief, she kissed her remaining ring. At least her parents' love was still with her, and she placed it back on her finger. Her mum and dad's ring meant more to her than the heirloom ring did, and she smiled because she knew why. But that lost ring was probably expensive and could never be replaced. She had failed to keep it safe, and she felt guilty for letting everyone down. She'd let that woman down, but also her parents, who had gone to such trouble making the two rings fit together. Turning to the door to leave, she realised she had to go and face the music!

CHAPTER 39

13th December 1964

"Are you waiting for me to make your sandwiches before you play golf?" Catherine said sarcastically, as she walked into the kitchen.

"That would be lovely, thank you, darling," replied Joe without looking up from his Sunday magazine.

She turned to David, who also didn't stir from reading his Sunday paper. 'Men!' she whispered and grabbed the bread from the larder. As she cut the loaf, she thought about what she'd do with her free afternoon. Maybe she should go and tend to Win's grave; she hadn't been for a while. She stopped and looked up, deciding she'd visit Angeline for coffee instead. She knew Saul was away buying another restaurant near Angeline's parents in Thornton, Blackpool. Catherine reached for the ham, and as she sliced it, she admired how Angeline and Saul had expanded their business. Twelve Restaurant and Lounge Bar was now the best restaurant in Kent. As she filled the bread with the ham, she contemplated how her sandwiches were nowhere near their restaurant standard. Saul's exquisite food, combined with Angeline's hard work at getting everything to flow, had always been a recipe for success. She was sure the Thornton restaurant would be a winner.

Catherine's thoughts were disturbed by a loud thump from the staircase and Tia came storming into the kitchen. "You're up late, I was getting worried," Catherine said as she finished the sandwiches. "Jack's gone to football, and your dad's already home from church." She waved her arm towards David. "Uncle David's just having some lunch before they go to play golf." She turned back to plate the lunch. "Do you want breakfast, or would you like some of these sandwiches?"

"I'm OK," Tia replied breathlessly, grabbing the side of the table as she sat down. "I didn't mean to oversleep. I stayed up too late when I got back from picking Jack up last night."

Catherine placed the plate of sandwiches on the table, and the men grabbed them instantly.

"Mum, can you sit down for a minute? I have a present for you." Tia reached into her pocket and pulled out a jewellery box.

"It's not my birthday," Catherine said as she leant down and plucked a small white feather from Tia's hair.

"Oh, that must be from my feather scarf. I was wearing it yesterday."

"But your scarf is multi-coloured."

"It does have some white in it. Anyway, sit down, Mum," Tia said as she handed the box to her.

Catherine looked inquisitively at the jewellery box, but noticing Tia seemed to be watching her intently, she carefully raised the lid. Then unwittingly, she squealed as she stared at the contents. "Tia, where did you get this?"

she shouted as she took the ring out and examined it for the engraving.

"Is that Win's old ring?" David cried, choking on his bread.

She looked up to see Joe staring at her.

"Is it, darling?" he asked with a mouthful of food.

Catherine couldn't speak; instead, she nodded the confirmation.

"Tia," Joe snapped. "How did you get it?"

"Yesterday afternoon, I was shopping with Valery, and I saw it in the window of a second-hand jeweller's shop in Canterbury. It looked so familiar, and then I remembered."

Catherine stared at Tia. She was proud of the fact Tia had chosen to be a day student at Canterbury College. However, she suspected Tia's motives for living at home were mainly to continue to see George every day. Then Catherine noticed Tia was now slightly pink in the face, and her eyes were locked on the jewellery box.

"The heart shape looked the same as your old ring from Win," Tia said excitedly. "So, we went into the shop. That's when I saw the inscription on the inside, 'C and W Forever'. I knew it was the ring you lost all those years ago, I couldn't believe it, Mum. It was as though Win had wanted me to find it."

Catherine's eyes turned to Joe and David, who both looked totally stunned. Then she gazed back at the ring, feeling as if she'd seen a ghost. She felt sick at the thought that the child …

"It was in a shop, you say … for sale?" Her voice felt weak. Tia nodded while going even redder. Catherine guessed she was probably expecting her to jump up and down with joy at being given her ring back. But she didn't feel any elation right now.

"Aren't you pleased, Mum? You have your ring back."

"Yes, I'm thrilled. I just can't believe it, that's all. It's such a shock." Catherine felt anger rising from the pit of her stomach. How could the child have had no thought for the meaning of the ring?

Tia got up and gave her a big hug. "I'm glad it was me who found it for you, you deserve to have it back."

Catherine looked at the others again. Joe still seemed astounded, while David had turned white and was glaring at Tia.

"How did you pay for the ring, Tia? It's an extremely expensive item," Joe said.

"I have my savings from when I worked at Aunty Angeline's restaurant."

"That was only for a year, it wouldn't have—"

"Tia phoned me from a phone box," David intervened. "Um … I thought it was unlikely to be Win's old ring … but Tia was desperate to buy it. The shop, stupidly, wasn't asking much for it, which was another reason I thought it couldn't be Win's ring." He breathed deeply. "Nevertheless, I was going to Ashford anyway, so I agreed to pop to Canterbury and meet Tia in the car park beside the old town wall. I gave her the money."

Joe dipped his head in acceptance. "It was good of you to do that. I'll reimburse you."

David said forcefully, "No, you won't. It's Tia's gift to you. Not mine." Then he whispered, "She's going to pay me back."

Catherine spotted Tia glare across at David, she supposed he wasn't meant to tell them about the money. She turned and looked at Joe. "I guess someone must have sold the ring to the shop. It obviously wasn't that important to the person who had it."

Standing up, Joe put his arms around her. "Darling, it's only right that you have Win's ring back." Joe looked across at Tia and said softly, "Thank you for finding it and returning it to the rightful owner."

Now Catherine felt the tears start to fall, and she heard Joe utter quietly to David, "Would you mind if we don't play golf this afternoon? I think Catherine has too many memories ... of Win's death flooding back. I need to spend the day with her."

"I quite understand," replied David. "Anyway, I have something I need to sort."

"I'm sorry, Mum," said Tia as she moved to her side. "I wanted to cheer you up, not upset you. It never occurred to me that it would bring back the sad memories of your gran's death."

"It's alright, Tia. I am grateful to you for giving me Gran's ring back. You've no idea how much it means to me." Catherine wiped her eyes. "I've many wonderful memories of my gran, and now I can have her close again." Putting her arm around Tia's waist, she pulled her close. "Thank goodness no one else bought the ring before you did." She placed the ring back on her slender finger, beaming up at Tia as she did so. She stretched out her hand to admire her ring. Gran was back where she belonged. That other child didn't deserve her trust.

"I didn't realise the time," exclaimed Tia as she examined her watch. "I'm supposed to be at George's house."

"I'll give you a lift," David announced as he gobbled down the rest of his sandwich.

"It's fine, I'll drive there."

"But I have to pass their house on my way home," David persisted. "And it will save on your petrol," he added with an insistence in his tone.

Tia looked at the floor, "Ok, thank you, Uncle David."

CHAPTER 40

13th December 1964

Tia put down the phone as David brought in two cups of tea and put a plate of toast in her hand. "You didn't eat any sandwiches, so here you go," he muttered before moving his car magazines so they could sit down.

"I've told George I'm running late," Tia said as she sat down. "And why do you keep all these magazines, Uncle David?"

"I like to read, and when you live alone, it seems pointless to put stuff away. Well then, young lady," he added as innocently as he could. "As we discussed in the car, I think you'd better tell me the truth, and from the beginning, please."

"How did you know I wasn't telling the truth about the ring?"

"I can tell when people are lying." He gave a half-grin. "It was my job in the war."

She studied him for a while, then sipped her tea. "Yesterday, I took Jack to his football club's Christmas dance."

In a flash, David remembered – Maria had been talking about going to a football club dance with Will and Janice. It hadn't occurred to him that Jack would be going to the same one.

"I dropped Jack off in the afternoon, he was meeting a friend in Maidstone. Then I did go to Canterbury, and I went shopping with Valery. We also collected a book from our History lecturer." Tia took a bite from her toast. "I spent the evening with Valery, but I left early to drive back to Maidstone to collect Jack. I wanted to get there ahead of time because I guessed the car park would be busy with parents collecting their children." She stopped to eat some more toast.

"What happened next?" David asked, impatiently.

"I opted to wait for Jack in the car, so I put the light on and picked up the book my lecturer had given me, it's on tracing your family tree. There's a lot involved. I'm going to have to start it now if I'm going to get it finished in time for Granny Ada's birthday."

"Fine. But what about the ring?"

Tia didn't seem to hear the anxiety in his voice. "I needed to spend a penny, so I closed the book and went into the hall. Everyone was madly dancing to 'It's All Over Now' by the Rolling Stones. I love that song."

David wondered where Tia was going with this; the trepidation making his heart race. Had she met Maria? Was the secret out?

"I couldn't see Jack, so I went straight to the Ladies. When I washed my hands, I saw someone had left two rings by the side of the sink. I picked them up to hand them to the organisers, but then I noticed one of the rings reminded me of Mum's old ring. I saw it had an inscription

inside. As I read it, I had a flashback that Win's ring had—
"

"Was anyone in the Ladies with you?" interrupted David.

"It was busy when I went in, but as I washed my hands, all the girls left. I guess they wanted to get back for the last dances. So I put Mum's ring in my pocket. I knew I was taking it, but I consoled myself that I was only returning it to the rightful owner."

"Tia, that's stealing!" David said. "And what did you do with the other ring? I mean, you said there were two rings?"

"I couldn't take the other ring to an organiser; not once I'd taken Mum's ring. I left it on the sink, hoping the owner would return at the end of the dance. Then I went and looked for Jack." She took the last bite of her toast. "He was dancing with a girl."

"Did you find out who the ring belonged to?" He felt the sweat building on his forehead.

"No, and I feel bad about it, I know I stole it."

"Does Jack know about the ring?"

"No, he doesn't. Once we were in the car, Jack went very quiet. I thought he must be upset about the girl. Anyway, I didn't tell him what I'd done. I thought he'd tell me off for taking the ring."

"Your secret's safe then," he said with relief. He couldn't be cross with Tia. She'd taken the ring for the right reasons. She was so good-natured, just like Hannah had been. "But I think it's best if we keep this just between ourselves."

"Thank you, Uncle David. It means a lot to me that Mum and Dad won't find out that I stole it. That's why I put the ring in one of my old jewellery boxes and told them the story I'd made up the night before."

David felt awful now. His reason for supporting her wasn't just to protect her; it was to protect everyone from finding out the truth! David pushed up his glasses. "So, you said Jack was dancing with a girl. Why was he upset?"

"They were dancing to 'Do you want to know a secret?' by the Beatles."

David raised an eyebrow, Tia, and her modern music! He went to speak, but Tia resumed without looking at him.

"The girl looked familiar, but I just can't place her."

"Really?" He knew Maria had a look of Catherine about her. Tia noticed everything while Jack was oblivious to the world. "What did she look like?" he asked nervously.

"She had shoulder-length, sandy-blonde hair and beautiful light green eyes. She was tall like Jack, with a slim figure."

There was no mistaking who Tia was describing. He needed to guide her away from the truth. "She doesn't sound like anyone from here. Perhaps you know her from Canterbury?"

"Yes, I thought that. She was too young to be at college, but I suppose she might work in one of the local shops."

"That's probably it," he said, thankful Tia had come to that conclusion. Now he turned his concern to the thought of Jack dancing with his half-sister! Jack, like him, found it hard to socialise, but when it came to women, David had never had a problem.

"Did anything happen between them?"

"She had a boyfriend and to be honest, Jack seemed keen to get away. But I guess his pride was hurt."

Sighing, David sat back, thank goodness for Peter. His thoughts turned to Selina and Mark. He wondered if they'd reported the ring as stolen. He sat upright. If the police became involved, they might question everyone at the dance, and then the whole terrible truth could unravel. He had to make sure Tia didn't find out about Maria's connection, it would break her little heart. He had to stop that from happening.

"Right," he announced. "I'll take you to see George now. Then I'll go and see some friends of mine."

As David drove to Gravesend, he realised for the first time that Will and Jack were the same age, so they would be in the same Kent under-eighteens team. Jack was always in full flow about his football, he just never put the two of them together. As for the ring, it had caused more problems than it was worth – and it was worth a lot! He hated that ring, it was a constant reminder of his own deception. He hadn't lied as such, but he hated the fact there were things he hadn't told people. He couldn't inform Catherine and Joe about Maria; it would cause too many issues. And as for Selina and Mark, he'd lose their friendship if he told them the truth. He was in the middle here, and he had to find a way to sort this ring problem. He had to protect everyone concerned. His priority was to keep the secret safe – forever.

CHAPTER 41

13ᵗʰ December 1964

Selina pulled open the door to see David standing awkwardly on the front step. He walked forward without speaking. "This is a surprise," she said as she moved aside to let him through.

"I thought I'd pop round and collect that novel I lent to Maria. I forgot to pick it up last week."

She watched as David ambled into the house. She thought he often seemed so contemplative, he was such a pensive type of man. "It's not a good moment to ask Maria about that book," she said as he headed straight for the lounge, but he didn't seem to be listening. "Sit down," she added, knowing her voice sounded a little annoyed, but then David wasn't to know his timing wasn't good. "Maria's crying in her bedroom," she said softly, "and Mark's in Maidstone with a plumber friend of his."

"What's happened? I can hear her wailing from here."

"It's a long story," she whispered as she sat opposite him. "Maria went to that dance last night with Janice and Will. She begged us to allow her to wear her rings, and we agreed it seemed safe enough. But it seems Janice scraped her arm and so Maria took her rings off to wash Janice's wound. She thinks her heirloom ring must have fallen off the side of the sink and dropped straight down the plughole. She didn't see it happen, but the ring disappeared."

"She thinks it went down the sink!" David cried. "That's terrible news, poor Maria," he said with a sad face.

Selina was touched by David's distress; he was such a genuine man. "Mark and his mate have gone over to Maidstone to see if they can find it lodged in the U-bend or any of the pipes."

"Oh, no! Have they? I mean, it's good of them to go and look." David scratched his head. "And what about the other ring, the one you and Mark gave her? Did she lose that as well?"

"No. It seems she forgot to put her rings back on, then when she returned, only our ring was there, which is a relief." Selina pulled her hair up, tucking it into a loose bun behind her neck. She noticed David looking at her and blushing. She guessed he was thankful their ring was safe. She smiled at him, she knew how much he liked her idea of combining the two rings, and she guessed he was pleased their money hadn't been wasted.

"I'm delighted about that," he said, appearing to relax.

She sighed. "At first, Mark and I were sure someone had stolen the ruby ring." She frowned. "Mark said Maria was bound to assume it was her fault; you know how she never thinks badly of anyone. But when we spoke to the police, they said if someone had stolen it, then both rings would have gone. It was they who suggested we checked the U-bend and the pipes."

David seemed to stiffen. "I agree with the police; it doesn't sound as if it was stolen. I know how Maria can be

277

a little careless at times. For all her intelligence, she has no common sense, and she is so forgetful." He sighed deeply. "Perhaps you should have waited longer before giving Maria the rings, she isn't responsible enough yet."

Now Selina felt hurt, but she knew David always spoke bluntly, it was one of the things they respected about him.

"But my heart breaks to hear her so upset," he said with real feeling. "Can I do anything to help?"

"If only you could find the ring for her, that's what she needs right now." Selina felt her heart beat in unison with her daughter's sobbing. She stood up. "I'll go and look for that book of yours." As she left the room, she turned and saw David lowering his head to his knees.

"I've found it. Maria left it in the kitchen," Selina said as she passed the book to him.

"Oh, great, thanks," David replied with a half-smile.

Just then she heard Mark's key in the front door. "Any luck?" she shouted as she went to sit down.

"No." Mark's voice echoed from the hallway. "We undid the U-bend and every pipe we could find, but the ring wasn't there." As he entered the lounge, she noticed he was clutching his left arm. "Hello, David," Mark exclaimed. "I saw your car outside." Then with exhaustion in his voice, he added, "I thought you played golf on Sundays?"

"Not today. I came to collect the book I forgot last week. But it seems I've called at a bad time."

"It's not the best day we've had," Mark said. Selina noticed how tired he looked, even his scar seemed more pronounced than usual. Turning to her, Mark explained, "Mr Baldwin, that bloke Will got in touch with, was very helpful. He let us in, and he seemed devastated when we didn't find the ring. Apparently, his son's to blame for Janice's scraped arm."

"I'm so sorry you've been through all this today," muttered David.

"It's not your fault, David. I just wish we'd found the ring, then it would've all been worth it." Mark looked at Selina. "Can you make us a drink, love? I'm gasping." Then he flopped into his chair, grunting loudly while clutching his arm.

"Mark, you've done too much, haven't you?" Then, knowing he wouldn't answer in front of David, she stood and headed to the kitchen. She halted in the doorway and put her hand to her chest. "If only there was a way of getting that ring back. I'd do anything to make our Maria happy again." She turned and saw David frown, while Mark just nodded. As she left the room, she stopped at the bottom of the stairs. Everything was quiet. She peered back around the lounge door and said, "I think Maria's fallen asleep. If only she were little Briar Rose, then she'd sleep for a hundred years, and we wouldn't have to tell her the ring has definitely gone."

Mark's eyes looked red with fatigue. "I know, love. I'm sorry we didn't find it."

"Do you think we should inform the police?" she asked.

"No," shouted David. "I mean there's no point, they obviously don't believe it was stolen."

"David's right, love. They'll only say the ring must have washed away." She nodded at Mark, then glanced across at David. She was sure the big man had tears in his eyes. He was such a caring person and a good friend to them all.

CHAPTER 42

16ᵗʰ January 1965

Maria could hear voices downstairs so, grabbing her ring, she walked to the top of the stairs and told Lucky to be quiet. Standing for a second to place her ring on her finger, she heard Peter say,

"It's a surprise, but I'm taking Maria to a performance by the local Amateur Dramatics Society. They're doing 'The Importance of Being Earnest,' and I know she's studying it for A Level English." Maria tutted; Peter understood how to impress her parents.

As she strolled down the stairs, she could hear her dad's voice. "That's very thoughtful of you, Peter."

Then she heard her mum. "So, what's the play about?"

"I think the essence of the story is about a man who deceives everyone." Peter seemed to hesitate. "The plot's very complicated. But in the end, the main character, who's adopted, discovers his true origins and realises the importance of being who he really is."

Maria stopped in her tracks. She hadn't discussed the story with her parents. Now she realised that she should have done. Peter had got the point of the play completely wrong, but then he wasn't studying A-Level English! She galloped loudly down the rest of the stairs, nearly falling over Lucky as they both landed on the hall floor together.

"I'm ready, Peter. Sorry, I was so long," she said as she gave him a big hug. "Let's get going," she continued. "I can't wait to see where you're taking me." She knew she wasn't supposed to have heard the conversation, but she made a mental note to explain the play to her parents when she got back.

"Hat, scarf and gloves!" her mum said as she left the lounge. Maria ignored her, she wasn't going to wear that childhood stuff anymore, she was an adult now!

The cold January evening was enhanced by the stiff breeze blowing through the streets. It was freezing, so Maria speeded up their stride. Peter told her where they were going and discussed the complexities of how he'd got the tickets. Maria walked faster, watching as her breath expanded into the cold night air.

"What the play looks at," she started to explain, "is the importance of being a good honest person." She scraped back her hair with her freshly painted nails. "People think that those born into money are more important than everyone else, but what's actually important is who you are as a person."

Peter seemed to grasp what she was saying. She knew he'd understand; he was a deep and thoughtful individual with a caring nature. That's why she loved him. She giggled to herself. She also loved him because he was a good honest person.

As they marched along together, she decided that the heirloom ring was unimportant. It wasn't part of who she was, what mattered was her parents' ring, they had made her into who she was today. Peter had fallen silent, and she thought it was because he was mulling over what she'd said about the play.

Then he announced, "I've got a place at the Academy of Music and Dramatic Art, in London."

"That's great news," she replied, although her heart was screaming for him not to leave Gravesend.

He glanced at her as they walked. "I want to ask you something. Would you … would you also think about applying there next year? While I'm studying music, you could study acting. You could become a fantastic actress. We'll be a year apart, but we'd still be together."

This was music to her ears! Peter wanted them to be together.

"I love that idea," she said enthusiastically, but then she stopped in her tracks. "It'll upset Mum and Dad. They want me to be a teacher, a job that's respectable and pays well."

Peter took her hands into his. "Maria, you've just said money isn't what's important. You love acting. I'm sure your parents want you to be happy."

"That's perfect! When I explain to them about 'The Importance of Being Earnest,' I'll stress that money, and social class aren't important. Then I'll tell them about the Academy and how much I want to go." She kissed him. "Let's walk, it's bitter."

At last Maria could see the Town Hall looming in front of them. She ran through the door, seeking shelter from the cold. People were everywhere, and she guessed most had come to support the amateur group. Everyone was taking off their coats. She didn't think the room was very warm, but she took her coat off, not wanting to appear different from the crowd.

"I'll take these to the cloakroom. You wait here," instructed Peter. While she stood looking around the lobby, she noticed that everyone seemed to be wearing expensive-looking clothes. The building felt grand, with its high, beautifully decorated ceilings. It also had lots of large framed paintings and photos on the walls. A thick red carpet covered the large staircase as it swooped up through the hall. Peter was taking ages, but she could see there was a queue for the cloakroom. Feeling a little young and uncomfortable, she moved into a corner. She studied the boring photos of all the previous mayors of the town, and then her eyes fell on a different photo. It was of King George V presenting a trophy to a football player. She smiled at the thought of Will receiving a trophy from the young Queen Elizabeth II. How wonderful that would be!

"There you are," she said as Peter walked towards her. "The play's about to start, we'd better go and get our seats."

Maria sat and watched the play in disbelief. The actors couldn't remember their lines, and at one point the script was even brought out. "Our school plays are a hundred times better than this," she sniggered to Peter.

"It's the worst performance I've ever seen," snorted Peter. "I don't think I can sit through much more of this. Shall we give up and go somewhere else?"

"Where shall we go?"

He leant closer to her and whispered, "My parents are staying with my gran in Margate, and my brother's still away. We could go back to my house and snuggle up on the sofa."

"That sounds great." Then she added, "But I won't be able to stay for too long, Mum and Dad will be waiting up for me."

"That's fine." Peter's eyes sparkled at her. "Let's go and get our coats."

Now all she could think about was being alone with Peter. Nudging him towards the empty lobby, she said, "At least no one's noticed us leaving."

Peter opened the door and instantly put his arm around her waist. "I'll keep you warm."

She cuddled up to him to gain maximum heat.

Maria had been to Peter's house on a few occasions, but tonight she felt uneasy. Entering the house without his parents' permission felt wrong. It was a much larger house than hers, but the extreme tidiness somehow made it feel empty of life. She loved the homeliness of her own house; Lucky's toys all over the place, her dad's newspapers left in the lounge from the night before and her mum's slippers lying wherever Lucky had taken them! Peter took her into the lounge, and she sat nervously on the sofa as he knelt to light the coal fire, which had been laid ready for use. While the fire took hold, he went to the kitchen to make some hot drinks. She sat back, feeling the warmth while staring at the glow that was starting to flicker. Looking up from the flames, she watched as Peter put the cups by the fireside and sat down on the sofa beside her. As he put his arm around her, she moved closer into his chest. It felt so cosy and comforting. Leaning towards her, Peter gave her the prolonged kiss she'd longed for all evening. His kiss felt soft on her lips, then his hands began to move around her body. He nibbled her ear and caressed her neck with his mouth. It felt wonderful. Suddenly, he broke off.

"What's the matter?" she murmured.

"I'm sorry, it's just … I think we should stop."

She gazed into his eyes and realised what he was saying. "I don't want to stop," she said as forthrightly as she could.

"If we're planning to be together for a while yet, then I can't see why this is wrong."

"Are you sure, Maria? Don't you want to wait? It's a big step for both of us." His slightly scared expression seemed sweet.

She gently kissed his lips again. "I don't want to wait. We can learn together, and there isn't anyone I would rather learn with."

As they watched the fire dying down, she lay contentedly in Peter's arms, not wanting to dress and not wanting to go. She looked up at him.

"Even though I know we shouldn't have done that, I'm glad we did."

"Me too," he said as he kissed her gently. "I'm in love with you, Maria Tozer."

"I love you too, Peter Moss," she said as she cuddled into him.

Then he glanced at his watch. "Look at the time! I need to walk you home. Your parents will be worrying."

"But I don't want to unravel from the heat of your body," she said, burrowing deeper into his chest.

He pulled her closer. "I've got you, and I never want to let you go."

CHAPTER 43

25th March 1965

Catherine looked lovingly at Joe. Under the lamplight, he still reminded her of Cary Grant. "Why's Tia so long?" she asked, as she got up and peeped through the curtains for the tenth time. "Do you think she's alright?"

"It's probably just the London traffic."

She turned back from the window. "Angeline tells me George is saving hard. We're hoping he's saving for an engagement ring for Tia."

"You and Angeline need to give the two of them time, they're only young."

"But they're a perfect match," Catherine said as she took Joe's empty whiskey glass from his hand. "Anyway, I hope Tia's finished Ada's family tree today. These trips to Somerset House are exhausting for her."

"History's her passion. Although I don't understand why she enjoys looking through musty old books so much. It's not my idea of fun."

Catherine unscrewed the whiskey bottle. "Tia says she's found out a lot of information, but it's all too much for one chart, so she's going to put Ada's mother's line in one frame and Ada's father's line in another." Then above the sound of pouring alcohol, she said, "And Tia's found two large antique gold frames that she says are just right, so I've agreed to go and buy them." She screwed the top back on the bottle. "Her friend Valery's going to write them in calligraphy. They're going to look very professional when they're finished."

"I'm sure Ada will love them," Joe said as he took the glass from her hand.

Catherine sauntered to her chair and picked up her discarded knitting. She heard a car screeching onto the drive. "At last, she's home," she said.

The front door flew open, then slammed loudly. "Mum, Dad." Tia's voice roared through the house. "Where are you?"

"Tia, what's the matter?" Catherine asked, walking towards her.

Tia barged passed her. "I want to talk to my father, and I want the truth," she snarled.

Joe glared at her. "Tia, apologise to your mother. What's wrong with you?"

Tia slumped onto the settee, and Catherine noticed that her face was red with anger and her eyes puffy as if she'd been crying. "I should never have traced Ada's family tree," Tia said while looking at her father.

"Why not?" asked Joe.

Tia sat up and frowned at him. "When I'd gone back as far as I could on Ada's tree, there was still an hour to go before closing." She glared at Catherine. "So, I looked through the birth records for my own name. I liked seeing it there; it made me feel official. Then I looked up Jack's registration, and there he was too." Tia's glare intensified. "Then it dawned on me that it would've been my sister's birthday a few days ago, she would have been seventeen. I knew the child had to be legally registered." She looked fiercely at her dad.

Catherine couldn't breathe; she sunk back into her chair.

"I found an Angeline born to Catherine Lawrence," Tia continued. "But the entry for the father's name was Gregory Jones." Tia blew her nose and wiped her tears away. "The place of birth was Dover, Kent. I traced my finger to the column which gave the name of the informant," she glared at her dad, "that's the person registering the birth, and it read Joseph Jack Lawrence." Tia gulped. "I stared at that book, hoping that the wording would change. But it didn't."

Catherine felt as if a dagger had pierced her chest. She started to tremble uncontrollably.

Tia scowled at her. "Then I suddenly had a thought, and I ran down the corridor to find the death index records. It was nearly closing time, so I had to be quick. I looked at the list for the 27th March 1948, and there wasn't a death registered for an Angeline Lawrence from Dover." Tia stared angrily at her. "Is the child alive?"

Catherine looked away, then she tried to speak, but words wouldn't come from her mouth.

Tia carried on. "As I left, the porter held the door open, and I think he said, 'Goodnight,' but there was so much going on in my head." Tia wiped her eyes. "I walked to my car, feeling numb. I relived my childhood, those happy hopes I'd had about my unborn sister. The pain I'd suffered over her death and the constant nightmares that, even now, still haunt me." She snivelled. "The fear I had of Jack dying was all because of the death of my sister – an event that didn't happen." Tia pointed at Catherine.

"You're wicked, the lies you've told, and not just to me but to everyone."

Tia's wrath felt like a snake, planting venom in Catherine.

Then Tia turned to Joe. "And Dad, how could you lie to me as well? She had an affair and has a child that isn't yours." Tia turned on Catherine again. "So, what did you do with your illegitimate child?"

Catherine's head fell in shame; her worst fear had happened.

"Where's Jack?" bellowed Tia. "I think he needs to hear all of this!"

Joe stood up and grabbing hold of Tia's plump little arm, he spoke forcefully, "Stop it. Jack's still at football training." Catherine could see Joe's hands were shaking. "I'll explain. But I want you to listen and try your hardest to understand."

"What's there to understand?" Tia glared at Catherine. "I hate you."

"Tia, you have to listen to me and stop ranting." Joe sounded angry now. "There's a reason ..."

"Go on then, try to explain your lies," Tia said indignantly.

Catherine watched as, using one arm to steady himself, Joe leant against the fireplace. He seemed to be finding it hard to focus, and he spoke nervously, which wasn't like him. As he informed Tia about the night of the rape, he flinched now and again, his voice increasing and decreasing with his obvious pain. Catherine didn't want to remember that night. That madman had raped and attacked her. Now, not only was she being forced to relive it, but so was Tia. She felt tears welling up. She was upset, not for herself, but for her daughter.

Joe continued with his account, now explaining the adoption. Catherine put her head in her hands. She couldn't look. Tia hated her, and there was nothing she could do to change things. Catherine felt so worn and frayed. She'd put all her effort into protecting Tia from finding out about the unspeakable truth and now the nightmare was happening. When Joe finished, Catherine lifted her head from her hands, and she saw that the anger had gone from Tia's face. Instead, there was a look of sorrow in her expression.

Catherine stood up and went over to Tia. With a wavering voice, she murmured, "I'm sorry we lied to you; it was all such a mess." Then, putting her arms around the frozen Tia, she added, "We couldn't explain it at the time. You were far too young. I hated lying. I cried myself to sleep every night knowing the heartache I'd caused you. I love you so much …" She squeezed her daughter's body and felt it soften. "Listen to me, Tia. I hated the man who did this to me, and I hated his child. Abortion isn't legal, and besides, your dad wouldn't allow me to have one." There was no response from Tia. "The thought of looking at that child every day and being reminded of … I just couldn't bring her up as part of this family." There was still no movement from Tia, so Catherine continued. "I didn't do it to hurt you. Please don't hate me. Tia, you're a woman now, think about how you'd feel if it happened to you."

Tia's head dropped to her chest, then she whispered, "I'd want an abortion if it happened to me, and I can't believe abortion still isn't legal." She looked up. "Now I know why you've never let me walk through the cliff alley to George's house." Her voice strengthened. "I'm sorry for being so hard on you. I don't hate you, Mum, but I do hate the man who did this to you." Catherine felt Tia's kiss on her cheek. "But I wish you had told me, even if it was just when I was old enough to understand."

Catherine shuddered and let go of Tia's hug. But Tia squeezed closer, forcing Catherine's arm to go around her once more. She looked across at her dad. "So, would you have ever told me that I wasn't actually related to the child?"

"She would have been brought up as your sister," Joe replied. "What difference would it have made about who was related to whom?"

Tia seemed to ponder this for a while. "I would have wanted to know. But I guess you're right, Dad. Mum's my mother even though we don't share the same genes." She squeezed her mum's hand as she spoke. "So I do have a sister after all." She looked questioningly into Catherine's eyes. "Who else knows the truth?"

"As Dad explained, only old Doctor Bryant knows, and Uncle David." Catherine stopped as she recollected how often Tia had made David read her those Fairy Tales. "Uncle David was very supportive. Underneath that hard exterior, he's a good man."

Tia dipped her head. "I knew I'd heard the name Gregory Jones before, I remember now, Uncle David said something about Gregory Jones's funeral, but why …?" Then she looked up again. "Jack, should we tell him?"

Joe sputtered, "There's no need to tell him."

"Doesn't he have a right to know he has a half-sister though, Mum? In the same way that I'm his half-sister through you?"

Catherine interjected, "What good would it do to tell Jack? Please, Tia, don't tell him. The last thing I want is for Jack to be upset as well as you."

Tia frowned. "A discovered lie can be very painful, as I've found out." Then she stared into space. "I won't say anything." She fell quiet, then muttered, "But couldn't the three of us try to find her?"

"No," Joe said adamantly. "Nothing is achieved by going over the painful past. Your mother's suffered enough."

Catherine found herself nodding. "Tia, I gave up all rights to the child when I gave her away. Years ago, I told Doctor Bryant I didn't want him to find out where the child was, and I still don't want her found. I've thought about it, and the thing is, she may not even know she's adopted. I refuse to upset her and her family by coming into their lives." She squeezed her daughter again. "I can see it from the other mother's point of view. Imagine how I'd feel if Hannah suddenly appeared and started to interfere with your life."

Tia looked shocked, then she chuckled, "The thought of my mother rising from the dead is a little too much. But I see your point."

"So, we all agree, we won't try to find her?" confirmed Catherine.

"If that's what you want, but you do realise, Mum … the child is your real daughter."

"Tia, you're my real daughter," Catherine said. "You and Jack are the children I've put all my energy into rearing." She held up her hand. "You know that Great-Grandma Win, gave this ring to me the day before she died, but what you don't know Tia, is that she told me to pass it on to you. Gran said that a mother's love is about bringing up a child, and not just about giving birth to it." She took off her ring and put it in the palm of her hand. "Gran told me to wear this ring so I'd always know she was with me, now I'm saying the same to you. I want you to have this ring and wear it, so I can enjoy the fact that Great-Grandma Win and I are always with you." For the first time, Catherine realised how important family had been to Gran and guilt struck her. Gran would not have approved of the adoption; Catherine had given away Gran's great-granddaughter! What had she done? Now she understood that the child had been as much hers, as it had been Gregory's. But then Gran's words returned to her mind. "The fact remains, Tia, I haven't brought up that other child, so I'm not her mother in that sense. The child I gave birth to is now someone else's daughter, that's the true fact in all of this." She held the ring between her thumb and forefinger. "You're the daughter I love. Can't you see, Tia, you and only you, have the right to this ring." Tia sobbed hysterically, and as Catherine held her, she felt the warm tears falling onto her bare arms.

Tia murmured, "I'm not sure if I'm upset because I can't cope with you giving me your ring, or because Great-Grandma Win had wanted me to inherit it." Tia looked up at her. "But maybe it's all this legacy stuff. The very idea of you dying is an unbearable thought."

Catherine pulled back a piece of Tia's wet hair that had become stuck to her face. "While I live and breathe, I'll always be here for you."

"I do love you, Mum, and now I know how much you love me too." With that, Tia reached out her right hand, and Catherine placed the ring on Tia's chubby little finger.

CHAPTER 44

26th March 1965

David bit into his toast. He loved this part of the day, early mornings were peaceful. It had been a stressful week at work, but at last, it was Friday. Deep in contemplation, he jumped as his doorbell rang with one persistent tone. Feeling irritated, he got up. This disturbance was unacceptable, it was only 7.30am, he was not about to be polite to the intruder.

He opened the door, and Joe pushed past him. "Joe, are you alright?" he asked as, without a word, Joe marched straight for the lounge. Darting in front of him, David quickly moved his car magazines from his armchair. "Sit down. What's the matter?"

Joe fell into the armchair and put his head in his hands. "It's Tia, she came home last night and told us she'd found out that I wasn't the father of the child."

"What?" David said. "How's she found out?" His large legs wobbled as he eased himself down onto the settee.

"I was foolish. I never gave it a thought when Tia went to the records office to do Ada's family tree." Joe groaned. "It seems Tia delved into the child's records!" He looked at the floor as if in shame. "When I registered the birth, I couldn't lie, it was a legal document. I had to be honest about who the father was." Joe gazed up, and his eyes fastened onto David's as if looking for his approval.

David nodded, "It's the law."

Joe didn't move his eyes from David's. "We told Tia about the rape, but the other thing was, she said she couldn't find the death record for the child."

David felt his hands quivering. He hadn't considered the record office as a potential hazard; he thought he'd controlled everything so well. "I see. So, you told her about ... the adoption?"

"We did, and that's why I'm here."

"What have you said?"

"Most of it." Joe looked at his watch. "I'm worried that Tia will try and find the child. She said she wouldn't but ... well, you know Tia!" He stared at David again. "We told her you knew we had the child adopted, but I haven't said you followed the child that day." Joe wiped his brow. "I've always been happy just to know she was somewhere in Kent. I'm still not asking you to tell me where, and Catherine even said she didn't want the child found. The problem is," Joe scratched his head, "Tia will ask you about what happened. David, I'm begging you not to tell her where the child went. I know she might have moved by now, but even so; I don't want Tia checking."

David composed himself. "I won't tell her anything ... my enigma is impossible to crack."

"Good," replied Joe, with a huge smile. He looked at his watch again. "I'm sure Tia will be round to see you, she'll want to check out our story. So, I need to fill you in with what we've told her ..."

Joe glanced at his watch again. "Gosh, I've been here for an hour. We'd better go to work now, it's 8.45am."

"We're late," David said as he jumped up.

They both ambled silently to their cars, which were parked next to each other on the drive. Then, as Joe opened his car door, he looked across and said, "Tia's calmed down a lot since yesterday, she's much happier now. Not surprisingly, it helped when Catherine gave her Win's ring."

Trying not to show his alarm, David gave an understanding nod, then waved Joe off the drive. He realised that the movement of the ring probably didn't mean that much to Joe, but it meant a massive amount to David. Deep in thought, he got into his car. If the football connection brought the youngsters together again, Tia could be wearing that ring while talking to Maria. This was a risk he didn't like. His mind was racing, this was all getting too much.

Once he arrived at work, David sat at his desk, watching his staff running around and getting all stressed about things that weren't important. His head was pounding, and he couldn't concentrate on his job. He predicted that Tia would want to know more, she might even delve back into the records. And now that Tia knew about the adoption, she might even realise Maria looked like Catherine. What should he do? His head was spinning as he gazed around the office. He wasn't enjoying his job anymore; everything had paperwork attached to it and adhering to the new rules and regulations was a total nuisance. His motivation had gone, the younger men seemed so much more excited than he did. Joe's words were still going around in his head. He couldn't stand the noise in the office, he had to think. He got up from his desk and did something he'd never done before – he announced he was going home, as he had a headache.

He sat in his car and put the key into the ignition, but his head was throbbing. If Tia and that ring ever gave the secret away ... He felt guilty for not telling Mark and Selina the truth, the whole truth and nothing but the truth! To give Mark Catherine's child had seemed the right thing to do at the time. But he never wanted to be involved in all this deception. It had all got out of control, and he couldn't stop it. Reality hit him like a punch. He was the one who'd deceived Mark and Selina, so he was the one who had to put things right. He couldn't risk them finding out by some other route, and at least he could try to get them to appreciate why he'd never said anything before. When should he tell them? He presumed Maria would be at school now and Mark would be at work. Actually, it was right that Selina should be the first to know. Besides, she was also the one who might understand, Mark was going to be much harder to persuade. His heart was thumping as he turned on the ignition, pulled out the choke and headed from the car park, turning right towards Gravesend.

As he drove, he thought about how to tell Selina. He expected she'd be angry. He didn't want to lose her friendship, she was sensitive and understanding, she had many of Hannah's qualities. He remembered how Selina used to be so timid. He smiled, his thoughts returning to how Catherine used to be so demanding. It was true that Selina and Catherine were opposite in every way. Then, with a half-grin, he recognised that over time, he'd seen them both change for the better. He felt honoured to have been there for both of these women, and he loved all three of their children as if they were his own. Now his whole world felt in jeopardy.

As he drove around a bend, his attention returned to Tia. He should have known she'd be the one to find out the truth. He remembered her as a child, always noticing if things weren't right. He recalled Tia catching Joe out every time he tried to miss parts of her bedtime stories. David loved the fact that he was the person she'd trusted to read to her. It was then he had an idea; he thought it through meticulously. He wasn't used to this tactic, but maybe he should try and copy Tia's sensitive attitude to life. He was reasonably pleased with his analogy. It wasn't perfect, but it was a pleasant approach to the difficult subject he finally had to face. Chuckling at the irony, he now deduced that it was Tia who was the one who might just help to save the day!

CHAPTER 45

26th March 1965

As she looked at the clock, Selina saw it was past lunchtime. She hadn't appreciated how hungry she was so, putting down the washing basket and turning off her music, she went to make a sandwich before going to her mum's. Hearing a knock at the door, she stopped and turned to answer it.

"David. I wasn't expecting to see you. Have you forgotten something from the other day?" she said as she stood back for him to enter. "And thank you again for Maria's book on acting techniques. You always get her such brilliant birthday gifts."

David's eyes were fixed on the ground. "I'm sorry to land on you like this," he said glumly, "but something's happened, and I need to talk to you."

"You look terrible, David." His face looked ashen. She could tell something was seriously wrong. "I think a cup of sweet tea is needed. Come into the kitchen." She sensed that popping to her mum's was going to have to wait.

"You make the tea, and then we will talk," he said as he sat down.

She moved to the sink to fill the kettle, noticing that even Lucky had settled unobtrusively in her basket. David sat silently while the kettle boiled noisily on the stove. As she poured the tea, she considered how the quietness seemed to accentuate the situation. She thought about putting the radio back on but then decided against it. Instead, she handed him his drink and sat opposite him at the table. She could see he was apprehensive, so she waited for him to speak.

After a while, he said, "I haven't been honest with you all."

She sat upright. This was a strange thing for him to say, he was such a truthful type of man.

His voice seemed distant. "I should have explained a long time ago … it's a sensitive subject, and this isn't going to be easy for you, or me. I'm pleading that when I've finished, you'll try … try to understand."

She gazed at him. She hadn't a clue what he was going to say. "Alright, I promise," she said as sympathetically as she could. She watched as he gulped his tea and closed his eyes.

"I think this is going to be the best way to explain things," he said softly. She nodded, although she could see he still had his eyes firmly shut.

He opened his eyes and said gently, "Once upon a time, in a land far away, a baron, and his stunningly endearing wife, lived happily with their beautiful baby daughter, whom they called … Cinderella."

She sat back in her chair. His voice was velvety, and she found herself feeling like a child having a bedtime story. Perhaps David hadn't got bad news after all. She closed her eyes to listen.

"A terrible war broke out in the kingdom, and the beautiful baroness was killed. The baron was devastated, so his brother, Buttons, helped him to bring up the young Cinderella. When the war was over, the baron married a young French girl. Then shortly afterwards, a son was born, and their family was complete." He pushed up his glasses. "But soon after this ... an evil subject brutally attacked and raped the new baroness."

Selina opened her eyes with a start, and her heart pounded, but David didn't seem to react.

"The baroness gave birth to the evil man's daughter," he continued.

Selina placed her head down on the table and brought her arms over the top of her hair. She didn't want to hear the rest.

"The baroness was adamant that the rape had to remain a secret, and she wanted the child to disappear."

Selina wasn't sure if she should speak, so she didn't.

"They told Cinderella her sister had died, poor Cinderella's grief was unbearable. As for the baron, he couldn't handle the child's banishment from his kingdom, so he begged Buttons to follow the baby, just to make sure she was safe."

Selina sat bolt upright. "What?" She stared at him, his face seemed tight and twisted, he didn't look like David anymore.

He averted his eyes from hers and carried on, "Then some years later, Buttons had to return, but as he rode his horse into the bridleway, the Princess ran in front of him—"

"You're Buttons!" she shrieked. Her world was collapsing, things were not what she'd thought. "You aren't our friend at all!" She could hear her voice was sharp

301

and bitter. "You've been spying on us … for all these years. You had no right to do this." She grabbed her chest as if she needed to protect her heart from more hurt. This man was someone she didn't know anymore.

David looked calm. "No," he said vehemently. "I've never told my brother anything about Maria." Then his voice relaxed, "You are my friends. I owe Mark my life. I appreciate I should have kept away, but I liked you all. I knew if I told you my connection to Maria, you would push me away. Then as time went on, a bond grew between us, I didn't want to risk losing that." He added hesitantly, "Can you understand my problem?"

She didn't answer. Her body was juddering. Could she trust him? He looked at her forlornly.

"I've always considered my role in life as being to help and protect those I care for. I realised I had the chance to care for my step-niece, a function my sister-in-law had denied me. I also had a chance to help Mark, if ever he needed it." His eyes met hers. "You and Mark have become my family too."

She felt so mixed up, it was hard to take it all in. "So, why are you telling me now?"

David pushed up his glasses again. "Things have got complicated. It started when Maria went to the football club Christmas dance and met her half-brother."

"No!"

"It seems Cinderella arrived and saw them dancing together."

Selina went to speak, but David held up his hand.

"No one realised the connection, except me. But it was Cinderella who found Maria's rings by the sink." Selina gasped again. "Cinderella recognised her mother's lost ring – so she took it."

David's face contorted.

"Why didn't you tell us?" Selina cried. "You know how much heartache that ring caused to us all."

David didn't answer; he just cleared his throat. "Then yesterday, Cinderella discovered the truth while researching her family tree. She was told everything but was asked not to divulge it to her brother." He looked down at his hand, resting on the table. "Cinderella was then given the ruby ring." He reached out and touched Selina's hand. "Because of the football connection, there's a chance that Maria and … Cinderella could meet again. That nightmare of a ring could give it all away. So, I had to tell you." He stared into her eyes. "At this point, you and no one else knows the truth." Taking his hand away from hers, he added, "I beg you for forgiveness."

Selina felt her tears pouring down her face. David reached into his pocket and offered his clean handkerchief. She accepted it, and he gave her one of his understanding grins. He looked like their David once again. Selina sat back in her chair and studied him. There was such sadness in his eyes. She could tell he was sorry for what he'd done … or failed to do! She thought how childlike he looked, how harmless, and her temper faded. David had meant well. He did care, and it wasn't his fault he was connected to that woman!

She stood up from the table and walked over to where he was sitting. She bent down beside him and gently kissed him on his cheek. "I'm sorry I got so cross, it hurt to think you weren't a real friend." He looked up, and she could see his colour had returned. She continued softly, "Over the years you've always been good to us. I can see, more than ever before, that you're a true friend, and indeed our own guardian angel." Now he was smiling, and she noticed the relief in his eyes. "But I'm glad you've kept our details a secret from ... them." With a heavy sigh, she whispered, "But David, how will it all end?"

"As Maria's mother, I hand that decision over to you."

"Your acceptance of me as Maria's mother means a lot. You have no idea how that other woman has haunted me."

"You're Maria's mother. I've watched you mothering her for all these years ... no one else has done that."

Selina grinned, then she realised that she'd thought so often about Maria's biological mother, but never the family that was also involved.

"Mark isn't going to take this well, is he?" David said. "I'll stay and explain it to him. He's a good friend to me, and I don't want to lose that."

"No, David. I think you should go. The truth would be better coming from me." She cleared the teacups from the table. "Maria's at Janice's tonight, so we'll have plenty of time to talk it through. I'll try to explain it carefully. I don't want Mark to hate you either."

"But you will explain how sorry I am for my deception, won't you?" he said, looking so downtrodden. "Walter Scott was right; it is indeed 'a tangled web we weave when first we practice to deceive.' I regret it all so much now."

CHAPTER 46

26th March - 27th March 1965

Selina flopped into her armchair. Mark was going to be so hurt; she needed to try to find a way to ease his anguish. She wished she could ask her dad, he would have known what to say. Closing her eyes for a moment, she saw her dad's face in her mind. It felt so comforting to see him again. She was woken sometime later with a start as Lucky barked at the front door.

"Hello, Lucky," Mark's voice rebounded from the hallway. "And where are my other two gorgeous girls?"

Still only half-awake, Selina replied, "I'm in the lounge, and Maria's at Janice's, she went straight from school."

"Oh, yes, I forgot. I'm getting old, remember," he said as he entered the room. "And have you had an afternoon sleep, my dear?" he asked teasingly. She didn't open her eyes until Mark's kiss hit her lips. He sat in the chair next to hers and picked up the paper she'd put there earlier. "I've had a terrible time at work, love," he said, as he flicked through the paper. "How was your day?"

She took a deep breath. "David called round." She waited for a response.

"Why?" Mark asked, still looking at his paper. "Did he forget one of his books again?"

She rested her head back in her chair and half-closed her eyes again. "Do you remember how Cyril always lent Dad books? It's funny how David does the same for us." She expected an acknowledgement, but there wasn't one. She opened her eyes and sat up in her chair. "That's it!" she whispered to herself. "Mark," she announced loudly, "I've never told anyone this, but Cyril once informed Dad of something that shocked him to the core." Mark looked up from his paper, she had his attention now. "Apparently, Cyril served time in prison."

"No!" Mark looked at her in amazement. "But Cyril was such a decent bloke."

"He was, and it seems Cyril broke the law because he was trying to help his brother." She sighed. "I remember Dad saying he was glad Cyril hadn't told him at the start of their friendship, because he would have prejudged him and then he'd never have got to know what a good bloke Cyril was."

"Harold was a wise man."

Selina took a deep breath. "I want you to think of my father and Cyril when I tell you … about something David has confessed to me." She looked Mark in the eye. "You must be like Dad. You need to look behind the facts to see the good in people."

Mark put down his paper and stared at her. "Go on, love. I'm listening."

Mark sat on the edge of his chair, with his head in his hands. "I can't believe this! I saw him you know, following us in a red Triumph 1800 Roadster. I even remember you saying David's write-off was a red car. Why didn't I clock it at the time?"

"You didn't tell me you saw someone following us."

"I thought it was just the orphanage checking on us."

"Well, perhaps like with Dad and Cyril, it was better you didn't know the truth. You've formed such a good friendship with David, and you wouldn't have done if you'd known ..."

"Too right, I wouldn't!" Mark shouted as he went to stand up. "That man's no friend of mine. I trusted him, and to think he was using us to get to Maria."

"No, Mark, he wasn't. I told you he likes us. He knew he should keep away, but ... Mark, where are you going?"

"To phone him and give him a piece of my mind."

She followed him to the hall. "Please, Mark, calm down. David's been good to us over the years. I can never thank him enough for taking Maria to the hospital that night. He probably saved our daughter's life ... and for the second time if you count the first car accident! Mark, please, he's been a great mate to you, don't throw him away." But Mark was dialling the number. "Mark, please put the phone down and listen to me." David had evidently picked up the receiver, and she sank to the floor as Mark bellowed down the line at him. Then Mark's voice seemed to calm down.

"What, you influenced the adoption panel?" He fell silent. "Look, Maria's at Janice's until tomorrow evening, why don't you come over in the morning? Then all three of us can discuss this properly ... Good, in that case, we'll see you at 11 am ... Bye, David."

When Mark came off the phone, she jumped up and put her arms around him, kissing him gently. She wanted him to know she was pleased he'd invited David round. Mark pulled away and looked her in the eyes.

"Harold was right, prejudging people could stop friendships from forming."

She nodded in agreement, knowing her dad would have said those words … if the prison story had been true! She turned away; the end justified the means.

Selina hadn't slept, and now she felt her eyelids needed sticks to lift them up, but she made a pot of tea, while Mark and David sat at the table. She hoped the three of them together would somehow make the crisis seem more manageable, but deep down, she envisaged that it wouldn't be possible.

She heard Mark say, "It was all such a shock yesterday, but I'm glad you've told us the truth, David."

"I do want to be a friend you can trust," David answered in a relieved tone.

She put the teacups on the table. "David, I don't want any names yet, it still feels strange that Maria is part of your family."

"You and Mark are her family. We might be three people who aren't biologically related to Maria, but we are the ones who love her."

Selina touched his arm affectionately. "We need to discuss the future. What do we do next?" She picked up a chocolate biscuit and dunked it in her tea.

"I vote we do nothing." Mark drank his tea. "It doesn't matter where Maria's genes come from. She's our daughter, and that ain't going to change."

Selina put down her biscuit. "I can't eat anything." It felt hard to be brave, but she had to, for her daughter's sake. "I've thought about it all night, and I think we should tell Maria the truth." Selina had to put her demons behind her. "And once Maria knows David's connection to her, I feel sure she'll want to meet her biological mother." She gave a long sigh. "Things have altered. That woman won't be a stranger to Maria anymore, she'll be part of Uncle's David's family."

"No!" Mark glared at her. "We shouldn't tell Maria. Besides, I won't put her through meeting that hard-hearted woman. You remember what she was like."

"You've met her?" David's sounded jumpy. "When?"

Selina murmured, "At the orphanage, she waited to see us. She didn't want any contact with Maria; she said she didn't want to see the child again. She even asked us to promise not to allow Maria to try to find her."

"Unbelievable!" snapped David. "How could she have …? But I was there. I didn't see her. I just saw you two coming out with a baby wrapped in … Cinderella's old pink blanket."

"She left before us," Mark said.

David seemed unnerved. "That means you know what she looks like?"

Selina frowned. "I took in every feature and yes, I know Maria looks a little like her."

"This is awful, to think …" David stopped and looked edgy. "I mean for you to know the woman like this."

"The other woman is someone neither of us has ever forgotten," Mark said, as he eyed David and reached out to hold Selina's hand.

Selina winced. "I thought I saw her driving past once, but—"

"Did she see you?" interrupted David.

"No. Why do you think it—"

"I just don't think a meeting with my sister-in-law is a good idea." David's voice sounded quaky.

"I agree," Mark nodded.

She pulled her hand from Mark's grip and glared at him. "We have to think about what's best for Maria, not what's best for us. You know how much I want to be Maria's mother, but we all know I'm not her biological mother. If Maria does want to meet ... that woman," she turned to David, "then I would like you to set up a meeting."

David's face looked anxious. "I'll have to talk to my sister-in-law, but I suspect she still won't want to meet Maria. She has too much to lose; her son, her friends, and family. They don't know the truth."

"I don't care about what that woman has to lose!" Selina felt her anger rising; this was her daughter's future they were talking about.

"She's a stubborn woman," David replied.

"Look, David," Selina said. "You need to check if your sister-in-law will agree to meet Maria. Once we have our response, we'll have another meeting to discuss how we're going to give the news to Maria." She glared at the two men. "Are we all agreed?" Both men slowly nodded.

David shifted his glasses, sliding them back up his nose. "But there is something else I need to explain, and you're not going to like this either ..."

·

CHAPTER 47

28ᵗʰ March 1965

Maria felt as if her bedroom was protecting her from the world outside. The morning sun shone through her windows and, cuddling down into her chair, she listened to the war songs emanating from the radio downstairs. Winston Churchill had died in January, and the old songs had become fashionable again. She smirked as she listened to her mum, trying to sing 'The White Cliffs of Dover'. She definitely sounded different to Vera Lyn! As Maria glanced down at Lucky, she noticed the large box containing her childhood keepsakes. Her dad had been busily tidying the loft, and when she returned home, he said he'd put the box in her room for her to sort. Looking down at her mementoes, she resolved that she wasn't going to throw anything away. Her memories were important to her, they represented her happy childhood so, she pushed the box under her bed.

Peering in the mirror, she stared, heavy-eyed, at the pale face that gazed back at her. Glancing down at the dressing table, which she used as a homework desk, she picked up the application form she'd left there. Now that her parents had approved of her applying to the London Academy of Music and Dramatic Art, she needed to get on with her task. The essay page glared up at her. She started to focus, she wanted to do this well ..."*Shakespeare compares the world to a stage and life to a play. What lessons have shaped your life and made you into a character fit for life's stage?*"

She found herself falling deep into thought. She'd always been wise before her time, so this was just about putting her life discoveries into words. As she pondered her past, she reached over to take a sip from her cup of coffee, which she'd perched on her dressing table. She needed to make headings about her life, then she could structure her essay correctly. Where was that birthday present that Uncle Brian and Aunt Sandra had given her last week? Rummaging through her drawer, she pulled out the posh notebook still in its wrapper. Looking down, she twisted her ring. Where should she start?

Maria threw down her pen. At last, she'd finished her notes. She couldn't face writing her essay just yet, so she and Lucky strolled down the stairs.

"Approximately, what time? ... Alright, thanks." Maria reached the hallway and watched as her mum placed the receiver down very carefully, almost as if she thought the phone might break.

"Who was that?" she asked.

Her mum twisted round and looked surprised to see her. "Oh, it was just Uncle David. He's got that book I wanted ... he said he'd bring it over later."

"Maria, have you finished upstairs?" her dad asked as he appeared in the hallway. "Only I want to put those shelves up in your room."

"You go ahead. I'm going to have some lunch."

"You look pasty, Maria." Her mum's concern showed on her face. "Did you stay up too late at Janice's last night?"

Her dad laughed as he walked off upstairs. "Maria's young. Stop worrying, love."

Her mum nodded and took Maria's hand. "The spring sun is shining, and the birds are singing. When we've had our lunch, shall we take Lucky for a walk?"

Lucky jumped up, barking loudly.

"As long as I'm back in time to start my essay and get ready to go out. Peter and I are going to the cinema with Janice and Mervyn tonight."

"You're never in these days!" her mum sighed. "But it's good that Janice has Mervyn now, he seems a decent lad." Her mum suddenly looked troubled. "At the football party – you didn't dance with Mervyn, did you?"

"No. I avoided dancing with anyone, well except Jack, but he doesn't count. He's just a friend of Will's, and I was doing him a favour because he wanted to impress ... he wanted to make ... some girl think he was popular." Her mum looked very uneasy, and Maria wondered if she was cross with her for dancing with a boy when she was going out with Peter.

"Jack, that's a solid name," her mum said softly. Then she gave an understanding nod before heading for the kitchen. Maria followed, while also glancing at Lucky, who'd slouched back onto her bed in the hall.

After lunch, Maria collected Lucky's lead, while her mum went upstairs to tell her dad they were going out. "Let's put your lead on," Maria said to Lucky. The dog started barking and wagging her tail. "I've got our coats," Maria shouted up the stairs, but there was no reply. So, she

313

tied the whimpering dog to the door handle and went upstairs to see why her mum was taking so long.

She heard her dad say, "Are you sure you don't want me to come with you?"

"No." her mum replied. "This is a mother, daughter thing."

As Maria walked into the room, she saw her dad was holding his arm. She guessed that putting up her shelves and sorting the loft last night had caused his arm to hurt. She knew he hated any form of sympathy, so she and her mum had learnt to accept his suffering without saying anything.

"We need to go before your dad starts shouting at these shelves," her mum said, throwing her dad a naughty little schoolgirl smile. "But when we get back, I'm sure the shelves will be finished, and your dad will be pleased with himself."

Her dad put his right arm out and grabbed her mum. "I do love you, and I'm proud of you."

Her mum pulled a face, but Maria could tell she was delighted by his comment.

As they left the house, Maria asked, "Is Dad, OK? I know he always does too much when he's worried about something."

"He's fine. He's just in one of his sorting moods."

"But that's my point, he sorts when—"

"I do love the trees," her mum interrupted as they walked towards the woods. Maria knew her mum treasured the countryside. She always looked at people's gardens and wished she had one of her own. When they reached the edge of the woods, Maria let Lucky off the lead. She loved her dog to be free, even though Lucky was hard to catch afterwards.

Putting the lead in her coat pocket, Maria pointed across to the side. "Look at the sun shining through those trees over there. It's beautiful."

"It's good to be away from the town." Her mum fell silent for a moment. "If you hadn't become our daughter, you might have been brought up somewhere better than Gravesend."

"I love this town. There isn't anywhere better."

As they climbed over a broken tree that lay across the path, her mum went in front of her. "Do you ever wonder what it would've been like if your biological mother had kept you?"

"No. I never think about it. That woman didn't love me. Why would I think about another life that might have been unhappy?" Catching up with her mum, Maria walked beside her again. "What's brought this on? Are you alright?"

"Everything's fine. I just wonder sometimes how you feel about finding your mother, that's all."

Maria stopped. "You are my mother!" After her day of reminiscing, Maria had found an awareness that felt stronger than ever. "My mother is not some strange woman whose genes I share. My mother is the one who has cared for me and nurtured me and has been my mother for all of my life." She trod on a twig, and there was a loud crack.

Her mum took her hand, and Maria saw tears flowing down her face. "I'm sorry, love. I just needed reassurance."

Squeezing her mum snugly in her arms, Maria said, "You and I are mother and daughter. We have a history together, and nothing can change that." Even though Maria was now taller than her mum, hugging her made her feel warm and safe. They carried on walking through the woods, with Lucky sniffing at everything and running madly around.

"But do you ever think about the woman who gave birth to you?" Her mum persisted. "Do you wonder what her family background might be?"

"I wonder who she is and where she lives, but that's about it."

"So would you want to meet her?"

"I guess it might be interesting. It would be good to know a bit more about her ... I suppose it would be like a mystery story coming to an end."

Wiping her tears away, her mum said, "I've always dreaded the thought of meeting that woman again. Right from the first moment I saw you, I couldn't bear the thought of ever losing you back to her." She paused and blew her nose. "In fact, losing you has always been the demon that's plagued my soul."

Maria felt her face tighten and in a childlike voice, she said, "But as a young child, I was frightened of losing you! I used to think you'd leave me like that other woman had done. To think we both had the same fear of losing each other!" She pulled her mum into another huge hug. "Honestly, Mummy, we're a right pair." She hadn't called her mummy for years, but somehow it seemed appropriate.

Her mum pulled away. "I'm not frightened of losing you anymore."

Maria giggled. "I do love you. You daft old woman!"

With that, her mum reached up and gave her a pretend clip around the head. "Not so much of the old, thank you!" she tittered.

When they reached the edge of the woods, her mum looked at her watch. "I've often noticed that hole in the fence over there, why don't we climb through and walk home across the graveyard."

"Are we allowed to do that?"

"I don't see why not," her mum said as she climbed through the hole. "Come on, love, it'll be a different walk for Lucky."

Maria followed her. "Can Lucky stay off the lead?" she asked. "People in the graveyard might not like her running about."

"I've seen many dogs charging around in here." Her mum beckoned to Lucky. "Lucky, you can come with us, but when it's time to go home you know we'll catch you."

As if Lucky knew what she'd said, she ran off into the graveyard, making sure she was just out of reach.

They stood at the top of the hill, and the church and its massive graveyard stretched down in front of them. Maria noticed that the gravestones gradually appeared smaller as they progressed down the hill. The gravelled path formed a frame around the edge as if holding the graves within its arms. She could see the car park halfway down, and the second part of the graveyard rolled away steeply below it. The graves seemed to go on forever.

"Maria," her mum whispered. "As we walk down the hill, do you mind if we wander around the graves? I'd like to look at the stones."

"OK, if you want to. I'll keep an eye on Lucky." She watched as her mum started walking between rows of graves, looking around as she went. The thought of dead people haunting the place had always frightened Maria, but she sauntered across the grass, trying to keep away from the people putting flowers on graves or walking along the pathway. She didn't like the idea of visiting a grave. Then she felt thankful her Grandad Harold had been cremated.

She scoffed, only the rich could afford burials anyway! She noticed Lucky was keeping a small distance away from her, so she walked forwards, hoping to persuade the dog to come closer.

"Maria! I thought it was you." She jumped as she turned in the direction of the voice, then squealed as the person grabbed her in a bearhug.

"Jack!" she exclaimed. "What are you doing here? Are you with Will?" she asked as she looked around. She called across to her mum, who was already walking over to her. Lucky appeared from behind a stone, watching but keeping her distance. "Mum," Maria shouted, "this is Jack … Will's friend, from football."

Increasing her pace, her mum quickly reached her. She didn't speak at first and just stared at Jack. Then, looking mystified, she finally said, "I'm very pleased to meet you … Jack."

CHAPTER 48

28th March 1965

David heard his bell ring, not once but twice. "Tia, come in," he said as he opened the door with pretend surprise.

"Uncle David, you've been out," she said accusingly. "I've called loads of times."

"Well, I'm in now, but you'll have to be quick. Your dad and I have arranged to play golf." He pointed to the lounge door. "I've only popped back from church to collect my golf things and make a phone call."

As he sat opposite her, he anticipated the inevitable quiz that was about to come. He stared at the ring sparkling on her finger, and he hated it for all the damage it had caused. He'd always tried not to overthink the link between the two families, but now the ring seemed to illuminate the truth as it shone out at him. It was a cruel reminder that the two families were not separate. He glanced at Tia's hands and saw how she had Joe's small, chubby little fingers. They were very different from Maria's, which were long and thin, like Catherine's.

"Uncle David," Tia began, "Mum and Dad have told me all about the adoption." She looked at him, obviously waiting for a reaction, so he quickly supplied a gasp. "I want to know your side of the story …"

*

"Aren't you ready yet?" David said as he entered Joe's front door. "I've been ages because …"

"After church, everything changed," shouted Joe. "Catherine wanted me to help dig up some pansies from the garden so that she could plant them around Win's grave."

David smirked. He knew how much Joe hated gardening. Catherine and Jack were the gardeners in the household.

"You've only just missed them," Joe said. "They've all gone to the grave."

"But at church, you said Catherine was going on her own."

"She was, but when I'd finished digging up the dreaded pansies, Jack arrived back from football. He offered to help plant them at the grave." Joe seemed to be searching for something on the hall table. "Jack went off to phone his friend from Gravesend. Then Tia appeared home and said she wanted to go as well. She'd been out this morning; I guess with George."

"What friend from Gravesend?" David said as he stared at the phone, then he added, "Tia came to see me this morning. She wanted to know about the adoption."

Joe was rummaged through the coat rack, looking through his pockets. "Really? I guess you didn't mention …"

"No, of course, not."

"Who did Jack phone?" David stuttered.

"The captain of the Kent team, he's meeting him later." Joe turned and went quickly into the sitting room. "There are my house keys," he said, picking them up from the table.

Following Joe into the sitting room, David's head started to spin, and he fell into the nearest chair.

"Are you alright?" Joe asked as he stood over him.

"I think you'd better sit down, Joe. You're not going to like what I have to say."

Joe plonked himself on a chair. "What is it?"

David looked up at the football photo above the fireplace. "It's everything … But it starts when Catherine put the baby up for adoption. You know how worried I was about what would happen to the child." Joe nodded. "Well, I used my political contacts to get myself information on the people being considered to adopt Catherine's child."

"You didn't!"

"I read the reports that were sent to the adoption panel, and I discovered that the young chap who pushed me away from that rockfall in Gibraltar was one of the applicants."

"So?"

"The report on Mark was excellent. So, I instructed my contacts to 'persuade' the panel to choose Mark and his wife as the child's parents."

"You shouldn't have …"

"When you begged me to follow them I agreed because I felt responsible for the child. I wanted to check the couple were good with the baby." David pushed up his glasses. "I kept a safe distance so I couldn't see much, but I could see they really cared for the child. After that, I had no wish to return. I told you they lived in Kent, but I didn't want to worry you about where they lived." He gazed at the floor. "I did end up having to return to the house some years later." He looked up. "Over the years, I've formed a very strong friendship with the family."

"No!"

"The child's delightful, Joe. She's such a thoughtful girl. She's another niece to me." David saw the look of horror on his brother's face. "None of them knew about my connection with you ..." David gulped ... "but the other day when you said Tia had found out, I deemed it was time to explain the truth to the parents. Joe, I didn't know Catherine had met the parents. If I'd known they'd all met each other, I would have told you that they lived—"

Joe interjected, "Catherine's met them? When?"

"When she handed over the child," David muttered. "Anyway, after Win's death, Catherine didn't visit the grave, so I wasn't too concerned. Then five years later, she decided to start visiting – that's why I had to return to see if the child still lived there, and I ... Joe, Win's grave is near to the child's house."

"Good God, man!" yelled Joe. "You know how often Catherine goes to the grave. They could have met at any point."

"But they didn't." David shuffled his feet and fiddled with his shirt sleeve. "However, the crux of the matter is that the child's mother wanted me to ask Catherine for a meeting. I knew Catherine wouldn't agree, so, before I left to come here ..." his back stiffened as he straightened up ... "I phoned the child's mother." Joe yelped, but David continued. "We agreed she wouldn't tell her daughter anything. She wished to check if the girl wanted to meet her birth mother. So, if the daughter said yes, I suggested the mother could walk through the graveyard with her daughter and bump into … She asked for an approximate time when Catherine would be there."

"How dare you!" yelled Joe. "This isn't fair on Catherine. You should have asked her permission … and Tia and Jack are with her! Can you phone the child's mother and stop her?"

David stood up. "I'll try," he said as he rushed to the phone in the hallway. He dialled the number, but there was no answer. "I think it's too late, they must have gone," he shouted.

Joe leapt out of his chair. "We need to stop this from happening. Let's take your car, it's faster than mine. You can tell me more on the way."

David's foot pushed further down on the accelerator. His cunning plan had gone wrong, he had to prevent this meeting from happening. "I believe part of the new M2 motorway is open, we'll try that route," he said as he drove. "It should be quicker than the way Catherine usually drives." As he steered, he hastily imparted some of the facts about Maria to Joe. He'd only just told Mark and Selina that he hadn't disclosed any of their details, but he knew the game had changed and the rules had to be adapted. Joe listened, seeming to take it all in. When David stopped talking, the noise of the speeding engine felt louder than ever. Looking in the rear-view mirror and turning into Gravesend, David said, "Are you speaking to me yet?"

"You've been there for Maria, which is more than Catherine and I have done." Joe went quiet for a second. "I think it is time for Maria to meet Catherine." He glanced across at David. "There have been too many lies," Joe muttered. "For the child's sake, the wrong has to be made right."

David gave a wide grin, at last Joe was considering what was best for Maria. He felt his grip on the steering wheel relaxing.

As he pulled into the church car park, there were a few cars around, but David spotted a space against the gate leading into the churchyard. It was out of sight, but they could see Win's grave in the distance.

Joe sat upright. "I think we've made it, there's only the three of them at the grave."

David nodded. "I can't see Selina, and remember, if Maria doesn't want to meet Catherine, then Selina won't bring her."

"Maria will want to meet her," Joe said with certainty in his voice. He grabbed the door handle. "You stay in the car. If Selina sees you, she might sense something's wrong. I'll think of some excuse to get Tia and Jack back to the car. Then we can tell Jack the truth, and you can fill Tia in with the rest of Maria's story. That'll leave Catherine alone to meet Maria and her mother, just as you planned."

"This is like being back in the old days."

Joe grunted as he closed the car door. "No. This time, we're playing with the emotions of the people we love."

David watched as Joe started trotting along the narrow pathway, which led from the car park down towards the lower part of the graveyard. Win's grave was in a small dipped area at the end of the churchyard, some way down the path, then across to the middle. David had always thought it was a secluded plot, away from the main graveyard, which openly stretched out to his right. He hoped the long, curvy path with the sun shining through the trees was helping to shield Joe's entrance. He could see Jack, Tia and Catherine were all engrossed in their digging and were unaware of Joe approaching. David didn't understand Catherine's desire to cover Win's grave with flowers, a memorial garden seemed futile to him. Jack stood up, stretched and said something to Tia. Then he started sprinting across the main graveyard and up towards the church. David leant over his steering wheel, his eyes following Jack's route. He was heading towards … Maria and Selina! David could see them clearly, ambling through the middle of the graveyard. David scrambled out of his car and ran to the edge of the car park, waving frantically at Joe. He hoped no one would see him, but he had to get Joe's attention. Joe was staring at Jack running through the graves, then he turned to the car. David indicated towards where Jack was going, and he watched as Joe's eyes followed his directions. Then Joe looked back at Catherine and Tia, who were still busily planting the flowers, and he changed course and marched forcefully through the grass, towards his son.

Thank goodness, thought David. His heart was racing. He remembered how much Joe had loved Maria, and as Joe hastened towards her now, he felt himself bursting with anticipation. He speculated that Joe had probably wondered what she was like. David had so often wanted to tell him. Most of all, he'd wanted his brother to meet Maria, but he'd always resigned himself to the thought that he never would – yet now it was about to happen. He saw Jack turn to his dad, and then the introduction happened. David could almost sense his brother's happiness from where he stood. He sighed; the reunion was wonderful to watch. Then he heard someone running, and before he could turn, he felt a tap on his shoulder. Twisting around, he saw a very breathless and red-faced Mark.

"What's happening?" Mark panted as he bent forwards. "I was getting ready to come over, and as I cleared my tools from Maria's windowsill, I spotted your car heading towards the church car park." He breathed deeply. "Has something gone wrong with the plan?"

"I did try to phone," David said, with a big sigh. "It all got rather complicated." He slapped Mark on the shoulder. "They haven't met yet, but it looks like Selina's proceeding with the plan. Let's get in the car; I have a lot to explain." As they walked, David added, "We can see the grave from here, and if Catherine refuses to be civil, you can rush over to support Selina."

"I'd planned to watch from here anyway, but I didn't expect they'd be meeting already," Mark said as he got into the front seat. "Thank goodness I've made it in time." He peered through the windscreen. "So, her name's Catherine then …"

CHAPTER 49

28th March 1965

Selina found herself studying Jack. He didn't look anything like Maria, but he sounded so much like David, and his stance was the same too. She could see Jack was beaming at her daughter, and she couldn't help but instantly take to him. He seemed genuinely fond of his sister.

"I'm here with Tia and my mum," Jack announced to Maria. Selina's heartbeat increased; that wasn't what she'd been told. "I'm off to see Will in a bit. We're meeting in a café for coffee. Is the town very far from here?"

"I know the cafe," Maria giggled. "I'll take you if you like."

Jack was about to speak, but an Irish sounding voice boomed from behind him. "Jack, I need to borrow you for a moment."

Selina swept round to see a silver-haired, middle-aged man approaching. She stared, thinking his face looked remarkably like Jack's.

"Dad, what are you doing here? I thought you were playing golf?" Jack put his arm around Maria's waist, "This is my friend, Maria, and her mum."

The man was now standing beside Jack, and he threw Maria the biggest smile Selina had ever seen. "Hello," he said, then he turned to Selina. "It's lovely to meet you." She felt taken aback as he vigorously shook her hand as if she were an old friend. Turning to Jack, he announced, "Golf was cancelled, so I thought I'd come and give you some help with the pansies. I've some more plants in the car, would you give me a hand to carry them over to the grave?"

Selina felt her daughter take her hand. "We'll wait here for you, Jack. Then I'll walk down to town with you."

Jack's dad pointed to the lower end of the graveyard, "You two ladies could wait with my wife and daughter if you like."

Selina panicked. David obviously hadn't known that the whole family would be there, she needed to abort her plan. "I'm sorry, but I think it's time for us to go home now," she said, as politely as she could.

"Mum," Maria said. "you can go if— "

"Please don't go home yet," interjected Jack's father. He looked at Selina, and she felt as if his eyes were trying to tell her something. "My daughter ..." he cleared his throat. "I'm sure Cinderella and her mother over there would love to say hello." The man gave her a wink, and she felt herself turning crimson as she realised, he knew. She peered across the graveyard, and she could see two women frantically gardening around a grave. The man followed her gaze. "My wife is the one in the blue coat with the fur collar. She was supposed to be here on her own, but at the last minute, both children decided to join her. My brother was worried," he glanced towards the car park then back to the grave, "but my daughter's fine. I'm sure she'll love meeting you." He looked at Jack. "I just want to borrow my son," he said, winking at her again. "We need to have a chat while we fetch some more plants from the car." We'll join you at the graveside in a while."

"Are you sure?" Selina asked, worried.

"Yes, I'm sure. I think it's the right thing to do." Smiling at Maria, he said, "What I mean is, I'm certain they'll be pleased to meet a friend of Jack's."

"I'm certain Maria would like to meet them too," Selina said, and she found herself almost chuckling at the conversation they were having. This was such an amiable man.

"That's good then," he said, and he touched Maria's arm. "We'll see you in a while, once Jack and I have got some more plants." He winked again at Selina, before sauntering off with his arm around his son.

"Honestly, Mum," Maria muttered, "why do all middle-aged men wink when they talk to you."

"They don't," Selina said, staring down at where the young girl and her mother were working.

"And what was he on about?"

"He was just being friendly."

"He seemed strange to me. Anyway, I've only met Jack's sister once before. We don't have to go over, we could wait here for Jack."

She gave Maria's hand a squeeze. "I know we don't have to go over, but we should say hello." Then she let go of Maria's hand. "Come on then … let's do it."

As they walked down the hill, Selina saw the young girl look up. The girl waved and ran towards them.

"Jack said he thought it was you," she shouted as she got closer to Maria.

Maria waited until the girl reached them. "Yes, I've offered to take him into town."

329

"Where's he gone?" the girl asked as she looked around.

"Oh, your dad's arrived, and they've gone back to the car to get some more plants."

Tia's face changed. "That's strange. I wonder why Dad's not playing golf. I bet the club was closed or something." Then she smiled at Selina.

"Sorry, this is my mum," Maria said. "Mum, this is Tia."

"Hello," Tia said. "It's nice to meet you."

"It's nice to meet you too, Tia." Selina liked this girl's polite manner.

Tia grinned and pulled her gardening glove further up her wrist. Turning back to Maria, she asked, "As Jack's run away, I don't suppose you'd like to help us with planting pansies?"

Selina watched as Maria stretched out her fingers. "My friend painted my nails last night. I can't spoil them, well, that's my excuse anyway." Maria giggled.

"That ring … it's lovely." Tia stared at Maria's hand.

"My parents had it made for me," Maria said.

Tia's face turned a shade lighter. "It looks … gorgeous. Can I have a closer look at it?"

"It is amazing," Maria said, beaming as she took off her ring.

As Tia studied the ring, Selina tapped Maria's arm. "Let's go down and say hello to Tia's mother." She started to march off, concentrating on walking down the slope. She could see the woman was now planting flowers at the front of the headstone. The whole grave looked covered with pansies. She laughed to herself, where did Maria think Jack was going to put the rest of the plants he was supposed to be fetching? She halted before reaching the bottom of the grave and, wiping her eyes with a hanky, she turned round to check her daughter was behind her. She could see Tia standing above them, staring at Maria.

"Wait for me, Mum," Maria said, running up to her.

Taking Maria's hand once again, she held it tighter than she'd ever held it. Selina turned to stare at the woman, who was bent down by the headstone. She felt her body stiffen. She wanted to hold on to this moment because she foresaw that everything was about to change. She forced herself to move, guiding her daughter to where the woman was patting a pansy into the soil. As they stood opposite her, the flowers felt like a great divide. How she wished they could stay on this side of the fence forever.

But then the dreaded woman looked up. "Well, that's finished," she said as she stood upright. She cast them a quick smile while she took off her gardening gloves and started brushing the earth from her coat. Then she stopped abruptly as she stared at a tiny white feather, floating slowly down from one of her gardening gloves. She watched it land silently at her feet, her gaze remaining on the ground.

She was still the tall, slim woman Selina remembered, smartly dressed with a headscarf around her hair. She could just see a lock of red hair that had fallen across the woman's face. Her long-feared demon had appeared, and Selina gripped even tighter to Maria's hand. She knew that in her heart she didn't want to let go, this all felt so painful. She had to force herself to do this, she had to for Maria. Tia arrived at the grave, and her posture seemed tense. Selina had to speak, she had to ignore her fear …

"Seventeen years ago, I made a promise to you …" she began.

The woman looked up and stared at her. Selina watched as her facial expression grew taut, but she forced herself to carry on. "For my daughter's sake, I'm now breaking that promise. You see, I now realise it's important that my daughter knows who she is and where she comes from. I hope you will help her to discover …" she paused, looked at Maria and smiled … "the importance of being … Maria."

Selina felt she had to do something; she needed this woman to respond positively. She prayed for help as she slowly raised Maria's hand up, above the pansies and towards the woman. At first, there was nothing, then, as if everything was moving in slow motion, the woman's hand came out to hers, and Selina placed her precious daughter's hand firmly into the other woman's palm. "This is … Maria," she croaked. Then she looked at her daughter. "Maria … this is the woman … who gave birth to you." Selina let her own hand fall away, and she forced herself to take the most painful step of her life – she stepped backwards, to leave them to talk across the grave of flowers.

CHAPTER 50

28th March 1965

Catherine was left staring into a face that was a younger version of herself! She noticed Maria was looking at her intensely and she guessed she too was trying to take in the enormity of what had just happened. She felt numb. The world had stopped spinning, and she felt as if she was falling off. She had to control herself, but this wasn't easy.

"I'm pleased to meet you, Maria. That's a lovely name." She held her hand firmly while examining every part of the girl. "I'm Catherine." She was unsure what she should say. "I've often thought about you." She wobbled as she lost her balance, and her hand fell away, but her eyes remained on the girl. "You have my face after all! You have my eyes and my mouth. Your hair is still the colour of ..." Then she looked down at the girl's body. "You have the same build as Jack." She turned around. "And where is he?" Nobody answered her.

Looking stunned, the girl asked, "Jack ... is he a relative of mine?"

"He's your half-brother. However, unlike Tia, he doesn't know of your existence." Catherine turned to Tia.

Tears were cascading down her daughter's cheeks. She guessed this was as hard for Tia as it was for her. Catherine stepped over the pansies, tripping over her own feet as she went, but Tia didn't notice, she was busy throwing her arms around Maria's waist. Catherine smiled at the sight. Tia was so much shorter than Maria, but she understood, the hug was a big sister's dream come true.

"We've found you," Tia cried. "You've no idea how happy that makes me." Catherine could see her daughter's eyes were glazed with joy. Tia looked up at Maria. "You won't know this, but Catherine isn't my biological mother, not like she is yours. Even though you and I are not biologically related, you're still the sister I should have grown up with, the sister I loved and lost. If I've learnt one thing … it's that biology isn't everything."

For a moment, Catherine stood and marvelled. Now she saw that Tia really did understand that love is what matters in life. Catherine's head stopped spinning, and her body relaxed. She felt as if the world and its gravity had reverted to normal. She strolled up to Maria and whispered, "Do you hate me for what I did?"

Maria answered quietly, "I used to … but not anymore." Then she seemed to contemplate something. "I know who you are now, and for that, I'm pleased." Moving away from Catherine, Maria turned and took the hand of her mother, who was still standing behind her. "This is Selina, and I'm very honoured to be her daughter. I have wonderful parents, and I wouldn't change that for the world. I am very lucky." The dog ran up to her and barked as if in agreement, then quickly ran off again.

Maria placed her arms around Selina and pulled her gently into her. "Come here, Mummy," she whispered.

Catherine watched as Selina's body eased into her daughter's arms. She could see they had a close bond, one that meant they understood each other. There was a connection that no one else could ever share. She smiled as she realised that was exactly how it was between her and Tia. She looked across at Tia, who was busily taking off her gardening glove. Catherine turned back to Selina. The woman looked the same, but her nervy demeanour seemed to have vanished. "I'm pleased to meet you again," she said as she shook Selina's hand.

"I never thought I'd say this, but yes, it's right that we've met again," Selina replied.

Catherine noticed Tia was holding up her finger with Win's ring attached. "Now I understand why this ruby ring was by the sink at the football club dance," Tia said to Maria. "When I saw it I took it to return it to Mum. I didn't know it was yours ... I'm sorry."

"Tia, you stole it?" Catherine said in horror.

Tia didn't respond, she was too occupied trying to pull the ruby ring off her finger. She held it out to Maria. "Now, you must have this back." Catherine could see the ring in Tia's hand sitting beside another, more delicate ring. The large ruby from her gran's stone caught the sun and sent a flicker of red light onto Win's headstone. Catherine gasped, sensing that her gran wouldn't want Tia to give her ring away.

But before Catherine could speak, Maria said, "No, Tia. The ruby ring is yours because Catherine is your mother. My mother gave me the halo ring, which represents her love for me, and that's my heirloom." Maria took the delicate ring from Tia's hand and left Gran's ruby ring behind.

Catherine looked at Tia and whispered, "Remember what matters, is not just the giving of life … the giving of love is just as important."

Tia seemed unsure, and her hand remained outstretched. "But my mum gave this ring to you before she gave it to me."

"I made a mistake, which I have now corrected," Catherine said in shame. "Maria is right, the ring is yours, Tia, because the ring represents what you and I have shared."

"Tia, there is something else," Maria interrupted. Catherine held her breath as she saw Maria lean across and take back Gran's ring. Then to her amazement, Maria placed her halo ring around it. She put them both on her finger and held up her hand. The two rings now looked as if they were one ring.

"They fit," bellowed Tia.

Selina laughed, "It's the glass slipper!"

Maria cast her mother a strange look, then turned back to Tia. "My ring was made to fit around the ruby ring. So now we each own a ring that can be joined to make one. In the same way that we are joined as sisters." She looked at Catherine. "We are all one family, united by two separate rings and two separate mothers."

Catherine stared in disbelief as Maria dismantled the two rings again and placed Gran's ring back in Tia's hand.

Maria closed Tia's fingers around the ring. "Your mum is right; it's mothering that's important." A tear fell from Tia's cheek and landed on Maria's hand.

"I promise there will be no more sad tears for the sister I lost," Tia whispered.

Catherine couldn't help but feel so proud of both her girls. She put her arms around Tia, and as she hugged her close, she felt the joy bursting from her daughter's heart. "Your sister is here," Catherine murmured in her ear. She looked up at Maria. "I've hated the lies I've told, and now finally, I can tell everyone the truth. My friends and family will be hurt that I didn't tell them ..." she held out her hand, "but Maria, I want you to stay in our lives now." Maria nodded while Catherine bent down and picked up the tiny white feather that had fallen from her glove. Then, placing it firmly in her pocket, she turned and smiled at the gravestone. "I know you're with me," she whispered, "and I know you're happy now."

CHAPTER 51

28ᵗʰ March 1965

Feeling hesitant, Maria asked, "In your note, you wrote that you knew the man who's my biological father?"

Catherine shuffled her feet and muttered, "We knew each other from our school days. His name was Gregory Jones." Her voice dropped. "He never knew about you, and I'm afraid he died last year. His mother still lives in Dover ..." She looked uneasy and fell silent.

Maria thought Catherine had such a posh accent, just like everyone in Dover seemed to have. She watched as she tenderly stroked the gravestone.

"My grandparents lived in Dover but originated from Gravesend." Catherine looked around the graveyard. "My grandfather was a local football hero here." Then her eyes fell on Maria. "But he was a banker by profession, and early on in their marriage, his work moved them to Dover." Tucking her hair behind her headscarf, she added, "My grandmother, Win, fell in love with Dover, but Charles never did. When he died, Win brought him back here to rest in his beloved hometown." She looked at the stone again. "Gran wanted to be buried with him so they could be together, forever."

As Maria examined the headstone, she saw in large letters *'CHARLES JOHN DEMORE'* and further down it read *'Was joined by his beloved wife WINIFRED CATHERINE DEMORE.'* Now she knew who C and W were!

"So, Maria, your relatives were from Gravesend," her mum said gently. "It's almost as if you were meant to return to this town."

A shudder went through Maria's body. Her mum and that spiritual stuff again. It was such rubbish to think that her dead ancestors were guiding her. As Maria stared across at Catherine, standing there in her coat with a costly fox-fur collar, her mind turned back to 'The Importance of Being Earnest'. It occurred to her that Oscar Wilde's play reflected her own life. It wasn't her birth family's fortune that mattered, life wasn't about birthrights, what was important was the person she'd become.

Looking around the graveyard, Catherine asked, "Where has Jack gone?" Maria suddenly realised the woman's voice had a twang of a French accent. Of course, that's why Jack spoke French. It was all becoming clearer now.

Pointing to the car park, Tia said, "He's with Dad collecting more flowers. But they've been ages."

"Why's your father here? And we don't need more flowers," exclaimed Catherine.

Maria saw her mum flash a guilty look towards Catherine.

"I'm afraid it's my fault," Selina said. "Your husband knew this was going to happen." Maria felt her mum's arm slide around her. "I'm sorry, love, but that's why I checked with you earlier to see if you wanted to meet ... Catherine. I wouldn't have gone ahead if you'd said no."

"But how did you know Catherine was here?"

"Your guardian angel told me she —"

Catherine interjected, "How could you possibly have known we were here?" Her brow gathered into a scowl. "And how could Joe have known about this meeting?"

With that, Tia started waving her arms towards the car park, beckoning her dad and Jack to join them.

Catherine added, "This is going to be difficult. Jack has a half-sister he knows nothing about."

"Don't worry, your husband's already told him," Maria heard her mum say softly.

"Joe wouldn't have told him, not without asking me first," snapped Catherine.

Maria smiled to herself. Catherine was self-assured and confident, just like she could be at times! Her mum frowned, and Maria knew she'd noticed the similarity as well. Then her attention was drawn towards the path, Jack was sprinting down the track. She'd never seen anyone run so fast; his football training was paying off!

"It's OK, Maria, he knows everything," her mum whispered.

Maria's head was whirling. "What's going on, Mum, how ...?" but Jack reached her before she could finish her sentence. She felt him grab hold of her, and then her feet left the floor.

"Maria ... my sister," he yelled. "It's incredible!" He twirled her around in the air.

She clung on firmly and screamed, "Put me down – big brother!"

He obeyed, then held her in his arms, muttering in her ear, "You're alright with me as your brother, aren't you?"

She broke free from his grip and punched him playfully on the arm. "Don't be silly. I now have you as well as Will to look after. I'll always be there to help you both … just you watch me."

Jack mumbled, "I think I love my new sister." Then he roared, "You and I, brother and sister, who would have thought it?"

Tia peered across at Jack. "Looking at your two lanky bodies, it's pretty obvious!"

Jack tossed her a look of brotherly affection. "Oh no, now I have two sisters to nag me. Life's so unfair."

Maria watched as Tia walked towards her. "When I first met you," Tia said. "I thought you looked familiar, but now I realise you have a look of Mum about you." Then she stopped short and stared at Maria and Jack together. Maria guessed Tia suddenly felt left out. She reached out her arms engulfing both Tia and Jack in a hug.

"We're a team now, like the three musketeers!" she said warmly.

"Dad's told you then?" Catherine retorted as she stared at her son.

"Yes, and don't be cross with him. I'm pleased I know and to be honest, I think you should have told us years ago." He went over and hugged his mum. "I do understand, though, and I do love you." Smiling, he added, "By the way, Dad, Uncle David and Maria's father are talking in the car park."

Now Maria was confused. Did he mean her Uncle David? And what was her dad doing there? She went to speak, but her mum just gave her a knowing smile.

"Trust your dad to check on us."

Catherine, however, was still talking to Jack. "What's Uncle David doing here? And how does your dad— "

Quickly Maria's mum interrupted. "We only live over there," she said, waving towards their house. "Would you all like to come for a cup of tea? It would be good to talk things through properly." Her mum pointed back up the path. "Our house isn't far; it's just past the car park, up the road and towards the church."

"That's perfect," said a very cheery Jack. "We'll stop in the car park and collect the others."

"Catherine," her mum said assertively, "would you mind asking Maria's father to take you all to the house and put the kettle on the stove? Maria and I just need to get our dog; she never comes back once she's off the lead. It can take ages to catch her."

Catherine looked as if she was about to say something, but she stopped and put her arm around Tia. Smiling, she said, "Thank you. We'll see you both in a minute or two." Maria understood Catherine was giving her some time with her mum. Then she noticed Tia cuddling into Catherine's arm. Maria felt a bond that only her and Tia would ever comprehend, neither of them had the genes from the mothers they loved.

Jack turned to Maria, and with concern in his voice, he asked, "What about Will? I'm supposed to be meeting him."

"You can phone him from mine. If he's already gone, I'll ask Janice to go and let him know where you are." She chuckled. "Will's in for a shock, isn't he?" As Jack nodded, she added, "But then again, I think Will's more perceptive than we realise!"

They all strode away, and Maria felt her mum's arm slide around her waist. She nestled into her grip. She needed her mum right now, the events of the last hour felt too consuming. Maria contemplated that indeed, she did have Catherine's face and build, along with her self-assured and confident nature. She cuddled into the woman who had nurtured her to be understanding and caring, the woman who really understood her. Maria now realised the two rings did represent what had made her into who she was today – she had to admit she was a combination of both women.

As if reading her thoughts, her mum whispered, "I've always said nurture is important, but today I've learnt that nature is too, both things affect the circle of life." She giggled. "Or should I say, the ring of life."

Maria sighed. "I still think that eighty per cent of my life has been you and Dad helping to define who I am. That heirloom ring only represents part of me, I'm glad I've left it with Tia. The heirloom ring signifies family, and it's her heart that's with Catherine." Raising her own ring, she added, "And mine's with you." She beamed. "This is my heirloom because it's us who are a family." Squeezing her mum closer, she said, "Thank you for sorting today, I know how painful it's going to be for you and Dad to have Catherine in our lives. But my mystery is getting solved, and somehow it feels like a closure. I don't have to imagine my past anymore."

Her mum looked up at her. "Maria, the most important thing in my life is you. Any pain I might feel along the way is nothing compared to the pleasure I get from seeing you happy." She cupped her hands around Maria's face. "I think this has helped us both. Now I fully understand that to be your mother has made me into your mother."

Maria smiled with satisfaction. She knew how much her mum loved being a mother. She grinned; her essay notes were right; her life story really did show that love is powerful and significant in shaping lives. She also knew she had shaped other people's lives too! For every action, there was a reaction. She was indeed … a player on life's stage.

"Shall we go and catch your naughty dog now?" her mum asked as she broke away. "Look, there she is." Her mum indicated towards a gravestone in front of them. "I'll walk to the left," and nodding towards the right she added, "you go that way and try to make Lucky run towards me." Maria reached into her pocket and took out the lead. "I'll take that lead," her mum said and started to stride away.

Deep in thought, Maria wandered off in the other direction. As she sauntered, she felt a sudden twinge in her stomach, like a butterfly fluttering inside her. She stopped, and the feeling went away. Walking on, she felt a wave of nausea. She stopped again. She remembered how pale she'd looked in the mirror, and how she'd been feeling so sick in the mornings. She must be going down with a tummy bug. Walking on, she tutted as she realised her period was due. Obviously, that was why she was feeling so ill. Then she thought about it. She hadn't had one for ages … not since … she stopped still.

She heard her mum shouting, "I've caught her, love."

But Maria couldn't answer her. Her legs gave way as she slid slowly down to the ground. Sitting on the grass, she felt the tears start to well. Her mum and Lucky were by her side in an instant.

"What's the matter, love? Has it all been too much for you?"

Maria started wailing and shaking her head. Her mum knelt beside her, twisting the handle of Lucky's lead around her shoe. "Oh, my love, it's going to be alright," she said as she hugged her firmly.

Sobbing uncontrollably, Maria saw her future changing before her eyes, and she didn't know what she was going to do. Through her watery mist, she looked up at her mum. And then she saw her answer … she was going to be as good a mother as her mum had been to her.

The End

Printed in Poland
by Amazon Fulfillment
Poland Sp. z o.o., Wrocław